Love in Idleness

'There is something almost fin-de-siècle about Mendelson's debut novel – it reads like a late 19th-century exploration of a young woman's development, and echo of a period when young women were stepping out into the world for the first time, independent "bachelor girls" and modern women all . . . Mendelson is assessing both the value and shame of a young woman facing a new age'

Lesley McDowell, *Scotsman*

'Mendelson has an ear for unexpected vocabulary and occasional outrageous and startling simile, but her real talent is poetic, for barbed language and a sense of metaphor that's unerring . . . "The air is sticky with distractions" from start to finish of *Love in Idleness*'

Ali Smith, *Glasgow Herald*

'It is refreshing to find a novel offering a different twist on someone female and single, trying to live and love in the unfriendly metropolis'

Joy Sable, *Jewish Chronicle*

'Charlotte Mendelson displays enough zest and flair to convince in a branch of fiction that is often slackly written. If nothing else, she deserves credit for her authentic – even sympathetic – portrayal of solitude'

Nathalie Fraser, *Times Literary Supplement*

'Charlotte Mendelson is one year short of 30, but closeness to youth in a first novel allows you a youth's-eye view'

Anna Shapiro, *Observer*

'Mendelson writes sharply and perceptively' ***Sunday Times***

'Charlotte Mendelson's debut novel is an exploration of the pursuit of passion. No lesbian bodice-ripper this, but instead a well-crafted work of literary fiction with a subtle Sapphic undercurrent . . . If you subscribe to the notion that less is often more, you'll find *Love in Idleness* an intelligent and gripping first novel with a pleasurable ripple of sexual tension'

Beverly Kemp, *Diva*

'This is a gripping coming-of-age novel that depicts the often turbulent relationship between mother and daughter'

Shine

Charlotte Mendelson was born in 1972 and grew up in up in Oxford. Her second novel, *Daughters of Jerusalem*, won the Somerset Maugham Award and the John Llewellyn Rhys Prize, and she was shortlisted for the *Sunday Times* Young Writer of the Year Award. Her third, *When We Were Bad*, was shortlisted for the Orange Broadband Prize for Fiction 2008. Charlotte lives in London with her family.

Also by Charlotte Mendelson

Daughters of Jerusalem

When We Were Bad

Love in Idleness

Charlotte Mendelson

PICADOR

First published 2001 by Picador

First published in paperback 2002 by Picador
an imprint of Pan Macmillan Ltd
Pan Macmillan, 20 New Wharf Road, London N1 9RR
Basingstoke and Oxford
Associated companies throughout the world
www.panmacmillan.com

ISBN 978-0-330-48298-1

3 5 7 9 8 6 4

A CIP catalogue record for this book is available from
the British Library.

Typeset by Intype Libra Ltd
Printed and bound in Great Britain by
CPI Mackays Chatham ME5 8TD

For Joanna Briscoe,

with love + ∞

Thanks to:

Valerie Thomas, Craig Raine, Christie Hickman,
Clare Naylor, Emily Charkin, Emma Bryant, Eleanor Clarke,
Tamara Oppenheimer, Rebecca Salt, Lynne Drew,
Alexandra Pringle, Pat Kavanagh, Stephanie Cabot,
Maria Rejt, Ilu and Berti Kertesz,
Rachel Mendelson, Theodore Mendelson,

and most of all to my parents, with love.

One

Everything had been decided the last time she'd seen Stella.

Exams have just finished: a sodden anticlimax of drinking and disarray and maudlin promises. It is Saturday – the first of her adult life. She wakes late with a headache and the sun in her eyes from a gap in the skinny orange curtains. After a ceremonial and strangely unfulfilling walk through the Meadows (goodbye roses, goodbye famous ugly statue), and a numbly everlasting train ride, she limps the slow mile from the station to her parents' house. A pyre of Edinburgh possessions already lies in her childhood bedroom, collected by her mother, impatient as a bailiff, several days before.

Four years ago she made the opposite journey. As she weaves through hormonal swarms of slack-uniformed teenagers, affecting nonchalance for the tourists, she considers her progress.

CLOTHING
Then: Mormonish skirt, avocado smock. The fruits of hours of anxious speculation.

Now: Black trousers, tight striped T-shirt. Possibly too tight.

DEMEANOUR
Then: Icy terror and blushes, alternating in streaks.
Now: Raddled savoir-faire.

LUNGS
Then: Pristine.
Now: Carefully soiled.

LIPS
Then: Four inexpert molluscy kisses.
Now: Five more kisses, some recurring.

BODILY EXPERIENCE
Then: Unsolicited breast-groping. One knuckled fumble in a field.
Now: Four terms of ardent monogamy. Three best-forgotten random incidents. It's the same body, and not the same.

Even Anna isn't impressed with her score. But, without gerontophilia, how will she ever improve it? As her feet sink into the gravel she once again despairs of reaching the point when she stops keeping count.

It isn't an important moment. She's only survived finals – not won anything, barely strayed out of touch. It isn't reasonable to expect a heroine's welcome, but she prepares her expression anyway. The front door has been repainted, this time in rich navy, lickable as chocolate. There's a new French house-number, charmed from melting Parisian bureaucrats. Rust from its short-lived predecessor still stains the lintel. At least they haven't changed the locks, she smirks to herself, as her key slides smoothly in, and freezes.

Her throat burns with instant disbelieving tears. She tries again. The key really will not move. They *have* changed the locks.

There are no alternatives. No child of her mother's would calmly ascribe a problem to ironmongery. That's not how they dealt with things in the Old Country, and that's not how they deal with them here. It's family feuds, a birthright denied. Injustice, and exclusion.

She storms down the path to the back of the house, tearing through her options. Break and enter? Ring from a phonebox? As she rehearses asking what she did wrong, she hears her mother's voice, like a pirate hornpipe to shipwrecked sailors.

'*Dar*ling?'

She always calls her Darling in public. Darling in private means Anna's father.

Anna is prepared for a scene in front of her mother's friends. In front of strangers, even. This is not an overreaction; they have changed the locks. She is right to be furious. As she rounds the corner into the cool of the garden, her blood is up.

'What's going on? What are you doing? The keys . . .'

Her mother is sitting at the white cast-iron table. Somebody else is standing, smoking under the elm.

Anna stops shouting. The garden hums. She wipes her face with her sleeve and turns towards the table, slowly. Her eyes are on the elm's green shade.

'Oh . . . I thought you'd changed the locks. I didn't realize . . .' She waits to hear it's all a mistake.

'Yes, we had to,' says her mother. 'Since that business – well, too many people had keys.'

That business was a drugs bust. Anna's sister had been

house-sitting while the grown-ups were in New York (their father giving readings, their mother despoiling Bloomingdales), and had declared herself At Home to the county's crusties. The neighbours, who include at least two solicitors and a woman said to be second-in-command at MI5, hadn't complained about this mini-Glastonbury until her boyfriend had parked his bus in a disabled space. Even Anna's sister had commented on their parents' uncannily calm reaction. She claims their mother has started boasting about it to her London friends.

Now Anna's mother is telling her something about new keys. Finally the bright shadow walks over from the elm, and smiles at her.

'Hello, Anna.'

Shyness is so strange, thinks Anna. Girls, or women, so often say they have it, even the ones with confidence like chainmail. Her own sister is offensively silent with everyone over nineteen – except Stella, their aunt. With Stella she is charming and hilarious and rude. They leave each other elaborate messages via Anna's mother, whose voice clicks with irritation as she passes them on. Whereas Anna, who can talk back to anyone, Anna, whose parties have featured adults, Anna, notorious for unexplained friendships with lecturers twice her age, is with Stella an anxious child.

And here she is.

They don't look like sisters. Anna's mother seems almost as young, until you look up close. She was beautiful. Now the smoking and the thinness have overstretched that fine skin. It's too matt, too yielding; just beginning to drift and pinch under her eyes, beside her mouth. But neither age, nor the expensive boredom of her clothes, can dull her celebrated cheekbones and jaw, her dark, deep, shadowed eyes. Her hair is more silver than brown now, and she wears it in a low, loose knot, but it still has the shine of cold water and a million brushstrokes. No, when you look she *is* beautiful. Only her nervous hands, which are starting to liver-spot, and her creased neck give the lie to those men who ignore Anna's snarls, and say, 'You must be sisters.'

Stella is different. Not just because she's a decade younger, or because the entwining waves of her reddish-brown hair are cut short around her neck, or because her skin still palely glows, still holds itself to her bones. But her thinness is different, less anxious. She doesn't have a smoker's lines, or a smoker's hands. They have the same wide mouth, but without her sister's Chanel-sticky sheen, Stella's lips look soft as marzipan. Their eyes are brown, but while Anna's mother's are larger and darker, there is something about Stella's – long, cool, crescent-lidded – that pin you, smiling, in her gaze. Her silver jewellery is from North Africa, not central London. And, unlike her sister, Stella courts the sun.

She's in it now, leaning back in the only chair not sheltered by a huge canvas parasol. Anna blinks: the brightest Virgin on the Green. Her shirt is dark grey linen, with the sleeves rolled up. In the heat her arms gleam, tanned and speckled – Anna's mother's are shrouded in cream viscose. She puts her hand to her eyes as if saluting, and squints into the light. Gold flares on her right ring finger.

'So, you've finished at last.'

'On Thursday. But there was . . . quite a wind-down.'

Stella gives a slow smile. She has good teeth. 'God, when

I finished my course I barely moved for a week. And then didn't slow down for another fortnight. You young things have no feel for degradation. I still dream about it.'

'I'm sure you do,' says Anna's mother. Anna looks at her quickly, but her mouth is smiling. Her sunglasses seem to grow every summer.

'And what are you doing with yourself now?'

'She's going to loll around for months, and then may grace London with her presence,' says Anna's mother. Anna's barbed stare bounces straight off her sunglasses.

The sisters are together so rarely that she never has a chance to watch them, to work out exactly what it is that soured their bond. Her current verdict is that it must be envy. Stella is a decade younger, stronger, sharper. Where Anna's mother is shrinking and sinking into a brittle parody of herself, all bone structure, lamb's wool separates and histrionics, Stella is ironic, and unimpressed, and somewhat dangerous. She is never nice for effect, unlike her sister, who doesn't have the courage to be seriously rude. She looks as if she doesn't think about what to wear but always gets it right. Anna's mother's dreary clothes still crackle with money spent and excuses made and sales assistants' careful lies. And after all, Stella mostly lives in Paris. No amount of antique balsamic and objets trouvés (trouvés at Liberty's) can disguise the fact that her sister is stuck in Somerset – land of the yokel, treacle-slow.

If only her mother wasn't here, and they could talk properly, alone. Stella may have suggestions; friends she could meet; advice and concern and interest. Or at least a small tough grain of comfort.

'I just want to go to London,' says Anna, hoping to

convey in one intense look all her aunt needs to know – her longing for what she has left in Edinburgh, versus her dread of rotting there with the other sad cases, umbilically tied to the greying town.

Stella gives a low laugh, holding her gaze. She's never interested in youthful traumas. 'Oh? A little Dick Whittington? And what are you going to do there?'

What should she tell her? There's no point trying to impress; Stella is famous for her sneer. She will see that, already, simply at the thought of London, Anna is helpless with anxious delight. 'I think I'll try to get a job in a bookshop. Then I'll see.'

'Well, that'll be fun,' says Stella, straightfaced. 'Do you know people to live with?'

'No, I don't – well, not for now. They're all going abroad, or going home. I'll just have to hang on.'

Stella shrugs and turns away. Anna's lost her; she was never her favourite, was a fool to believe the family lie. She watches her take another cigarette from the squashy pack in her breast pocket; a tendon twitches twice under the silk of her forearm.

'How're Mum and Dad? Did he see the specialist?' Stella asks. Anna's mother sighs, and begins to tell her how their father still has this cough, but gets irritable if you mention doctors, and their mother says he's impossible, and what is she, Magda, supposed to do? Given that no one else is helping? 'To them I'm still a girl.'

'Then I'm just a baby,' says Stella. Anna's mother's eyebrows lift. The cigarette is completely white, an airily poisonous tube. Maybe she will go indoors and Anna and her aunt can have a secret smoke at the end of the garden, in the shade. Except it's probably Algerian, and Stella will die laughing as her niece chokes on the fumes.

The conversation shifts again ('*Unbelievable*,' her mother will say. 'She has *absolutely no sense* of family responsibility'), and Stella begins to describe a recent run-in with the nation's second-favourite newscaster. The sun is sinking into the chestnut tree. Anna sits quietly at the table and starts picking at a leftover salad. A leaf of something curly and expensive uncoils unexpectedly, and slowly pings a drop of vinaigrette straight at Stella's shirt. Oh God, thinks Anna, then breathes again as it hits her aunt's pale brown hand. Stella looks up at the sky, then at her niece.

'Anna, be careful,' says her mother. 'Can't you see she's wearing linen?'

'It's fine. It didn't hit me,' says Stella. She grins at Anna, like a tiger after lunch. The back of her hand has an olive sheen. Anna wavers a smile back. She's been home for five minutes and already her composure is crumbling. She looks down; under the shrunken matelot T-shirt, her breasts are gargantuan. It's very hot even here in the shade. She is a red-faced grotesque nautical child.

Stella says, 'Do you want to come and live with me?'

Anna gasps, as if in pain. 'What – in Paris?' Phantoms of a possible future unfurl like streamers – browsing with Stella in angular designer shops, stirring couscous for dinner parties, walking in dappled light beside the Seine. The first flowers of Edinburgh nostalgia melt like wet ashes.

'Yes – I'll buy a bunk bed. No, idiot, I mean in London. You could stay in my flat in London.' She gives her sister a cursory smile. 'House-sit. I'm hardly ever there.'

Anna is crushed and reinflated in one airless breath. She looks from Stella to her mother.

'Well, I don't know,' her mother says. 'It's very kind of you. Isn't it, Anna?'

'Of course it is,' says Anna, which was not how she'd meant it to come out. 'I mean, thank you. Wow. That would be . . . amazing.' Her heart lifts, as if all the plants in the garden have collectively sighed their oxygen into her lungs. Stella's flat – staying in Stella's flat. The favourite's reward. 'I'd love to. Oh – can I?'

Now she sounds like a baby. After all, it isn't up to her mother, whose face is strangely clouded and thunderous. 'Shall I ring you to . . . discuss it?'

'You do that, Anna.'

She's never rung her aunt before. Somewhere to stay in London. Staying with Stella. Oh my God.

Two

Their last attempt at a family holiday is a mistake. Anna's father won't stop his heart-attack feasting, despite her policing of the cheeseboard. Her mother spends the fortnight reading *The Times* in the only comfortable cane chair, criticizing Anna's London plans, and smiling falsely at the neighbours. This is their sixth holiday in this house, and she still hasn't bothered to learn their names. Anna sits in her shuttered bedroom, plotting infantile revenge for her mother's every slight. She longs to ask her father to reign her mother in, but self-preservation has taught her to keep quiet. Talking to him about her mother is like complaining about a favourite to a Gothic overlord. He will listen, almost mildly, fingering the beard he shaved off twenty years ago, and make small concessions, acknowledge certain weaknesses. Then you push him too far, breach an ancient unreasonable law of chivalry and honour, and his sympathy retracts, swift as a sting. You fall from his grace like Lucifer.

After a night full of dark dreams of wide seas and angels, she wakes and remembers the unimaginable – it is the second of

September, and she is here, in London, at last. Her bedroom is full of light. She closes her eyes, trying to emboss her mind with this moment, and notices that her stomach is growling.

Fifteen minutes later, however, she finds she can't eat her makeshift breakfast. No exams, no heartbreak, but still she stares at her porridge like a nervy Goldilocks and cannot lift her spoon. Obviously it is the excitement. There is nothing to read; there is no music. She has nothing to do for the rest of her life. At this little table, waiting for the world to begin, she feels like Eliot's secretary, setting out food in tins. So she carries the bowl into the sitting room and sits at the end of the sofa, feet drawn up on the cushions, wrapped in an ugly brown kimono from the back of the bedroom door. Thin London light slithers through ancient glass and drenches the room.

Last night, as they drove here through a sudden rainstorm, Anna had watched her mother through half-closed eyes and imagined coming home when it all went wrong. The thought had turned her guts to vinegar. For two months she has oscillated between alarm – What if the flat is horrible? What if no one speaks to her again? – and jiggling excitement. She is going to the centre: the metropolis, the fount of life. Any existence is hers for the taking; there is no limit to what she could become.

Above the fireplace is a poster from a 1973 summer exhibition: *Steinberg – 'Immeubles' – Fondation Maeght.* Onion domes and spindly bridges crowd the frame like a map of Elysium, but no people, no place names, no clues.

When Stella's keys had arrived she'd torn apart the envelope looking for a note. There was only the Chubb and the Yale, and an old-fashioned tie-on parcel label saying *Have Fun.* What sort of fun did Stella want her to have?

Outside in the steaming street, a woman is shouting, 'Get off. Get off. Get *off*.' Anna vaguely wonders if she should move to a wobbling window and offer help. But what could she do, a girl, alone in London? Throw porridge? She moves one foot under her and sits on.

And last night, when she'd finished hauling her bags up the stairs, she'd begun to look for a proper note in the obvious places: the doormat, the chair in the little hallway, the tables, the stairs, her own room – nothing. Like wet feathers falling from a hot blue sky, disappointment settled over her elation as she climbed into bed. Looking up through darkness, the stars above the midnight ceiling gleaming just outside her vision, she snatched back the hand of friendship. Stella can be cruel; everyone knows that. If that's what she wants, she can be landlady only, kept at an efficient arm's length. It's better that way. Glittering grains of a brand-new hatred formed and gathered as she turned towards sleep; like salt, or sugar.

So, what had she expected? Without noticing she has begun to pick her heels, another of the habits she monthly swears to relinquish. She discovers a satisfying ridge of yellowed scurf and begins to prise it from the tight-packed whorls. It's too deep; she winces with the first tug, but goes on pulling. Too late to leave it now.

From what she has already seen, the flat is perfect; an absurdly harmonious adult space. She had visualized every possible permutation: a skylit cupboard where she will dye her hair and smoke, or a high-ceilinged suite of rooms on Piccadilly, in which to be languorously but thoroughly wooed. But this room – the tired lilac chaise-longue in the alcove, the knotty floorboards and huge aubergine rug, the walls the colour of ostrich eggs – is more welcoming, more indubitably right, than anything she could have imagined. Here, at last, she will come into her own; despite not knowing what to do now, and her friends' unhelpful absence. Despite, or perhaps because, as her father said last night in the wisteria dusk, waiting to wave goodbye, 'You know this is your home, though, don't you? You know you can always come home?'

Maybe it is this, the instant lava of emotion certain thoughts of her father always inspire, that is keeping her pinned here to the wine-coloured sofa. Graceful scrolls and curlicues of skin slide against her ankles. A tiny spring of blood outlines the three neat edges of the new wound on her heel.

Her feet wince on the kitchen tiles despite the swelling heat. Stella has painted the room an unexpected sky blue; it is bright but cold, an icicle lit by windows at both ends. As fragments of oaten jellyfish swirl above the plughole, she looks nervously round for a plunger. Her mother has left a carrier-bag of bleach and scourers, but Anna cannot ring for drainage tips and risk a housewifery course, or a visit.

A large Sabatier rests shark-like by the sink. She slides her finger down the heavy blade at the exact angle for testing sharpness. This one's a slicer. Her mind slips to grey stone, seeping oil in a warm basement. She could move one degree closer, but now is not the time. Still, it may be best to move away. She shuts the door behind her.

I am house-sitting, she tells herself. Stella's business is not my own. Nevertheless, she has Stella's Paris number, and there may be things her aunt should know. The answerphone, she discovered last night, is blacker, dustier and more immense than any she has ever seen, and far from self-explanatory. Now, in the interests of housekeeping, she glances at it again in passing, and to her horror sees an emerald light glowing discreetly beside the handset. Her mouth is dry; someone's thoughts have been here with her all this time. Tentatively she presses the largest button. An echoey male voice fills the vestibule.

'Stella, it's Richard. You probably think you've got rid of me, but I've been away – back last night. Don't know if you're in Paris or London, as you're not answering either, but give me a ring if you're around. You know I can't wait to see you.'

The light has gone out. He sounds like he's smiling.

What should she do to the tape? Clear it and risk losing ancient archives, or leave it full and useless? The instructions must be somewhere. She really ought to try to find them.

Who is this Richard, ringing while she lay asleep?

She dresses in clothes from the top of her suitcase: sailory trousers, a long-sleeved T-shirt, chosen at home for this, her first day. She brushes her teeth with hoarded French glittery toothpaste while standing at the open bathroom window, surveying roofs above the dimpled glass. She does not touch the medicine cabinet, the bottles by the bath, the plant with heart-shaped leaves trailing over the corner cupboard.

In the oval mirror behind the basin her face is startlingly pale. Freckles float just above the skin in a cloud of cinnamon.

The sun will ignite her hair in an attention-seeking fiery haze as she steps outside. When Stella comes back they might discuss this hair, how to deal with and enhance it, and could linger on the conspicuous fact that only they, of all known family members, have this dubious blessing.

The catch on the heavy door clicks behind her. She treads silently downstairs, past her unknown neighbours, and out into the glaring noise of the street.

She has furtively memorized her path to the Charing Cross Road in a sepia *A–Z* from her mother's bookshelf. But it isn't the same with the people, the shops, the roaring buses. She loses herself again and again. Eventually, with the help of three Danish tourists and an obviously deranged man who intercepts her on a zebra crossing, she heads in the right direction back down the Tottenham Court Road, past shockingly sub-legal shops full of mysterious hardware.

London is full of maniacs: Japanese girls in Lolita stockings and complicated hairstyles, tall men in tight *Tomorrow's World* textiles, women in television-screen glasses and pinstripe suits. Her eyes have become multi-faceted, hyper-receptive, like a fly's. Everything, even the pavement, drips and sweats in Technicolor. Her shins hurt from her mules, the sun blares against her corneas; she is untanned and shabby and uninteresting and everyone looks, then looks away. Her excitement is evaporating like ether in the heat. Perhaps it's job-hunt nerves: a sort of primitive focus. She imagines dramatically spearing a rabbit and has to bite her lip to avoid smiling like a lunatic, before remembering she isn't in Somerset. Here you can cry and laugh as much as you like, and no one will tell your mother.

Goggled cyclists dip through the crowds like arrogant piranhas. Two men with sleeping-bag boas approach and, feeling streetwise, Anna reaches back to grip her bag. However, before she can blink, or focus, something unseen empties her breath and slams her sideways. Am I shot? she thinks, as her knees smack concrete. Her ankle catches the kerb, and she almost falls in the path of her assailant, still pedalling, who screams 'Wanker' as he skids around her. Her kneecaps burning, she stumbles up and finds herself in the path of a taxi, horn blaring. Her mind freezes. The world stretches and goes slow. '*Move*' roars through the filthy air as the pavement rises to meet her, and a huge mudguard tears past her ear.

Her knee will not bend. Somehow she is leaning against a letterbox. She has survived, and people pass in a dirty stream, regardless. Anna gapes. They must have seen, surely. She is clearly the girl from the road, yet no one has paused, or spoken, or looked at her. They *must* have seen.

There is a grey gash in her trousers through which her knee blazes. What will she catch? I am alive, she notices. And, appallingly, crying.

In a café selling plastic-looking cakes and listless sandwiches, she buys a bottle of blood-warm water and sits facing away from the street. The fat man behind the counter keeps looking at her, so she can't look up, and the table is dirty so she can't look down. Her hands are shaking. There are no handsome artistic men to comment on her courage – although of course you can't trust any who smile at you in public places – or rumpled lady novelists looking for protégées. She dabs at her wound with a one-ply napkin to reveal, under the grime, a livid seeping graze. She needs, urgently, someone to save her. By rearranging the torn fabric her trousers' ruin is at least discreet, but the kneecap seems to have hardened; how will she walk back? The fat man smacks wet lips like a lecherous fish. She stands, clanging her chair into the nailed-down table, and hobbles through the yawning door.

The first bookshop Anna bravely enters sells coffee-table smut. She edges downstairs to find the real books, and emerges, dramatically, through a beaded curtain into a low-lit video underworld, sliced by racks of magazines. A slow second drops before she sees the defensive indignation on every turned male face, the pictures on the covers. At the same moment a pallid man with a crew-cut asks, 'Looking for something?'

She backs out through burning air to the clean street. Safer to stick with the chainstores. Cautiously, wiping unseen contaminants from her fingers, she approaches Waterstones on the wrong side of the street, like a heavy gazelle stalking a cheetah. After failing to absorb the window display, she limps into Fiction, looking alert in case she's been seen. Her father, who thinks two decades of bookshop signings have taught him the tricks of the trade, has already primed her:

'Simply march straight up to the front desk and ask for the manager.'

Naturally, she switches off when he gives her advice – a reflex which, in the wake of his inevitable and daily-dreaded coronary, she knows she will regret.

'Dad, I can't. Maybe I'd better write.'

'Remember what I did?' Of course she does. In the spondees reserved for telling her father he is being boring, she repeated: 'You Went Round To Mum's Flat Right Away And Said You'd Been Wrong And Asked Her To Marry You.' On this story of primal courtship, twenty-three years old this March, is based Frank Raine's creed of Seizing the Moment.

The trick of choosing the moment, however, still escapes

her. Waterstones is full of balmy air and silky alluring novels. Her trousers billow in the air-conditioning, damply outlining her thighs. She queues behind a blonde woman who keeps saying 'No, no, *alopecia*'. As she leaves, Anna smiles at the cold-sored assistant, who does not, or perhaps cannot, smile back.

'Can I have the manager please? Or manageress?'

The assistant bellows over her shoulder, 'Cath, there's . . . a person here.' People turn, children stop, paperbacks bend from the shelves to stare. The door lurches open, and a tall woman with a little-girl fringe leans back on her chair through the doorway.

'What?'

Anna walks as normally as possible up to the edge of the till and smiles, vigorously. 'Hello. I was wondering about a job.' At home she'd somehow imagined she'd enter and at once be spotted as the future of British bookselling. Now she suspects new complexities.

The woman surveys her like a last-chance foster-parent. 'Come in.'

Anna wavers to the door and steps in, leaving it ajar behind her.

'Shut it.'

'What? Oh, sorry.' She is blushing like a virgin from the provinces.

'Age?'

Her mind blanks. 'Twenty-one. Oh – no, sorry. Twenty-two. God.'

'Experience?'

'Of . . . bookselling? No, none at all.' Anna laughs like a mad girl; the blush begins to spread. She waves her hands to distract the woman from her ragged knees. 'I mean not really, not yet, but I'm very keen to get some. I just . . . *long* to work in a bookshop.' There are naked scaly stumps where the woman's fingernails should be. Should she accept a job from somebody so obviously uncontrolled?

'You long to?' Now the woman laughs. 'Why?'

Anna's pre-planned answer seems a little pat. She improvises: 'Well, you know, I love reading, and I'm quite . . . informed, and I suppose passionate, about books, and I feel, you see—' (she looks brightly at the manageress, who does not blink) '—ttthat I have a lot to offer in . . . well, encouraging people to read. I *am* good with pe—'

Perhaps they're looking for honest brownish-redheads. Perhaps not. The manageress turns to the door, then looks again at Anna. 'Look. You're hardly what we're looking for. I can't imagine what . . . You need experience to work in a busy store like this.'

'Oh. Sorry.' The windowless room closes around her. She grasps the warm metal door handle. 'Thank you.'

Behind her the woman is still speaking, but Anna turns her back and strides stiffly through the shop, head if not exactly high, then forward, as if she's used to this. The swarming street outside is a sticky mess of noise and sun and immobile chattering tourists.

She needs someone to tell, who will insist that she was better than she fears. As she attempts to cross the road her mind, almost shiftily, reverts to the man on the answerphone. He can't be Stella's boyfriend, because surely he'd know she's away. But he sounded too charming to be a friend. Maybe he's an *occasional lover*. The thought sends a chemical wave surging through her heart. An occasional lover was what they'd always dreamed of at school, spinning heavenly lives as they lay on their backs on the hockey pitch. A man for passion who wouldn't stifle, ideal until they met The One. Then would begin the serious business – novel-writing at kitchen tables, feathery marital beds, a garden full of plum-trees and interesting children.

Would her aunt have an occasional lover? She'd be bound to – probably more than one. Maybe this Richard is just a beginner, trapped near the base of Stella's doubtlessly complex romantic pyramid. But he had sounded confident, a man who knows he's high on her list. His voice – low, warm, intimate – is the Platonic ideal of lovers' voices, unknown but recognizable from the place where souls are forged and fissured. If he isn't Stella's lover he certainly wants to be.

It is only when she has filigreed the water label in her pocket that Anna faces her recent employment failure. She did everything wrong. Somehow she must learn, quickly, perfection.

How do others manage? How had editors and agents seen that behind her father's gloriously tattered jumper, and the seventies revolutionary moustache, was the future king of Dark Ages detective fiction? And Stella – how did her mother's little sister become someone whose documentaries are shown on television? Even her mother's a credible adult, although in her case it's mostly a question of being imperious and knowing about Roquefort. That won't help Anna now.

As she stands in the middle of the street, waiting for a gap in the enormous traffic, Anna wonders if her father would say 'Don't be defeatist', or 'Don't hope for too much'. She excels at both. Three laughing men in a white van are waving at her to cross. Should she snarl or smile? Her smile comes out as a snarl; the worst of all possible outcomes.

The other side of the road is paradise and hell combined. There she finds everything and nothing: no Tampax, or plasters for her knees, but all the nipple-attachments and neoprene record bags and teriyaki and absinthe she could ever need. The streets are thick with tired women and pierced men and sexless tourists. Another corner, past a theatre – a fire station, a Chinese herbalist, and she's completely lost. She turns slowly in the street. This is a new world.

She rounds an unfamiliar theatre, showing a musical about Napoleon, and finds herself back where she started, but opposite a huge BOOKS *etc.* – a London-only culture emporium, nothing like demure James Thin's. She tries to feel cautious, but knows it is a sign. However strongly she feigns indifference, her haruspex precedes her everywhere, scanning the sky for omens.

This time the front desk is at the side, the manager sniffs derisively at everything she says, and they are only recruiting in IT. Hoping to catch Fate offguard she asks directions to Blackwells, but they have nothing until December, and she has forgotten her telephone number, which does not impress.

Three

Objectively, this has been one of the most unsuccessful days of her life. Usually she can outwit failure: she scents it even before it arrives. After one of many anxious late-night conversations with his troubled ten-year-old, her father had memorably announced, like a doctor giving a last prognosis, that Anna was her own worst critic. The scrupulousness, the garrety ascetic perfectionism that implied had made her secretly proud. But today has confirmed failings she hadn't dared imagined.

There was Luke, of course, but that was love, and love is different. When they fell apart, four terms into the beginning of something, Anna had wept into her Alpen and known she was unwantable. But as the bruises round her heart had healed she'd begun to remember: how she had looked in vain for signs of courage; how his solidness had numbed like frostbite; how he had revealed, like Salome, a hidden talent for deceit.

And at least that had been nothing to do with her brain. This, however, must be. If only they'd give guidelines, she thinks, as she retraces her muddled steps. Anna has always paid attention to survival techniques. If pursued by a crocodile one should run in zigzags. Urine is a disinfectant. A mirror may be used to attract passing aeroplanes, and probably also crocodiles. Eye to eye with an alligator, or losing limbs to gangrene, these lifesaving tips may slip her mind, but at least they're in there. How is it then that with sixteen years of education, and dedicated background reading, she can't seem to manage urban life?

Now what is she to do? Where is the manager who will hire her? The only other bookshops she has seen today are the kind she and her friends used to stand outside and laugh at. *101 Mediterranean Pelmets*, *The Art of the Catamaran*: what made her think she was immune?

She reaches a Greek bank and wonders, fleetingly, if she should move her account there for friendly cashiers and plate-throwing parties. Someone is being sick against a poster. Everyone she passes looks hostile, tragic or deluded. I want salad days, she thinks, whatever they are.

When she arrives back at the flat nearly an hour later, wondering if she should buy a compass, a light is winking on the answerphone. There is a blister just below the ball of her foot, her knees are shrieking, and she needs the lavatory. Almost too late she hobbles upstairs to the bathroom and hunches, panting faintly, over the loo as she lets loose an enormous piss-stream, like a horse. She washes London grey from her hands very slowly, listening to the water noisily refilling the tank, and speculates about the message.

At Edinburgh, it seems, she was always running like a hounded heroine, through toast-smoke and disoriented survivors, towards the telephone to discuss that evening's plans. Now, however, her list of possible callers is humiliatingly short. It's probably her father, calling from his madman's study with a brief chin-up nose-to-the-grindstone message of courage in adversity, like you'd send to the troops just before Passchendaele.

She pads silently back downstairs, as if trying to catch the answerphone offguard, with a premonition that it is Stella, offering encouragement and hope. Cautiously she approaches the huge machine. Her finger leaves a circle in the dust.

'Darling [her heart leaps briefly, then stills again], it's your mother. I hope you made progress. Have you rung Andrea Lefschitz? Or your uncle? You're expected to see him, Anna; I'm not telling my mother you weren't in the mood. Anyway, Dad says don't forget: be firm but polite, and Sasha says "hang in there, sis." That's it . . . bye, darling.'

That's it? What about 'we miss you'? She hunts in the kitchen for a cup. The cold tap makes extraordinary clunking noises; what damage can she have caused in half a day? Gently knocking the fronts of her thighs against a cupboard she looks out into the street, sipping cloudy summer water. Opposite is an identical terrace of tall black brick houses – Georgian, if that means flat with interesting windows. Compared to the gentle crescents of her childhood, Bloomsbury is an elegant prison. She takes another mouthful of tepid water and slops it around and over her tongue, sliding silk against roughness. It's past five. Where has she spent all those hours?

And then her mother's message catches at a limp and sunburned dendrite: Andrea Lefschitz. Andrea Lefschitz is Anna's mother's most horrible friend. And now she has some terrible idea that Andrea, who apparently spends most of her time ('and can you blame her?') in her self-architectured London flat, could take Anna out.

'But *where*?' Anna had asked. 'Am I supposed to ring her up? Oh God, did you actually say I would? That is *so embarrassing*.'

'Honestly, Anna, you'd think I'd asked the Russian ambassador. I just said Andrea darling, could Anna call you when she's in London?'

'Oh *no*.' Now it sounds as if Anna asked her to ask. 'Do I have to? What would we do, anyway? Go drinking? Look around her Armani archives? I don't think so.'

'Jesus, Anna. I'm just trying to help – it's not as if you have friends in London, after all. I thought you might *like* to see mine. You'll be grateful for them, you know, when you've no one to talk to but Stella's bloody collection of African pottery.'

And now it is beginning. Andrea Lefschitz is just the first and worst of a long list of social engagements, which her mother expects her to work through, gratefully. Is every sodding phone call going to be like this, Anna wonders, beginning to tug at the frayed cuticles of her left thumb. Hasn't she noticed I've escaped?

Her mother's prickliness taints the flat's new air. She should have known she'd never escape it; it has followed her here, with the other silent certainties Magda's daughters take for granted.

These include:

1) *Mornings.* Never speak before nine, unless bearing tea. Anna cannot imagine how mornings had been when she and her sister were young, insisting on Dairylea, peeing in supermarkets, puking posset on their mother's bony shoulder. Would she have snapped before they learnt how quickly her moods could change? After all, as Anna occasionally reminds herself, her mother isn't mad, or cruel, or nasty. She's just difficult.

2) *Aspersions.* Do not cast them. On how much she's just spent on 'timeless' suede court shoes, on the beauty of her latest espresso machine, or the source of the spectacular mille-feuille at one of her 'little dinners'. She does not believe in domestic glasnost. Toe the party line.

3) *Apologies.* Do not expect them. Her legal code is fixed and far from lenient. If she errs, it is within her divine right as a mother to do so. Anna's grandmother Ava is Russian, and the female line is formidable. Anna suspects the Visigoths could have learnt a thing or two from her mother's family. She has not yet dared to ask her father about miscegenation between Northern Europe and the Volga, but every now and again makes daring references to Cossack hordes and the blood of Christian babies. Depending on her mood, as most things do, Anna's mother either laughs tolerantly, which always encourages Anna to go too far, or chooses not to, and frost appears on the inside of the windows.

4) *Arguments.* You're on your own. In intergenerational fights the parents always side with each other, although it's usually their father who has to show his colours. When Anna rows with Sasha, the parents have a policy

of non-intervention, like the UN. It's about as effective; their skirmishes are just as vicious, the battlefields razed and sown with mines. When they were younger the conflicts were far bloodier, and appeals for mediation were always rebuffed. 'Life isn't fair,' their mother would announce, retreating from the gory sawdust like a sated Caesar. Anna would retire to her room in a voodoo fury to brood on the malefactions of her brazen and amoral sister.

5) *Secrets.* They do not exist. Those that do are Magda's field. She locks them tightly, but cannot quite resist leaving a trail of aniseed.

There is no one to phone. The sitting room does not suggest television. Anna, who reads while cleaning her teeth, has never felt less literate. Sidling over to the stereo, ready for ironic dancing to Fleetwood Mac or some self-improvement with Moroccan lute-playing, she sees a terse notice taped to the front: BROKEN. DO NOT USE. Trust Stella not to have bothered to fix it. Now what is she meant to do?

Last night, looking for the lavatory, she had opened the wrong door. In the snap of light she caught bookshelves and straw-coloured walls, then a huge bed: Stella's room. The door banged shut as she raced back across the hallway. Behind her Stella's room hummed with life.

She has already uncovered dried pasta and a jar of sauce; her French had failed her at the crucial word, but she'd watched it for a full minute and nothing had seemed to be moving. It is labelled 'Auriole'. As she wanders vaguely around her new bedroom, like a failing creature treading water, she touches the dusty edges of picture frames and paperback spines' decaying bark, chanting 'Auriole': a hopeless charm.

Everything sounds better in French. If only she *was* French, for the savoir faire, and the accent, and the mastery of face-packs. Stella could be French quite easily. Just looking at her aunt, just being here, it is obvious that at no point has she ever not known what to buy, what to say, whatever makes one an adult other adults admire.

You sound like a child, she warns herself.

There was a time when Anna would have given her life for an hour alone in this flat; looking for clues. Somewhere in those shady and private rooms, she had been sure, would be the bracelet, the novel, the type of cereal which would give her the knack of womanhood. She had believed the hype of children's stories. How could there not be a jewel granting utter desirability, a book of knowledge, a food which would make this horribly plain child, gobbling rather greedily, everything a girl should be? Even now, despite the interim, a part of her still cannot believe there is no secret key.

'It's Richard; Richard Spence. Is Stella there?'

Is her 'Hello?' so unlike her aunt's? She decides not to spare his shame. 'Oh, yes, hi. You rang just yesterday?' Stella can't know many Richards, after all. They'll be outnumbered by Raouls and Claude-Augustes.

'I did.'

'Well, she's . . . away.'

Should she elucidate? If he knows Stella so well, why is she ignoring his calls? He might be a troublesome ex, or a stalker. She imagines the consequences of helping him; his quietly thrilling voice on a Paris intercom, and then the family, standing in a cemetery around Stella's grave, baleful looks and dark glasses, her mother's silent fury.

'Away? Is she now?'

Anna pauses, hearing his smile; his white teeth. How can she sound alert yet vague; off-putting yet inviting confidences? Maybe he'll entrust her with the secret burden of his passion, and she can help him pursue and win her aunt. 'Yes, she is, actually.'

'When's she back, do you know?'

His motives are clearly either murder, or romance. What would Stella want her to do? 'I don't know. I'm not sure. Not for a while, I think.'

'And you are?'

He'll laugh at 'niece'. She can't say 'friend'. 'I'm . . . a relative. Anna.'

'Oh, are you indeed? That's a subject Stella likes to keep coy about.'

'Oh. Really?'

'Don't you want to know who I am?'

Is he flirting with her? In a microsecond her brain has split in two, both outcomes projected with telefilm clarity in the bone-white space behind her eyes; either the fending-off of his Lothario embrace, or Stella's admiring fury when she hears of their romance.

'OK then, tell me. Who are you?'

'I'm a friend of Stella's – although not quite good enough to speak to her in person. Or perhaps too good . . .'

There is an inviting silence. Anna makes an involuntary whimper of indecision, and he laughs.

'Don't worry, cousin Ann . . . Anna, I'm not going to break your sacred family bond. Look, if she calls could you just mention that I rang?'

'Fine. Yes.'

'Thanks. How's the flat?'

'It's . . .' She peeps through the sitting-room door. 'Probably the same as last time you were here,' she says, cleverly. 'Unless she's redecorated. When *were* you last here?'

'A lifetime ago. Is it still zebra-print with mustard shagpile?'

'Yes. And, um, sharkskin barstools.'

'And hessian in the kitchen?'

'Mmm,' says Anna delightedly. She loves London; how easy this is. 'That wonderful Ryvita-plated look.'

'She is my style guru. Anyway, I expect we'll speak again.'

'Yes. I expect we will.'

Keeping quiet, as Richard said, is something Anna's family know all about. How else but under a mute asbestos layer could Anna have achieved such dangerous self-containment? On easy subjects their articulacy is notorious. WASP outsiders, once assimilated, entertain with stories of initial shock at the family's noise levels. But sex is rarely alluded to. Death, never. And pain is private, voiceless, tightly bandaged.

Only this summer Anna, hoping to have reached the age for confidences, had tried to draw her mother out. They had been reading the papers, calmly. Monitoring the air for friction, Anna had decided to chance it.

She lowered the colour supplement, furtively trying to pluck and smooth its creases. Her mother looked up and caught her identical eye.

'?'

'Mum . . .' Her mother is definitely oversensitive about

Stella. She zips away from every enquiry like a fleeing submarine. It makes it impossible to ask casual questions; every one is lobbed back, laden with guilt and thunderclouds. Is this reticence due to dislike, or her passion for privacy? If dislike, why? And whose privacy?

'I was just wondering . . . you know, in case I put my foot in it . . . is there anything I don't . . . that I should know, about Stella?'

'Stella who?'

'Oh, come on. Your sister.'

Her mother exhaled steadily, a paradigm of maternal self-control. 'Oh, *that* Stella. I thought you meant someone in the paper. Have you got the colour section? I need to see where Nigel buys his rolling pins.'

It's easy to forget about her mother's little shop; her references to it always seem to be calculated for effect. Only when talking to her own parents does she ever play it down. Anna once mentioned this to her sister, who rolled her eyes and said, 'What do you expect? They've slogged for fifty years in their own minuscule shop. Mum's pisses on them.' Since then Anna has been her grandparents' defender, scorning her mother's toy on their behalf, even as they claim to be proud. But now Anna realized that an Algerian tea-jug or professional-thickness milk-pan, casually left on Stella's table, might impress far more than student Tefal. 'Incidentally . . . I don't suppose the shop has any spare – well, household items you'd like to donate to Stella's flat?'

'I doubt it. Ask Fenella.'

But Fenella and the assistants never bother to be polite to the owner's daughter, and Anna will not beg. 'I might.'

'The colour section?'

'Oh – sorry. Here, have it. Well?' she asks.

'Well what? I wasn't listening.'

'You know. Stella. Like has she had a secret baby? Or is she a spy, or something?'

Anna felt clever. Hidden infants and the secret service are exactly what she had concluded her mother is trying to hide.

Icicles pierced the space between them. 'Don't be ri*dic*ulous.' As if already scanning her past life from her Bloomsbury eyrie, Anna now noticed, more strongly than ever before, a feature of her mother. Despite the English schools of her youth, she has somehow absorbed some of her own parents' deeply foreign inflections. Now there was a fiercer note in the air, the frosty intolerance of a race of fur-lined horseback women.

'I'm not being ridiculous,' said Anna, taking care to keep the italics out of her voice. 'I just meant, you know—'

'What, Anna?' said her mother, picking up the Travel section. Her quills rattle as she moves; unlike Stella, who uncurls like smoke. 'What is it you wish me to report about my sister? What you don't know is her business. Why do you always have to unravel everything?'

A chill Baltic wind swirled round their ankles. 'I *don't*,' said Anna in a small cross voice. Now it was obvious that she should.

Here, like a Regency surgeon before his first cadaver, she has a chance to prove some theories.

So why isn't she roaming free, pawing open drawers, dissecting evidence heaped on tables? Anna is a mistress of self-persuasion. She has learnt to justify most things if they will make her feel better – any food, any guilt-allaying ritual, any private torture. This urge to explore, however, is unexpectedly strong; too strong, she senses, to indulge. She will not tear around harvesting information, glutting herself on grown-up life. This is only a flat, after all; and Stella is ordinary. There is no need for Anna to be this peculiar stranger: so fascinated, so anxious, so uncontrolled.

But excitement, like itching powder, pulls at her skin. Hard as she tries to stay immune, the cupboards and shelves still call to her. Who knows what she may discover here? Stella will forgive a little reconnaissance. She will take her pleasure – slowly.

Four

Anna decides to go to bed early, like a self-governing infant. The spaghetti has boiled to a glaireous mess, like the entrails of sea-creatures. And she had tried eating it to a programme about orphan abuse in Cardiff, the possible moral benefits tainted by her hopes of impressing someone with her courage. She frets at her solipsism as a weeping child actor is attacked with boots and belts.

Before she gives up and goes to her room, however, there is something she must do. Like Pandora, blooding her fingers with the smell of iron as she peeks into darkness, Anna returns to the kitchen.

Once, when they were walking through Selfridges' China and Glass department, trying not to elbow shelves of decanters and cut-glass hedgehogs, her mother had remarked, 'We'll get Stella's present from here. If for once she can bear not to eat off antiques.'

'*Does* she?' Anna had breathed, visualizing swollen cushions, faded silk screens, ancient crazed porcelain in gold leaf, rose and pistachio.

'Not literally,' her mother snapped. 'Most of it is rubbish. She just thinks it's smart if nothing looks the same.'

Anna had vowed that when she became old enough to have her own plates, they would be mismatched perfection, each more ornate and covetable than the last. Now, in Stella's kitchen, she begins to realize how much she had taken for granted. Instead of piles of random china, two decades of junk shops, souks and the Galleries Lafayette, everything is plain, and co-ordinating, and very very clean. It's as if Stella bought a Habitat newlyweds' kitchen set. She looks through the drawers for an answerphone manual, in case she has to erase, or retrieve, but her aunt must have tamed the machine long ago. There are only unremarkable tangles of spatulas, orphaned corks and nameless metal objects. Why has Stella purged this kitchen? Her rented Parisian attic must be piled with possessions that matter, like a shrine.

Anna's bedroom is full of night, even with the velvety curtains open. She feels up and down the wrong side of the doorway, like a blind girl, until she finds the light switch, wondering how long she can delay ringing her uncle. Her bags are still piled in the middle of the carpet: clothes smelling of home, novels she hasn't had time to read. John Cheever, *Anna Karenina*; she takes the crumbling paperbacks out of their box reluctantly, and piles them in the corner at the foot of her bed. In this warm new room, distant stories of martini-clinking golf widows and ballroom politics have lost their appeal. Maybe she should look closer to home: Flaubert, or Lawrence of Arabia.

Perhaps she will feel more settled when her room is colonized. She unpacks slowly, filling a chest of drawers and a narrow wardrobe with cotton and corduroy, denim and wool. Almost everything she has brought falls into three discrete categories:

A: Clothes she likes wearing. All without exception dark as winter, frayed at seams and cuffs, worn to peachskin with a silver bloom.

B: Clothes she can bear to wear. These are her summer wardrobe: floppy trousers, long-sleeved T-shirts, narrow skirts. They are hot, of course, and inappropriate for the dawn of adulthood, but what else can she wear? People would stare.

C: Clothes she has brought anyway – clothes for a future life. These are mostly inherited from her mother: heavy silk shirts, black shiny trousers, a long midnight jacket with a rose-petal lining.

'Mum,' she had said, as her mother passed her the jacket a fortnight, a lifetime ago.

Anna's mother looked up. 'What now? Anna, I'm giving you these. Not making you take them. Try not to whinge.'

'I'm not whinging. I'm not. But you know I can't wear navy. It looks disgusting with my hair.'

The cellophane crackled like thin ice. 'Whatever I give you,' her mother said, shutting the door to her monumental wardrobe, 'is never good enough. It's always too small, or too *middle-aged*, or clashes with your bloody hair. You're *not* fat, you're *not* a child, and you're certainly *not* making the best of that hair, as I'm sick of telling you. Most people would kill for your colour. You don't deserve it if you won't flaunt it.'

Anna scowled, and took the jacket, and knew she had a point. Seven years ago she was begging hairdressers to shear it off, leaving her dizzy with cold-eared relief. Age and Luke and her mother's insistence that her hair is a national resource have started to change her; the muddy-copper waves are nape-length, and growing.

The clothes in Category C are for being exotic in at parties, or striding through her offices at *Vogue*, or idling, poised but relaxed among the japonica of astonishing villas, slowly swinging a linen calf against the side of a hammock. They're for a glamorous version of her mother; expensive, creaseless, polished, yet exciting. When she looks at those sleek skirts and blouses, she longs for that unimaginable future when, soignée in costly adult garments, she floats between dinner tables and twilit gardens, pursued by the men of her dreams.

Anna's uncle does not figure in this picture. Her future should be unimpaired by family obligation. However, hard as she tries to crowd it out, her mother's warning has been picking at the quiet. In an unaccustomed burst of family feeling, she now picks up the phone to her uncle, and suddenly feels vaguely obscene. Her steaming limbs are draped in Stella's roughened and frosted navy towels, and phoning in towels is dangerous. It makes you bold. She made a cartoon face of horror, for her sister's absent benefit.

As a brotherless girls'-school early teen, she had often fantasized about handsome, moustachioed and very gentle friends of her uncle, marooned in Bath due to diplomatic crises, or a curious desire to visit Markus's lovely niece. Markus had unknowingly been touched with matchmaker's glory; he would help her find her saviour from virginity. However, as her adolescence had progressed, it became clear that his had not; that instead he was retreating behind an increasingly impenetrable phalanx of twitches, verbal tics and personal grooming failures. She has somehow failed to see him once in four full years of university, and in that time, she fears, he has been growing odder.

Then, in the last weeks before London, she decided to ask about her uncle. It was better to do it now, here, face to face. She would need to watch for veils and shadows, for the displacement around whatever was unsaid. Somehow, however, the time was never right. In the end, her mother had mentioned him.

Anna's suitcases lay half-packed two floors above. They had been shopping, harmoniously: Anna had found a parking space, her mother bought her a bra, four books and two pairs of silver earrings, they had done trolley-dancing in the aisles of Marks & Spencer, and now were unpacking the endless carrier-bags, impeded by Anna's father who had drifted downstairs and was forgetting where to put onions.

'Is this jumper for me?' he had asked, his distaste touchingly ill-concealed.

'Hardly, darling,' Anna's mother said, cheerfully. Her mood, Anna suddenly noticed, had been improving daily. 'It's for Markus's birthday. Would I buy you such a wholemeal thing? I thought Anna could take it to him when she gets to London.'

Anna's hand conspicuously froze as she passed her father a bag of almonds.

'*I* could?'

Her mother turned. Her father's eyes were coded.

'Nothing,' Anna said, ever the problem child, endlessly breaching the feudal forcefield which hums around her parents. Her mother grabbed her pile of tights off the kitchen table and, stepping over the shopping, slammed upstairs. The door clicked behind her.

'What?'

Her father seemed about to be angry. If he shouts now, thought Anna, that's it. I'm going up to my room and I may never come down. She tried to look as tearful as she felt.

He relented with pitiful speed. 'Oh, I don't know. You know she's funny about Markus. I think she thinks . . . Oh, never mind.'

'*What?* You can't leave it like that.'

'Well, there was a patch last year, when you weren't home much—' Anna looked away, 'when your mother decided that Markus was schizophrenic.'

'God.' Anna is a child of the nineties. Loonies have haunted station platforms as long as she can remember. At the first dishevelled mutter she knows to double back, keep out of line. Now she imagined her uncle hearing voices, and what they might tell him to do.

Her father would know how bad it is. He, however, was looking unimpressed. 'He hasn't got rabies, Anna.'

He is far too low-key to know when to panic. 'But Dad, he might be . . . difficult to approach. Volatile.'

'He won't be. And he's your uncle, so visit him. Anyway, it turns out that he isn't schizophrenic after all. He's just . . . a bit off-kilter.'

What does one wear to ring a probably not dangerous but neglected uncle? Anna surveys the chest of drawers, and notices another category: faded scoop-neck tops, cotton trousers, plimsolls. They are clothes to accessorize with nonchalant smudges; clothes for light manual labour which ends in bed. She unearths a huge red T-shirt and reaches for the telephone.

Expecting it to ring unheard among dusty crates of paper,

she sits down to wait. A voice answers almost instantly; Anna scrabbles to her feet.

'Oh, hi . . . Markus?' She sounds breathless. He might think she's an obscene caller.

'Yes?' The voice is unrecognizably normal: a carer, come to make sure he isn't choking on his tongue, or a psychiatric nurse, looking for danger signs in butterfly blotches.

'Is Markus there?' she asks dubiously. Maybe she's too late.

'Anna, it *is* Markus.'

She laughs nervously. 'Oh, yes, Markus. Silly me.' Maybe she's antagonized him. 'I think we might have a bad line.'

'Oh, no, it's me,' he says cheerfully. Self-knowledge, thinks Anna; must be a good sign. 'You've caught me in the middle of a Liquorice Allsort.'

Anna almost sighs with relief. 'Are you well?' She tries to keep her voice cheerful. No sudden movements.

'Yes, yes, very well. Very well. Now, how's Magda?'

This is the last thing to discuss with Markus. How could she begin to describe the peaks and trenches of their pained ambivalence with a man – worse, her mother's brother – who for all she knows is unfit to buy a newspaper? 'Mum's – you know, same as ever. Anyway—'

'Well, well, yes. Now, come over? Would you like to come over? Your mum said you're going it alone so would I rally. Say, Tuesday, dinner? About seven? Marvellous. Bye then.'

What will his flat be like? What will they talk about? Oh God, what will he expect her to eat? 'Markus?'

The line is silent.

Anna undresses in semi-darkness, behind half-closed curtains. Her room is a baking velvet womb. She tries lying under the duvet but in seconds she senses her sweat is seeping through Stella's cotton and on to the mattress. Without a barrier between her and the air, however, she will not be able to sleep. She arranges a frill of duvet over her back and side, and lies on the concertinaed sheet listening to herself gasping: a self-conscious whale with wilting fins. The duvet flops on her curves like a huge tropical cloud in a bag. Hot night lies on her skin like oil. Turning over, turning again, she listens to the huge sounds beyond the quiet street and waits for air, or sleep.

An hour later she is still waiting. She has also begun to realize what she's done. She hasn't found a job and doesn't know how to. Stella has left no word saying when she'll be back in England, and she can't face Andrea Lefschitz just yet, not to mention Markus. There's no one else she can go and see. Panic rises off her body like fumes.

Sleep has become unimaginable. She should read. But her books seem dead and childish now, and those Stella has left here – green Margery Allinghams, dove-grey Evelyn Waughs – will not lull this crowding panic. Desperate for entertainment, she weakly climbs out of bed and fetches her new address book from the floor. A month ago it had seemed a good idea to prune its predecessor, casting off the fallings-out, allies lost to academe, drugs or accountancy, exes of friends and friends of exes. Considering how few of *those* there are, it's amazing how many crossed-out names are casualties of romance. Or lust, or whatever designates all that emotion and fumy single-bed sex with Luke. Their closeness before it began, and the nastiness of the fall, has wiped out legions, like typhoid. Her mind flits to him like a disobedient child; she jerks it away.

She can't uncross those names, not now. She tries to

imagine knocking on doors in Bruntsfield or Newington, or Edinburgh's other soot-soured back streets. She would have to say: 'You know how I dropped you because I fell for my dream boy who wasn't? Will you have me back if I promise it's forgotten?'

Slowly turning the pages of her optimistically large address book, hoping for just one name to kick-start her spangled social future, the uncomfortable truth looms nearer. In an inexplicable fit of optimism she has abandoned hilarity, debauchery and the possibility of romance for silence, clean living and pathetic need.

She has two remaining options out of the ten million here: Luke's shy brother's shyer ex-girlfriend, and Nicola Zveig, an unpopular acquaintance. But even Nicola has been flatsharing with a friend of half of BritPop since July, and heart-to-hearts are impeded by her growing friendship with Patsy Kensit.

As she lets the waxy pages fall, uncontactable faces materialize before her, infecting the London air with former failings. She stares at the final blank leaf for some time. There's no point beginning again; no marmoreal society hostess, holding out a fan of invitations, is going to emerge from the whiteness. Only when a plug of tiredness begins to form between her eyes does she shift, and remember herself. She kicks the address book off the duvet, buckling its corner against the clawed foot of the chest of drawers. Her limbs are heavy in an aureole of heat, incandescent in the apricot haze. She moves her hands slowly down her shining body, jolting her mind away every time it hooks on Luke.

At two or three in the morning she wakes with a knee-jerk shock. Somewhere in her dreams she has heard a noise. She lies flat on her back, eyes staring blindly into the teeming blackness. Her mouth has fallen open. She breathes silently, feeling her stomach press and fall against the crush of duvet. Her ears strain against distant sirens.

What was it she heard?

She is entirely, unequivocally, alone. No shouting now could save her. Brick and plaster separates the houses; this carpet will hush her cries. No one in the street would stop. In London everybody screams.

The stillness thickens. Stop it, she tells herself. This is ridiculous. You are not eight years old at midnight, waiting for the dropping-down of unspecified horrors. You are too old to be scared of the dark.

But this isn't just infantile fear. Her body holds the echo of a sound.

It is too dark to see a lock. Was there a phone by the bed in Stella's room? Should she run in, stiff-kneed, and try to find it? Or should she follow the shadows down the staircase, praying not to meet him – or them – half-way up. And what could she do anyway, without a gun? They could snatch away a knife, press a callused hand against her pleas . . .

She waits in the roaring silence, braced for another noise. There is nothing until she begins to turn on to her side to face the door; then, disbelieving, she hears a distant click.

This is it. Something terrible is about to happen. But how can she not know what to do? How is it that two decades of parents and teachers have failed to tell her how to save her life? Anna has many fears; one of the worst is about to come true.

They will not catch her in her bed. If she creeps to the top of the stairs and sees a sliding shape, a glint of metal, she could make a dash for Stella's room, barricade the door with heavy furniture and ring the police. Or throw open the windows and yell for help. Or something.

As noiselessly as she can manage, every twitch and rustle like a radar signal in the night, she eases herself minutely off the clinging sheets. She has no idea where the floor squeaks; she touches heels, then soles, then toes to the carpet, slides her bottom off the bed and remembers she is naked. The kimono hangs on the door like a lurking ghoul. She'll probably set one foot on the stairs, fall over the hem and land in the feet of the laughing intruders. Hitching it up around her ankles, she stands for a moment, hand on the doorknob, waiting. Are they listening to her listening, just outside? She stretches her neck, ear practically against the wood, deaf beyond the sound of her breathing. Holding it in for a second, she thinks she senses movement. If she stands here any longer she will have a seizure, and then they might as well come in. She pulls the door wide.

The hallway is empty; there is no light or movement at the foot of the stairs. Foot poised above the top stair like a gun-dog, she cranes into the dark, eyes and ears pushing against stillness. No sound. Unconvinced, she stays a minute longer, arm stretched towards Stella's door for silent flight. There really is nothing there. But she will not be able to sleep until she knows.

Step by trembling step, she begins to creep downstairs. As she approaches the vestibule, eyes enormous, mouth a dry O, breathing imperceptibly as though by osmosis, her ears, tuned to the frequency of crashing horror, fail for a second to detect a smaller sound. Then her heart gives a sudden sickened bounce. There is fizzing in the tangled blackness.

Comic-strip bombs, fuses sparkling, materialize before her sightless eyes. Then, clearly in the drumming night, she hears a click: the sound of a safety catch.

Anna has never seen a gun. She inhales, horribly loudly. Is it too late to run back up? As she turns her head longingly towards the stairs she sees a tiny emerald floating beside her thighs. At the same moment, she hears another click.

Oh thank God. It is the answerphone.

Relief surges through her rigid flesh like water. Oh thank you, thank you God, you lovely lovely man. If she had a crucifix now she would kiss it, no matter what her grandmother would say.

She fumbles the wall for a switch. That ugly squatting machine has saved her. Blinking, blinded in the fierce gold light, half asleep, heart sprinting, she caresses the button with a trembling finger. At the same moment a horrible realization catches her mid-beat.

No one rings her in the middle of the night.

The machine clicks once again. There is a brief, noisy pause, then nothing.

She stares at it, incredulous, willing it to lurch into sympathetic life. With damp fingers she prods 1471, but retrieves only an echoey announcement.

'Why?' she asks. 'Why *don't* you have the caller's number?' What sort of telephone doesn't record? Old panic ices her back and chest. Confused by light, sleep-thickened, she stares dully at the machine, then grinds back upstairs to bed. She will decide what to do tomorrow.

*

The next morning Anna wakes late. There is something odd about the quiet. She lies still, a pouring shaft of mote-filled light pinioning her to the bed like an alien abductee, listening to the absence of bells. Fleecy threads of her dream disappear as she tries to catch them; a forest, and an alarm. Suddenly she knows she heard the telephone. Lurching out of bed she rips the kimono off the hook and races downstairs towards the answerphone, despite the silence. But the black machine squats like an immense malevolent toad on its little table: no inviting lights, no messages or retrievable number, no sign of life.

When at last she emerges from the house, flushed and overheated after several abortive wardrobe crises, the sun is blazing hot and high over the looming buildings. She finds a chrome sandwich shop and perches high on a stool to eat an unaffordable salad-box and a yoghurt full of grains like weevils. The crowds seem even more glutinous and dogged than before; it's only Thursday, but already there's a weekending drive in the air. How will she survive it here alone?

At university it was easy: at every cobbled or stained concrete turn you met friends of friends, neighbours, enemies. They were inescapable, even when she was heartsick and dangerous, needing isolation. London's strangeness is like a disease: she's dazed with it, her resistance ebbing. Swimming alone through the noise, her ears reverberate with booming silence.

She tramps up and down Charing Cross Road a second time, trying to find appealing-looking bookshops in which to be well-paid and air-conditioned. Eventually she decides on four and, despite their dirty floor-tiles and smell of mildew, is rejected by every one. A shopkeeper calls her a bitch after she rejects a half-squashed pear; two women ignore her requests for directions; a boy steps on her foot as she wavers at Cambridge Circus; and as she tries to blink back brimming tears she wonders why, over one short summer, she has turned into a shivering mouse. She stands again outside the BOOKS *etc.* window, and prepares to smile shyly at a pair of friendly-looking girls with dyed blackish hair and interesting glasses. They stand apart, looking with heads identically inclined at a display of Oxford Classics; Anna moves between them, just behind, and they all look together in a height-graded line of three. Perhaps this is how they'll always be: Anna in the middle, happily conspicuous. London friendships must happen like this all the time; how else do you meet? She only notices that they're speaking German when the taller one takes the other's tanned elbow, and they walk off without looking at her, little rucksacks bobbing. She's like a soul in purgatory. She wants to go home.

Lost again. Gower Street must be somewhere on her right, but the roads leading to it are all plastic blaring tourist routes full of ersatz brasseries with names like 'Tweed' and 'Debonair's', or silent sunless terraces, spotted with blue plaques for anaesthetics pioneers, where thin-blooded postgraduates scurry between underfunded libraries and basement common rooms. Anna takes a side-street in a spirit of adventure – will her future husband be sitting on a wall? – and abruptly finds herself in shade. Standing under the flaking branches of an unexpectedly large and leafy tree she squints into the sun, looking for a sign. The nearest shop specializes in thermal underwear ('Ask inside for Outsize and Surgical'); through its swinging door she sees it is improbably busy. Wondering if she could claim a weakness for longjohns if the need for human contact becomes overwhelming, she walks slowly under green dappled light and awnings, trying to look interesting and at ease.

Any second now she might find a delicatessen, or a newsagent, or a café, and there will have a chance meeting. She watches for undiscovered bookshops, creeper-hung jungle clearings of old-world kindness, but her eye keeps sliding towards intimations of other lives – black and purple jazz albums, rubber bras, military trousers, dresses like the skeletons of leaves.

The streets are full of ghosts: an ex-teacher's streaky bob; brown bicycling legs and a black cow-lick like a friend's once-desired brother. Between these echoes she is braced for real meetings – straying lecturers, rejoicing acquaintances, even Luke, penitent and thin. In only forty hours she has remade this city: a dreamland, peopled with doppelgangers, its buildings shadowed with the ley-lines and enamel plaques of her uncertain future.

A taxi like a snouty hearse slams to a halt just beside her. A woman in a dark linen suit climbs quickly in, her clutch of stiff paper carrier-bags caught for a second on the door. It could almost be Stella, unexpectedly, secretly returned. Momentarily her guts slip and settle at the thought of colliding on a corner, jumping from a bus, glimpsing that shining henna hair beside a counter. Stella would wave from a spindly Parisian chair, half in sunlight, half in shadow, behind a patisserie's open door. Anna would join her, flush and heat mysteriously dispersed, and in the shade of late afternoon they will drink tisanes and crumble golden flakes and almond splinters between rosy fingertips, talking and talking, into evening.

Oh, for God's sake, thinks Anna. It's only been a couple of days. You barely know the woman. Find someone your own age to bond with.

A shop window glints under a candy-striped awning. From the street it's hard to see whether it's fairly busy or hopelessly overstaffed. A man with very short silver hair is displaying biographies in an artful domino.

When he looks up Anna is wrinkling a greenfly from her upper lip. He narrows his eyes and looks away, and her reflection shows a gargoyle leer. She tries to smile an apology, but the muscles in his turquoise polo-shirted back twitch disdain. He stands, and at last she realizes it is a bookshop. What is wrong with her brain? On an obscure impulse to make peace, Anna follows him in.

'Yes?'

She inhales surreptitiously and tries another smile, but her voice is croaky with disuse. 'Hello – I'm sorry about . . . everything. Have you got a job?'

'I'm sorry?' Exaggeratedly symmetrical creases dance above his brows. His eyes and shirt match exactly.

He can smell me, she thinks. She is standing in a miasma of fear and hopelessness. Try not to watch his nostrils. 'Oh God. I mean, I know you have a job. You work here don't you, no actually what I meant was is there a job? You know, that I could have?'

His eyebrows have a life of their own. One shoots up inches above an acid eye and lingers, quivering. With an effort Anna returns her own eyes to his.

This is an emergency. Destitution, prostitution, waitressing in an American-style diner on Southampton Row begin to beckon. Deep within her something shifts: a bravery gland, vestigial but intact – her genetic heritage.

'OK,' she says, her damp palms flat on a guide to evening classes. Her voice steadies. 'Is there a job? I'd like to work here.'

The man looks surprised again, this time more authentically. 'Would you?'

'Yes.' She attempts an invisible swallow.

'Well, I'm the manager.'

Anna looks briefly deep into his ice-chip eyes. 'Hello.'

He gives her a rapid professional smile. 'Yes, hi. Now, there is a job, as it happens, right now, but I don't have time to interview you. Have you any references?'

Does he mean from other bookshops? Or general moral guarantees? 'Well . . . no, but I could get some . . .'

'I don't expect it matters. There *is* a job: full-time, Tuesday to Saturday. Can you come in at one on Monday?'

'Well, yes. For an interview?'

'*Yes.*'

'Oh . . . yes.'

He nods.

'Bye, then.' She is briefly unable to see the exit.

There is a small pause. 'Oh, dearie?' The man must be speaking to her. She wobbles round, and smiles nervously.

'Yes?'

'I won't eat you.'

'Thank you,' says Anna, and races for the door as her face ignites.

Thank you? She will avoid the shop on Monday; even bypass the street altogether, pacing London in ever-widening circles as fresh humiliations multiply and spread. What must the turquoise man think of her now? What did he say as the door rang shut behind her? Perhaps as she walks in for her interview, staff and customers will unite behind her in a swelling wave of laughter, roaring and hooting, snarling at her heels until she stumbles home.

When every fragment of her shame has been dissected, she barely has the energy to climb the stairs to the flat. Her skin has a pall of London filth; she longs for a bath, but without food her nerve will fail entirely. Already envisaging a vast tuna sandwich she heads for the kitchen, then falters, appalled.

She is not alone.

A black plastic bag is drooping off the tabletop. An empty glass refracts blue water beside the sink. There is a newspaper folded on a chair, and snaking over its headlines lies a thin grey cloth.

The air in the icy room implodes and is vanquished. Anna is frozen, ripe for attack. The clock's tick is a dying heartbeat. How much longer does she have?

With a muddied impulse to clarify her life's last details she glances again at the water glass. Purple floats on its shivering surface. Her stomach thuds. She has been left a souvenir.

Whoever it is may be upstairs now, rifling through her rings and paperbacks, deriding her underwear. She must arm herself. She goes straight to the knives.

The pulpy contents of the glass are sinking fast.

It has petals.

Air rushes back into the room like a firebomb's change of heart. Someone has left her flowers.

The newspaper is today's, and neatly folded. The cloth is an unknown gauzy scarf, startlingly silver. In the carrier-bag is a pair of rubber gloves, a chopping board, some cotton wool and a box of apricots.

She has willed Stella here.

The scarf is exquisite: a web of melting ice. The packed slats of the chopping-board were born for charcuterie and vanilla pods. The apricots, pressing fatly against their balsa slats, smell of forgotten orchards.

Pink with relief, deliciously prolonging the seconds before she calls out, Anna kneels to open the refrigerator. It is stuffed with packages.

She sits back and marvels: honeycomb; raspberries; hummous and tzatziki pressing against tub lids in authentic swirls; a market stall of oranges, peppers and swollen aubergines; a baby loaf of rustic bread. If Stella comes in this minute she will read Anna's delight in the set of her shoulders. She takes out the loaf and sniffs it, smiling. Then she turns.

There is no one standing in the doorway. The bread smells oddly familiar. Her face falls. Her mother.

'It's me . . . Anna.'

'At last. I wanted to ask you, have you ever met Beccy Lefschitz's lawyer friend Julian?'

'What are you talking about?'

'Don't be difficult, Anna. Andrea's Beccy. Have you?'

'No – although I knew his brother . . . Why?'

'Well, you know that Beccy's in Florence?'

'No.'

'Come *on*, Anna. I showed you the brochure. Anyway,

Julian dropped by Andrea's flat to collect a book, and Andrea says he's a dear – much politer than his brother.'

'Mum, I'm not – what's wrong with his brother?'

'Oh – nothing, just a little problem with – he's a little wild, Anna, in Andrea's opinion.'

'Right. Is he in London, do you know?'

'He's a *drug* user, Anna. Hardly appropriate. Anyway, Julian, Beccy's friend, is such a sweet boy, and we – Andrea suggested—'

'Oh God. What?'

'Don't be so ungrateful. Andrea just mentioned that he's bought a wonderful little flat in Ladbroke Grove – not the best area, frankly, but apparently very "now", and at least you'd be near Andrea if you needed anything – and she knows it's a little awkward that you're staying at Stella's, and apparently – well, he's looking for a flatmate.'

'Mum. Listen. I don't want to be sold into domestic slavery just because some prig of Andrea's wants a skivvy – or a girlfriend. I'm fine. Please. Stop worrying – it isn't *awkward* here. And what I rang to ask was: have you been here? To Stella's flat?'

'Well, obviously, Anna.'

'Oh.'

'Who else do you think would have filled the fridge for you? A jar of gherkins and a rotting edam rind won't get you very far.'

'No. I just thought—'

'And those rubber gloves were disgusting, and I simply couldn't face the thought of the surface of Stella's chopping-board, and you know you can't hygienically remove cleanser with a flannel, and you'll need a paper if you're going to go to the theatre, won't you, and the scarf's for you – quite a bargain, though it's Selfridges so it should last, and—'

'And the flower – was that here when you—'

'Of course not. Were you expecting elfin visitors? *I* left it, Anna – it fell off some stocks I was taking home.'

'So did you . . . did you just drop by on the way . . . somewhere?'

'I drove up, Anna. I knew you wouldn't be managing.'

'Well – thank you, but you really shouldn't . . . I wish you wouldn't—'

Her mother sniffs dismissively. 'Anyway, I had to see a stockist in Fulham Broadway. The Balinese votive saucers are selling faster than we can import them.'

'Right. But Mum, don't you think maybe you should . . . should leave your set of keys here? As spares for me? I mean, I might need–'

'Don't be ridiculous. Stella gave me this set. *I* need it.'

'But why?'

'Enough, Anna. Have you seen your uncle yet? And we'd better speak soon about Julian.'

When her irritation has subsided, Monday's interview begins to fill the room. Raging optimism and alarm take turns to overwhelm her; she should tell her mother, but there's time for that. Celebratory, skittish, she bobs around the flat, looking for diversions.

It's time she developed eclectic reading habits. She decides to borrow one of Stella's books, and there, between pages four and five of P.F. Avery's *Night in Arabia*, she finds the end of a letter:

. . . what I'll tell you, but this time you don't. And it isn't because of who I am, and who you are, that I feel like this. But – listen, by any account it's horrible, and selfish, and incredibly cruel, and just wrong. I think 'what was she thinking of?' and then I just have to stop – I don't want to know. But of all people – I'm appalled that you could do it, and I don't know how you ever intend to undo the damage. But try, please try.

It is signed *M*, and she cannot mistake the writing.

She sits back down on the sofa, at the end furthest from the telephone, holding the page. Her hand is shaking. What has Stella done?

For all these years she's been right: there is a secret, and it cannot be spying, or a hidden child. It is worse. Has she horribly hurt her own parents? Or her brother? If Anna broaches it to her mother, walls of steel will slice her to quiet even before her question ends. Her father will close ranks. She can hardly ask Stella.

She rests her chin in the crook of an elbow, inhaling summer skin for comfort, and tries to think of a plan.

And so, later, she forgets to expect the telephone to ring, and it does. She is lying on the sofa watching a telefilm about bone-marrow-donor romance. As she falls off the cushions towards the sudden peal she has an image of Heidi, trapped in a rocky ravine, cheered by the bell of her favourite cow.

'Is that Anna?'

'. . . Yes?'

'It's Richard.'

'Hello again.'

'Yes – now, before you protectively ask my motives, I'm just ringing because I forgot to mention *why* I need Stella to ring – she hasn't already, has she?'

'No . . . I'm not expecting her to—'

'No, of course not. None of us are, more's the pity. The point is, I have two tickets for that French actor at the Almeida – very hard to get – and I know she'd kill to go.'

'Would she?'

'Oh yes. And although obviously I have her number, she is being very Stella-ish about answering. So if she rings, could you just tell her that I've got these two tickets, for next Friday, and I'm *longing* to take her. There.'

'Yes, I will.'

'I suppose she'd hardly—' He falters. 'I suppose I'd better start looking for someone else.'

'Yes, I suppose you should,' says Anna benevolently, thinking fast.

Stella's bedroom hovers like a flying carpet above her head; a weight of feathers and wood. She hesitates at the edge of the rug, toeing its border of rust and indigo diamonds and looking up at the ceiling. What is she under now? The wardrobe, thick with secrets? That stretch of bed? She ravels and unravels stained fringes with her toes. If Richard knows about the letter, what weapon could she use to make him tell?

Later, in her own bed, her thoughts will not be stilled. Richard's voice, Stella's unhelpful silence, have, combined, new power. Her mind beats gently at Stella's door. The sheet moves minutely, electrifying her skin, her fur. Now she'll never sleep. She thinks of them together.

Five

She has a postcard.

On the front is a mask; red eye-slits, woven hair.

On the back is Stella's writing.

Her eyes dance and skim over the navy letters: she is an archaeologist, wiping leafmould from the stone-face, scanning the sticks and circles of a lost language.

It could mean anything at all. She must be tired. The shivering fans of the chestnut trees outside the back window tremble in hot air. She touches the mask with her fingers; it is black and shining, with angular cheekbones. She turns the card over and begins again.

Dear Anna,

I think *your mother said you'd have moved in about now; can't remember. Haven't decided yet when I'll next be (briefly) back – maybe a couple of weekends' time – but you'll barely see me. Any major problems, just call.*

Stella x

P.S. When you do arrive, I need some help. I left a ring at someone's house – the family is called Glass – and I need it back: it's very valuable. Could you ring them for me – the number is in NW5 – and have them send it?

And that is it. Anna fixes her eyes on the final stroke until they strain and smart. Her feet are luminous among the blood-dark cushions. Now she is really here, now that her imaginings have, summertime-slowly, come to imperfect life, her fantasies fail her. Stella in this house? Impossible. She disinters herself from the sofa and goes into the kitchen; ignoring the nervy shiverings of her blood.

They'll pass in the hall on their separate ways out. The flat will feel less empty. How lovely to see her aunt.

She's still adrift and jobless, abjectly in need of company, and mad with the silence after less than a week. She goes for a walk, but still her mind will not pull away from her mother's letter in the silent sitting room or Stella's strange request; the ticking glacial kitchen; the secrets of the room upstairs.

What if Stella comes back today and finds her postcard discarded by her ingrate niece? She could arrive at any moment. Anna will have to be prepared.

Maybe she should answer it – simple, assertive, casually impressive. That is, if she can somehow acquire the address without arousing mockery, or suspicion, or any of the other unreasonable obstacles her mother seems intent on building between them.

Dear Stella,

She can't start like that; it sounds too formal, or intimate.

Better to launch oneself straight in, without thinking, (although how will she ever choose a postcard?)

Thanks for helping me escape. Could you send instructions?

What has happened to her self-control? By the time Stella's back, London will be easy. Now's her chance to set the tone.

I love it here, and the flat seems perfect, though I'm hardly ever there. Everyone's very friendly, and Mum's keeping away . . .

Anna and Stella meet so rarely that her mother is never fully discussed. Sasha, and Anna's father, are no good for serious discussions about What's Wrong With Magda; too doped, or devoted, respectively. Perhaps Stella's vision is equally too clouded to delineate her many grievous faults. Is it bad taste not to get on with one's mother?

When are you coming over?

She sounds too keen; it's not as if Anna wants her there for cringing bathroom etiquette and breakfast conversation. What if Stella wanted to have a friend – like Richard on the answerphone – for dinner? Or the night?

Hope Paris is sunny. It's fine if you can't rush back . . .

Every version sounds rude or pathetic. And is it so fine if she stays in Paris? Anna walks faster, as if she could physically prevent her aunt from hesitating a moment longer. What if she doesn't come? The prospect of countless days lost like this one blinds her like a ghost-train hologram. She does not suit being left to her own devices.

Why can't you just ring the Glasses yourself, or at least give me their number? And what have you done that made Mum so angry? What was so horrible and wrong?

The part of her brain that still expects stardom, that spent the summer imagining being plucked from the Bloomsbury streets to be famous, seems to have shut down. By the time she returns to Shawcross Street and finds the key to her aunt's flat, this sudden willingness not to be an actress or a writer or even, inexplicably, a model, has begun to seem ominous, a ticking symptom of mental decay. She has never, she now realizes, entirely lost her ego. Even at her rockiest she has always known how she looked and sounded, her self floating half a centimetre above her body, testing, calibrating, telling her trembling fingers when to stop.

There is no post for her on the doormat. Nobody has rung. She brushes angrily past the answerphone, smugly gleaming in the half-light. How do other people manage? They should never have let her come.

'You are being ridiculous,' she tells her faint reflection in the sitting-room window, superimposed on blackened brick-work and complicated chalky stucco. A fat tear falls on to the radiator and trickles down the white enamelled valley, gathering dust. She rests her fingers on the glass like a treefrog and tries not to picture the slender antique gleam snapped into icy blades, warm blood dropping on to the satin paint. What if Stella chose that exact minute to come back and walked in on her niece incarnadine, covered in self-pity?

Time loses its shape and vanishes. As the light fades she begins to run a bath and, risking her mother, strips where she stands, door open. Stella must possess bath products – where is she hiding them? Here there is only one small bottle, casting forest light on to the edge of the tub. She steps into the steaming water.

At least her new sweat will be clean. She kneels for a moment looking at her lap, all algae-tinged flesh and waving hairs, and realizes that she has been expecting bounty: not just columns of romantic crockery, but recherché beauty finds, life-changing poetry, ranks of photographs.

How can she live in a house she barely knows? There's time for that, she thinks as she slips below the surface, water lazily clinging and reforming round her breasts and neck and chin. She opens her mouth and lets a hot wave surge over teeth and tongue. Pipes hum and switch beneath her ears as her hair fans out behind her, fatly curving serpents red as arteries.

Emerging from a kind of swoon, Anna opens her eyes and finds that the day, splintered and blotted in the bathroom window, has darkened by a shade. Surface tension puckers around a pink archipelago of nipples and knees. It still seems mildly astonishing that she is now long enough to fill a bath from end to end. The silver dial below the taps is covered in steamy pearls not yet full enough to fall. She wipes it with a toe and sees a horribly distorted tangle of her own limbs in the clouded reflection.

One of her stardom daydreams deflates. As she had planned it, she would be sitting in a café, or turning, three-quarters profile, in her seat in a darkening theatre, when she would be spotted by someone, very thin ('Lucian won't paint skin and bones. What he wants is beautiful flesh'), who would take her to a garret full of light and turpentine. Here she would be painted, splayed on a groundsheet, to be hung in the Tate and worshipped. And one day he will let her have the picture and she and the man she lives with will discuss whether it should hang in their bedroom or over the kitchen table. Guests will gasp and turn back to her, eyes unveiled.

'Is that you?'

And Anna will see in their faces new knowledge of her hidden glories, and will watch as they drink their wine and try not to fixate on the picture of their hostess, naked and magnificent.

It seems appalling that this may never happen. But recollecting now how she has looked while trudging through London, fraying and clumsy, foxy-haired, it is hard to imagine that it could. Underwater her flesh is putrid, butter-soft; heavy sausage-limbs floating in greenish liquid. Her eyes return to the reflective hexagon, moving her head to catch a glinting curve of window, and catches herself thinking again of broken edges. Without peers, or responsible adults, she could sink here. She could easily drown. And if that starts there is no one to catch her.

Like a sea-swimmer thrown off balance by a huge wave, Anna is briefly blinded. Echoing water crashes about her ears before she emerges blinking into silence, amazing herself with every breath. She is going to have to save herself.

It's time she dealt with Stella's little errand, but there are five families called Glass in NW5. She begins at the bottom.

'Hello – do you know someone called Stella Salzmann? I—'

'Hello?' wavers an ancient voice.

'Sorry!' shouts Anna, and, shame-faced, tries the next number.

'Do you know Stella Salzmann? I'm calling for her—'

'Vot?'

'Stella Salzmann?' she enunciates.

'Not,' says a grumpy middle-European.

It's hardly worth trying again. But what would Stella say?

'Hello. I'm calling for someone called Stella . . .'

'She's out.'

'Who, Stella?'

'Nah. Mrs Glass.'

'Oh. Does she have a . . . large family?'

'Are you being funny?'

'I think I have the wrong number.'

Give up now, she thinks, dialling one more. 'Hello, do you know someone called Stella, at all?'

After a long pause a girl says, 'What?'

Discomfited, she tries again. 'I'm ringing for—'

'Stella Salzmann?'

'Yes! She's my . . .'

'Never heard of her,' says the girl flatly, and hangs up.

Anna blinks at the telephone. She checks the number: N. Glass, 127 Hershell Rd, NW5. Completely, undeniably, the right number. She cannot find the nerve to try it again.

Sirens stream down a road; very near. She crosses to the sitting-room window and stares out, rolling her forehead gently on the glass. If Stella had just given her the number, Anna woudn't be reduced to making prank calls to old ladies; by now she could have found the ring. Should she claim the number was ex-directory? That N. Glass said the ring disappeared? When Richard rings again should she ask him?

Another bath and she'll dissolve; it's too soon for bed. She could wait for the Glass family, regretting their momentary confusing rudeness, to enfold her to their North London bosom, but they may be biding their time. She could write to Bill, of all her friends the most unstoppably cheerful, but his clumsy post-Luke announcement of passion has rumpled the calm that lay between them. She could look for the rest of Stella's hidden letter, but there is the question of what she will find, and when to stop. All that's left is the phone, and with no one else around, that leaves her with her mother.

'It's me again.'

'I didn't expect to hear from you so soon.'

'Oh. Well, I spoke to Markus.'

'. . . Fine. Good. Anything else? Don't think I've forgotten about Julian.'

Poor Uncle Markus, Anna thinks, slowly cracking under his sister's Arctic frosts. 'Can I speak to Dad?'

She sighs patiently. 'Well, he's in his study, of course. But fine, OK, I'll go and shout for him, shall I? Bye, then.'

'Bye—' says Anna, as the receiver clunks and settles on her mother's bedside table.

She can hear distant shrieking. If her father calls her Chicken, as he still sometimes does, she will be lost.

There is another clunk, and fizzing. 'Yes?'

'It's me. Your beloved infant.'

'Hello, infant. How's it going?'

'It's not fantastic. I—' her voice sputters; she holds the receiver more tightly. 'Well, did Mum tell you . . . I rang?'

'What, before?'

'Yes.'

'She did.'

'Oh . . . well. Is work OK?'

'Yes. Bit of a rush, in fact – proof-checking.'

'Oh. Yes. Bye Dad. I miss you.'

'Keep that beak up, Chicken. We'll speak soon.'

Anna is watching the light from the window turning mauve. She has drifted about for hours; in forty minutes it will be time for a documentary about prize-winning vegetables. She has resigned herself to silence, is telling herself she will enjoy it, but when the telephone rings her heart skips like the shortest bridesmaid in the path of the bride's bouquet.

Her body seems to have paralysed itself. She feels her brain shouting at her nerves before her legs move. It could be anyone.

It is her mother.

In the background she hears the clinkings of spoons and forks on china, chair legs scraping the floorboards, the soft surrender of a cork. Despite their recent conversation, the thought of home rushes like an arrow to her failing heart.

'Darling, I can't talk long – the Newmans have come for dinner. But I had to call back to hear how the hunting went.'

'Oh.' With her mother it's important to sound upbeat. Not to bleed into the water. There's no telling what her mood will be today: whether that dark shape above you is a lifeboat or a shark. 'I might have found somewhere; I've an interview on Monday.' Her mother is a silent space. She offers more. 'They seemed quite . . . friendly.'

'Good. And how's the flat?'

'It's lovely. But I still haven't met anyone.' She wants to tell her: either it isn't what I hoped, or I'm not.

Her mother laughs brightly. 'Darling, come on. You've been there no time at all.'

Anna doesn't answer.

'It'll get better. But it must be hard at the beginning. Poor thing.'

That's it. She can't not cry when there's sympathy. It is the opposite of laughing gas, an aphrodisiac for tears. An involuntary moan escapes her, like a puppy's.

'Well, darling, why don't you come back for the weekend? It isn't far. Your father will collect you from the station in time for lunch. You need some mother comfort.'

Mother comfort is what she always promises. For other children this would mean hot drinks and platitudes. Not Anna. Her mother can do hot drinks as well as anyone, but that isn't the rare and precious thing. Real comfort is her at her finest: jokes, and making funny faces in restaurants, and her mastery of made-up languages. It happens infrequently now, and rarer still is Anna receptive; she feels herself tighten, and her mother looks away. But still she knows she'd cross continents for it, given the chance.

'Okay. Maybe. I probably will.' She begins to sniff, just loudly enough to hear, but her mother is already back at the party: Gerald Newman has just said something, and everyone is laughing. She says goodbye; as Anna puts the phone down her cheeks are already hot with easy grateful tears.

That night there is one more phone call. This time, thinks Anna as she sidesteps past the kitchen table, it'll be someone I can actually talk to.

She is wrong. It is her sister.

'Hey,' says Sasha, audibly exhaling.

'Oh God, hello,' says Anna. 'I'm a bit surprised.'

'Who did you think I'd be, sis? Put it over there.'

'What?'

'What? Oh, right, just talking to Lenny. Put it there, darlin'. Behind the plant.'

'Sasha, do you want to talk to me or to . . . him? Because I haven't—'

'Hold on sis, don't be a nightmare. Just my sister.'

'I'm *not*—'

'Shh . . . Yeah, love, yeah, that's lovely. A tenner. Thanks. Right, what was I—'

'Sasha,' says Anna, sternly. 'I'm going to go this minute if you don't—'

'God, look, I'm here, all right? Now listen.'

'I *am*.'

'Right, sis. I've got . . . a bit of a problem. Oh, yeah, how's London?'

'It's – the flat's amazing.'

'Bet it is. Stella would. And gorgeous men – any hanging around? Nick me one.'

'I don't think so,' says Anna. 'Now, what's the problem? What've you done?'

'*Nothing.* I've done *nothing*, sis. God. Why do you always—'

'All right, OK, sorry. Sorry. Now, what?'

'It's not me, anyway.'

Sasha's boyfriend is a haemophiliac with Sèvres skin and a mouth like wire. 'Is it Butch?' asks Anna. 'He *is* a problem.'

'Shut up. He's not.'

'Oh come on, Sash, he *is*. He smokes opium, for God's sake. He slept with—'

'Stop it. That's over . . . *months* ago. He's – yeah, bye love. Seeya – he's nice to me now—'

'Well he'd better be. I'd kill him.'

'Anna. Listen. That's not the . . . look, the thing is we need some cash.'

'Come on. What for? Smack for Butch? I'm not paying him to be crap to my sis—'

'Not for me. *Or* him. It's for Cally.'

'Oh. What, Cally from school? You're not still friends with her?'

'Like, completely. You know that.'

'Do I? Right. So, why?'

'She . . . just needs some.'

'Are you going to tell me what for?'

'I can't. I promised. But I've tried and tried to think of what to do, and I can't. It's urgent. Can you . . . can—'

'Sweetheart, I can't lend it to you. I don't have it. I don't even have a job yet'

'Fuck.'

'Does she need it for something . . . serious? I like Cally. I'd like to help if she really needs—'

'Yeah, it really is. Trust me, sis. I wouldn't spend your money on gear.'

'Oh?'

'Well, this time. Really. Please.'

'I'll think. Listen, I'm coming down tomorrow. Are you around?'

'Yeah. Maybe. Dunno.'

Anna opens her little window, and air washes over the crushed meringue of duvet. Three floors down is a small paved patch, backed by thin trees. Dark plants pour from walls and terraces. Before the last summer heat rises from the paving she'll be there, drinking made-up cocktails, laughing in the honeysuckle with her downstairs neighbours.

She lies back and basks in the smell of Stella's sheets. In Scotland she'd buy Persil without thinking, and everything smelt of family washing. Now she inhales above her pillow, and wonders if this is Ariel, and whether in Paris Persil has a name unconnected with herbs. She reflects on this surprisingly often, just as in the bath she remembers the eye-protecting halo she used to wear when her mother washed her hair.

'Am I as good as gold?' she had asked. She knew she wasn't, of course.

Her mother had laughed, her hand stroking suds from the otter sleekness.

'No, tell me. Am I?' Eyes tight shut against the answer.

'Of course you are.'

When Anna's life flits before her eyes will she think only of washing powder and No More Tangles? She touches the bones of her face, suddenly worrying about Alzheimer's, and then she is hunting for memories of Stella.

There is nothing for years. Anna can remember always knowing her grandparents, although she can barely imagine them outside childhood photographs: holding their hands over a cattle-grid, wheeling wet bicycles, splashing through a frill of sea water. There is a picture of Stella as a girl, in long dark shorts and an enormous jumper like a French boy, her future stretching in its shell. Anna's mother is nearly a grown-up, half smiling. She has a woman's body in wide trousers and a surprisingly tight polo-neck. Their parents stand with them in front of a seaside wall, already in their old people's clothes. Markus must already be at university, his world seizing up. But there are no pictures of Stella since Anna's birth, no proof that they were ever in the same places.

The first time Anna can remember her aunt is at a birthday. She was somewhere between seven and nine, but she doesn't recollect birthday-girl pride. There will have been hours of fractious preparation, helping her mother chop egg for sandwiches, tidying her bedroom, waiting hungrily for presents. But all that has faded. Instead she sees a climbing frame, covered with crawling children where, below the upside-down tomato faces, sit Anna and her lost friend Janey Maddicott in the grass. There is, as always, no sign of her sister. On the iron table near the house is a big blue plate of strawberries, which her parents and some others are eating slowly, dropping the hulls into abandoned creamy bowls. Anna looks over at her careless audience and there is Stella, laughing at someone else, with her dark eyes half turned towards her.

What would Anna have done when she saw it? Blushed and looked away, perhaps, and watched for that gaze all afternoon. Or started showing off, aiming childish charm too loudly at the table. She will never be able to ask the obvious questions: Did you notice me then? What did you think of me then? Had Mum already written you that letter? And were you visiting anyway, or were you there for me?

Six

On Saturday morning she sits on the Bath train, nibbling at her cold fingers and watching the rain-soaked fields. This first week has been bleached and stretched with crying. She has wept until she is light and frail. Her mother's silver car waits in the bus lane. At the sight of her huge sunglasses, flat black in the cold sunlight, Anna almost smiles. She opens the door; her mother turns her cheek to be kissed, and Anna slides into the warm air and old music and her mother's perfumed space.

'How are you?'

'Oh, you know . . .'

'Are you settling in?'

'Well . . . I'm trying.'

'Yes. Well . . . .' She strokes Anna's hand at a traffic light; it won't last, so Anna tenses her heart against it. 'It'll be all right.'

Anna makes a noise like 'yes'.

They drive though quiet squares and terraces, flat-fronted buildings fanning into impossible curves. Discreet cobbles shudder through her as they glide in dilute sunlight to the house.

They sit in the cooling car. As her mother climbs out she asks, 'Are you coming?'

'Yes,' says Anna, beginning to cry. She hears the door shut and sits on.

Of course her key works. She takes her bag upstairs to her bedroom, which is clouding with dust, and sits for a while, expecting to feel different. There is nothing in her except the need for food and voices. Despite the salt still drying on her freckled hands, her palm skips down the banisters towards the kitchen.

Afterwards she tells herself she couldn't have known. A weekend alone would have finished her off; she'd have been found raving on Gower Street wrapped in tea towels. But as she enters the room her mother's face quells her dreams of comfort. Rays of irritation freeze her at the door.

At times like this she wishes she could ask 'What?' accusingly, and give a hammer-blow to her mother's enamelled shell. If only *they'd* say something, she thinks. But their father floats above it, and Sasha, when roused, can storm off and charm her way back in an hour. When their mother snaps at Anna, Anna returns in kind, and there's no escape from the cold fog that settles in the kitchen.

She looks at her mother's back as she leans into the fridge. 'Mum . . .'

'What?' She shuts the fridge door and opens the oven.

'Shall I lay the table?'

'No one else has done it.' But that isn't the reason. Anna

shuts the cutlery drawer a little too loudly. Splinters of ice are already sliding through her bloodstream to her heart. She purposely gives her mother a dirty fork, then regrets it, fearing a huge bridge-burning row, or botulism. Silently, furiously apologetic, she puts it in the dishwasher and fetches a clean one. Her mother is still lowering by the hob. Anna looks at her narrow back, then looks away before she petrifies. There is no point retaliating. It may not even be something she has done.

But when, the third time she shrieks up and down the stairs, her father finally detaches himself from his box-files and Sasha from her friend's dribbling baby ('He's called Skye. Isn't that sweet?'), Anna's mother is friendly to them both. Only between her and her prodigal daughter remains this glassy wall. Anna picks at the fish and glares at her mother, who now hates her for leaving and for running home. She considers choking on a fishbone, discreetly hefts her knife in her palm. One thing is clear: she should not have come back.

'What is it, Anna?' asks her father tiredly.

'Nothing, Dad.' Should she say it's difficult in London? Or that it's harder to be here? He will not defend her against his wife's poisonous rage; like Anna, he knows how rarely its source can be found. She sniffs; her mother's mouth twitches downwards. She looks at her plate and swallows, but it's too late. As her mother scrapes her chair back and goes to find the pepper, a hot tear falls audibly on to the white china. Her mother shows no sign of having heard. Another tear falls as Anna thinks: could I control myself? Why does she make me react this way? Her chest aches in the universal weak place – just over the heart, where family barbs stick fast.

'Anna, what?' says her father again.

'Nothing.' She looks at her mother, and the tears fall faster.

It is like being fourteen again. She can howl with soggy self-pity until she's blue in the face, but cannot bring her father from his books on murder and marriage amongst the Visigoths, her mother from the telephone, or her sister from the room she shares with Somerset's travellers, where the furnishings seem carved out of ash.

Anna's old bedroom is already beginning to lose its heart. At the top of the tall and dusty house she had hidden, waiting to shine. The drawers have filled with teenage detritus: scoured magazines, novelty erasers, diaries, tapes of schoolfriends' brothers' music. Dusty Laura Ashley hats. Several dead bumblebees in matchboxes.

When she has cried herself calm there is nothing to distract her on her bookshelves. She will not go downstairs again, into her mother's icy annoyance. She looks out through the sheep-patterned curtains: the analysts, doctors and architects are quiet behind pedimented stone, playing educational games with responsive eight-year-olds. In this part of Bath there are never audible rows or broken bottles or shocking drunken parties. Anna has not kissed on this street, has never smoked here, and rarely been drunk. All she has ever done is draw on the pavement in coloured chalk, practise hands-free bicycling and speculate fruitlessly about teachers' sex lives, walking through the damp leaves home from school.

Sasha's music is battering through the wall, but Anna cannot brave the hash fog and crusties to entreat her for quiet. After an initial 'Hello, sis' and an offer of a backrub, Sasha has not risen to the occasion. If I were Sasha, thinks Anna, I bloody well would. But then if I were Sasha I'd be sleeping with Butch, who lives on a bus, and could free my mind with pills provided by a Catholic bishop's daughter. Several times Anna resolves, and fails, to go to her sister and ask, calmly, exactly what money they need, and why. Only the thought of sinister apparatus, or trouserless Butch, prevents her.

In the gloom under the bed is a paperback cemetery. She lies on her stomach to unearth one and there, behind a coverless Judith Krantz, she sees a gleam.

It is her penknife. She reaches out her arm and just touches it with a fingernail before, straining every muscle and tendon and bone to its limit, every atom of will, she wriggles out from under the bed. There are knives at Stella's, obviously, but here the history is thicker, and everything has a charge. She snaps off the light and lies flat under the sheet. Then, only then, does she let herself recall her old inventory.

The Knives in Anna's House

1. One Stanley knife, cold and rusty, in her father's workroom. There may be others, lost under sandpaper and bicycle pumps, but they'll be gummed up and dangerous.

2. One paper-knife on the big desk in the study. It's just a sharp blade in a plastic handle, about which her father is very possessive. The edge is grey with pencil lead and glue.

3. Various kitchen knives. Apart from the cleaver and breadknife, and the smaller ones with serrated blades, there are a few useful French ones with worn familiar handles. They are fairly sharp, and all very clean.

4. An old penknife in her father's sock drawer, with boot-laces, and broken watches, and a plastic yo-yo. It is minute, pearl-handled and blunt as a spoon.
5. One new penknife under Anna's bed. It can slice through paper sideways, and it's hers.
6. One cut-throat razor in the bathroom cupboard. There's nothing sharper in the house.

On Sunday it rains again, but more so. Anna sleeps late, as late as she can. If she could dig herself in, in this timewarped bunker, she will miss her first weekend in London, and her interview, if it comes to that. Delicious cowardice. She emerges for lunch, as a test-run, but her mother's thin civility has not thawed. The roast chicken has, obscurely, failed, a neighbour calls to complain about Butch's bus, and Anna's sister's plate congeals while she and Butch sleep on. I don't have to be here, thinks Anna, so relieved by this revelation that she almost repeats it aloud. Within an hour she is on a slow train east, teary with relief and disappointment.

She could have asked about the letter – if her mother was a different person, if her father could be trusted not to take sides. But this secret is beginning to warp the dye in the family photographs, and she cannot imagine where to begin. She determines to do something about it; that, or the Glasses. Tomorrow, she decides, she will find something out.

She has forgotten the veal-calf panic of the underground. A guard is mildly affable, and her gratitude is embarrassing. In the park during miserable adolescence she would walk for hours in the eddying shade of lime trees, hoping to be adopted by a bohemian family – handsome sons, a calm clever mother.

Now, standing in the tealeaf gloom of one of King's Cross's lower platforms, clammy in her drooping summer clothes, she imagines the guard's Dickensian family, crying 'Welcome!' to the demurely grateful stranger. 'Don't mind our simple ways! Have a lardy cake.' Surely assimilation is only a matter of time. Shortly she too will be a Londoner: marching in demonstrations, directing taxi drivers to Soho mews; retrieving amusing antlers from Portobello Market: a Bloomsbury Pearly Queen. Let it be soon.

At the foot of the stairs at Euston Square are three leek tops, lying in a perfect A. Is it a code? an offering? a mistake?

She has always been able to see, with reluctant visionary clarity, into her future. There are several options. The likeliest is unlucky in love, undervalued at work, trying to make the best of the single life. She's eccentric, arty, wild-haired in autumnal jumpers and chiming ethnic earrings. Her married friends advise her about her unhappy, dwindling affairs with caddish lecturers and minor writers. She has never painted a picture or had a baby or found a relationship that lasts. Slow decline to poetry readings, crystals and incense, too many cats. A horrible lonely desperate death in her cold ground-floor flat.

There are two alternatives. She may find herself in her late thirties, the long-term partner of a man she doesn't love quite enough. As her friends acquire the sheen of happy conjugal sex and motherhood, she will watch as any remaining bearable men are picked off, and her childbearing chances recede. She will settle into embittered and bickering middle age with the man, probably called Martin, who will dump her on her forty-second birthday for a woman younger, slimmer or more enigmatic than she could ever be. At which point scenario 1 takes over.

Or she will marry an okay man because he asks her, and will devote decades to not thinking about his affairs or her body. Her children will be unhappy and she'll cry in supermarkets. Then he'll fall ardently for a nubile sexpot at work. Scenario 1, again.

Variations are provided by a blissful union rent by tragedy (his death, usually), infertility, poverty, madness. Nothing glamorous, just low-level heartbreak. Obviously it will all go horribly wrong. It's just a question of how.

Now, however, she scents an alternative. As she walks back to the flat through the dinning London twilight, across glaring squares of traffic and grey hushed side-streets, she imagines being Stella, coming home. There is no husband, no paradisical garden, but it may be possible to have none of these and still find a life worth living. She can dance with saturnine suitors and summon them all to bed, drink without consequence, flirt with friends as summer evenings thicken. Stella's life is covetable, with or without her past. Anna will be fine if she studies her vigilantly. And finds the right man at the end.

As she tries to remember which way to turn the key she barely notices a lightness around her shoulders, a feeling of slipping in the dark space in her chest. A phone is ringing; with her foot on the first stair to the upper flat she realizes it is Stella's.

'Darling, it's Mum. Are you not back yet?'

As she opened the front door and heard the answerphone

starting up Anna's heart had clenched with possibility, then subsided. Now she crouches on the floor eye to eye with the machine, imagining her mother.

'I forgot to say when I saw you, which of course was very nice, I left a message for you on Marianne Brooks's answerphone. You remember Marianne, don't you, darling?' Her mother often treats Anna like a recalcitrant delinquent, wilfully unable to recall even the smallest personal detail. 'Andrea and I were discussing your future. I mean, a bookshop, darling – it's hardly high-flying, is it? And Andrea reminded me that Marianne's sister-in-law is very high up on *Cigar* magazine, and you know cigars are the next big thing – virtually essential in Manhattan. So we thought how wonderful if Marianne could organize a little secretarial job for you there, to put you – finally – on track. I'll help you find a suit. Well, darling, if you're sure you're not there, ring Marianne, and try to sound capable. And you *must* decide about Julian's flat.'

As Anna begins to run a bath she is practically growling. It's not even as if her mother has kept up with Marianne. Something happened between them, and as far as Anna knows they have barely seen each other since. The bathroom mirror is already blank with steam. She climbs into the bath like an oasis, sighing with relief. Water is becoming my natural habitat, she thinks as her head goes under.

Her breasts have never suited gravity. Now, floating, they are ivory spheres, crested with raspberry, warm under her hand. This is the perfect moment for a lover to walk in. Her nipple is hardening under her palm. She begins to imagine footsteps on the stairs.

*

Now Anna sits on her bed, trying to concentrate.

Things to do:

a) interview on Monday

b) buy food. Learn to cook it [she must act quickly, before her new life starts and social munificence is expected: coq au vin; Sachertorte; soufflés]

c) write to Sophie/Bill/Holly/Ruth?/Nick P/Helen. Be cheerful

d) see Markus/think of tactic re: Marianne Brooks.

e) find rest of letter? Ask someone if they know? Would Richard?

e) buy tape player?

f) meet people

g) Try N. GLASS AGAIN. Get Stella ring.

Her empty future bulges, dilated and transparent, every time she closes her eyes. She must remember to leave letters lying around, notes saying 'ring Holly when back from Russia'. Because Stella might arrive any minute, and must know her niece is only in limbo, becalmed before the storm.

And there is that, she thinks. Soon she will be back. As her brain sags and sinks, the bedroom grows noisy with aeroplane wings and taxi meters. Her aunt, elegantly aged, ushers in choruses of allies, lovers, friends, and Anna feels herself smiling, smiling: she will save me.

Graceful as a leaping panther, she springs from the step. Glossy ribbons of hair unscroll behind her as, tight-muscled and fleet of foot, she races for her goal. Her cheeks pink prettily in the balmy summer air. Her shapely bosom breasts the crowds which make way, marvelling at her lissom grace.

Anna is late for her interview.

After two wrong turnings she glimpses it, ominously circus-striped, at the other end of an empty street. This is her moment; to flee or to remain. There are booksellers in Bath; she could sink into that sticky womb and somehow live, protected and drowning, waiting to become her mother. Or she could return to Edinburgh and the shrinking circle of her vegetating friends, where every square and architrave still echoes with anticipation.

It is a choice between fog and oxygen. There may be a future here after all; a job for interest and money; friendship; conceivably romance. If she goes back now she will be stunted for ever. Would she rather be bonsaied or left in the forest? The Anna she wants to be whispers clearly: you have no choice.

Twenty minutes later she is free. Once she would have seen this as cosmically ordained; the right path chosen, doom magically averted. Instead she keeps her hands from tapping over railings, her eyes from cats and ladders, her mind well away from the infinite invention of signs.

She must also try not to beam, clap or skip, to rush back and cover the window with kisses. She starts on Wednesday. Her new world has begun.

As she crosses each paving stone she feels her future illuminate. She begins to sing '(I'm Going to Walk Down to) Electric Avenue'; a builder, waist-deep in a drain, looks at her in mild surprise. He must have seen losers sobbing daily;

at last they've found someone fit for the job. She gives him a watermelon grin.

She telephones her parents, who crow but sound distracted, eats burnt toasted cheese standing up in the kitchen like a busy person and, after resisting the urge to fiddle with the broken stereo, toasts herself in sloe gin from under the sink and tries dancing in a relaxed and urbane way round the sitting room to songs she only knows from her father's appalling singing: 'Some enchanted evening, you might see a lala, you might see a lala, across a lalala . . .' It is only when she trips over the ruched rug and stumbles hard against a bookshelf that her brief euphoria begins to melt and vapourize. The manager – disappointingly called Wilf – hadn't actually seemed to like her. None of the assistants had murmured encouragement as she left. Maybe no one else had applied. Maybe shopkeepers had watched pityingly, arms folded, as she gambolled unknowingly past their windows into a future of drudgery, or worse.

No, come on, she tells herself sternly. You're being unhelpful. This is good news. You deserve to celebrate.

In the next twenty-two hours she:

— goes out again for grapes. The shopkeeper looks at her scornfully as she fumbles for change, weakly muttering apologies. They are half-frozen, cold honey bullets, spiked with dry and bitter seeds.

— leaves messages with two friends' friends, and voicemails Sasha: 'So tell me the problem. And how much you – she needs. Hope everything's OK; don't do anything scary. Love you. I'll try to help. Does Mum know?'

— reconsiders buying a tape recorder, but the shame of being ripped off by smiling criminals precludes it, and she hasn't yet spotted an equivalent to Bath HiFi, where the manager knows her sister. Perhaps she should ask Stella.

— is called by Ruth, once her shyest friend:

> '. . . and anyway he's taking me out again on Thursday and the work's really good I mean knackering but fun and everyone's incredibly nice and hey did I tell you Vic and Clare from Sheffield are here too and we might all move in together and oh my money's running out sorry I missed you wish I had a phone at home but I'll . . .'

— shakes books at random and waits for Richard to telephone. Or Stella. Could she ring Stella?

— sits on the kitchen chair, the table, the bottom stair, her bedroom floor. Through the open doorway, Stella's bedroom waits.

— decides to try the Glasses again:

'Could I speak to N. Glass please?'

'He's not here. Can I help?' asks a different woman: older, less grumpy.

'Well . . . maybe. I'm calling about a ring, you see, that I think was left at your house?'

'Really? I don't think I—'

'Oh – sorry. My name's Anna.'

'Well, Anna, I'll find it and put it in the post right away. But I don't see how . . . What was it like?'

'The thing is, I don't exactly know. It's not mine, you see.'

'I don't . . .'

'It belongs to someone else – I'm calling for her. I think she assumed you'd know the one.'

'Who, then?'

'It's Stella. Stella Salzmann.'

There is a long, frozen pause. 'I never thought I'd hear from *her* again,' she says, and the line shivers. 'Who is this?'

Anna is now entirely thrown, but her tone is clear and proud. 'Her niece.'

'Well, *niece*,' says the woman, and the hiss in her voice fills the telephone, 'you can tell your aunt that she can forget about her ring, and let us get on with forgetting her.' And the line goes dead.

The room refills with air. Gently, she replaces the receiver. This woman knows something about Anna's own family. Could she call back and ask for details? Somehow she will have to explain the non-appearance of the ring. She has not fully discharged her duty. Her mind flirts with Stella's unimaginable sin.

It may be time to ask her mother for details. The explanation must be here, among the boxes, at the back of a drawer. If not, she'll have to find someone who will tell her. This isn't the kind of secret one can ignore.

She examines every postcard on the bookshelves. There

are several references to bad behaviour, but the perpetrator is never clear. One offers thanks for an amazing present, but a blue line scores it from left to right. There are shots of buildings, nineteenth-century textiles, Florentine counts in symbolic profile. One of these stops her short. Stella has sent it. Or rather she had meant to, but has changed her mind.

Forgot to tell you:

He asked again – obv. thought I'd forgotten. So I waited till head waiter came over, sat back and said "Ignace, I know you think women come when you smile. But I wouldn't suck your dick if my life depended on it." And I threw the ring at him and left.

Anna wanders over to the window and watches her mouth forming into an accommodating O. She imagines her own self speaking: imperious waiters stilled, the clink of porcelain, the dropping of Ignace's shadowed jaw. And how had it all begun? N. Glass could be a father, and Ignace his son, but why would Stella want the ring back now?

She practises in a range of accents: *Suck my dick. Stella, suck my dick.* Soon she will have to lie on the sofa again and consider it more fully. First she returns to another postcard: a Seurat of a sheepish-looking girl, too quickly overlooked.

Stella, I have to see you on Thursday. I know it's probably my last chance before she goes. Call me at work. N.

She turns and turns the card, squinting at the girl behind the dots, noting the more vigorous inky strokes of N's hand. It *could* be N. Glass, but surely it's too tepid, too bald, to ignite that level of quiet venom. Let alone her mother's letter. No; Anna suspects that the real drama lies elsewhere. Stella's life, she feels sure, is one of thrilling outrage. This flat must be full of it. Now is her chance to lay it bare; and learn.

Time Out lies open and water-ringed in front of her. All human life is here. She has pictured herself at every talk, has rejected (too long, too far away, too much fun to see alone) every available film; she has even read through ice-hockey matches and crossgendered workshops ('This week: issues around spiritual experience'). Eventually she turns to Entertainment: she will draw up a schedule to keep her busy from now till Wednesday, when she will emerge blear-eyed and hungry for her future.

But television fails her. She had anticipated evenings of film noir and cultish New York comedy, until she too develops a fire-escaped loft and protean sex-life. However, there are only programmes on voles and community health-schemes – late-night viewing, not alternatives to sunshine and conversation. Then the square-eyed god of television programming, amid the chill winds of heaven, lowers his rectangular head and takes pity.

3:00 *The Big Sleep*

After a wasp-harassed interlude in Tavistock Square and an olive and stilton sandwich, Anna is ready to watch. She lies on the floor kicking her shins against the sofa, picking at a plate of apple slices, and feasts her thirsty soul. The impossible plot, the clothes, the cars and the muttered wisecracks fill her with luxuriant envy. She wants to be all of them: Marlowe, darkly charismatic even in a raincoat; the girl in the bookshop, with him all to herself, with the scotch and the rain and the compliment all glasses-wearing girls dream of; gorgeously languid Lauren most of all, swinging a palazzo-panted leg on her Daddy's windowsill, the archetype of adult sex appeal. She fantasizes in glorious monochrome, alert for sparks of off-screen passion as Lauren and Humphrey hunch down between gunshots.

The sun again begins to tilt below the black houses, and children's television ends. It is not until after six, as she watches a serial-killer loner in a rural soap, that she remembers Markus.

It's in Streatham, which could be anywhere. His address is on a stained receipt: she can't quite allow him to be the first new entry in her book. She speed-walks to Warren Street, elbows oaring the chemical-heavy air, her bag banging tourists like a local. Markus doesn't drink; do men like flowers? Her father brings them home all the time, like a well-trained puppy. There is a stall by the station, but what would suit a barely-known uncle, dubiously sane? This is a nightmare of her mother's devising: dead cats festooning the cobwebbed hall; robes and incantations; hereditary daggers lying unscabbarded beside his plate. He may read an inadvertent challenge into her choice: she needs a laminated gift-shop card explaining the Lost Language of Flowers. Ninety per cent of murders are committed by people known to the victim, she recollects, finally choosing irises. They are beautiful, spread-eagled indigo and gold, but when she sniffs them there is only a wet-dog reek of damp brown paper and marshy leaves.

By the time she has crossed the river, and navigated her way between kebab shops to his dark front door, the flowers, which she has been using as a screen for discreet consultations of her *A–Z*, are soggy, bent and doilied round the edges. If she turns back, nothing on earth will appease her mother, who is legendarily sensitive to family slanders, particularly from within. Besides, now she has evidence. She needs someone to interrogate.

There's no need to be frightened, she lies as she raps on the glass. She and Markus will laugh about this, eventually, when he proves to be normal. Others will marvel at their odd but lasting bond. As, perhaps, will her mother.

'Anna.'

'Markus?'

If she had passed this man in the street she would have held her bag closer, looked out for flying cans of Special Brew, fingertipped him money only if feeling brave. Not have stayed for dinner. To think she virtually sprang from his loins.

She smiles, rapidly inventorizing. Her uncle seems to have expanded. It's not just that he's fatter, although jowls are beginning to show under the sooty stubble, and his half-buttoned shirt strains against a maternal belly. It is more that his head seems curiously inflated, as if his renowned brains have forced his remaining greasy hair into retreat up his bulging forehead. The corralled strands sit on the edge of his murky collar, smooth as a rat's tail. He winks one reddened eye like a lizard, briefly submerging it in a veiny cushion of flesh. 'Come in.'

He looks like an alcoholic baby, self-decorated with plug-hole hair. 'Lovely,' says Anna weakly, and follows him into the flat.

*

Half an hour later she has established several facts.

1. Markus is not continually trying to alert her to the presence of an intruder somewhere behind him. It is simply a new twitch.

2. His existing tics and habits have worsened – or improved, depending on perspective. The blinks and lightning grimaces have always made conversation arduously fascinating – now, she feels, it may be kinder not to look.

3. Due to the bewitching floorshow it is impossible to tell whether he is profoundly clever, or whether the pauses, gasps and stutterings merely conceal an ordinary brain. Markus has been told he's a genius so many times it's no surprise he's acting like one.

Edinburgh was full of boys like this: the watchful only children, duffel-coated from mildewed vicarages, taking notes in angry writing and ducking head-down into hall and chapel. Or wincing strangled academics, foxy in tobacco-spilled V-necks, pushing out ten-yearly monographs and spluttering through sherry parties, eyeing bursars' pie-crust wives. How galling, thinks Anna as she watches Markus's swaying back, her eyes half-shut to simulate concentration while blocking out the worst of his unspeakable kitchen. All his life he's been the brainy boy, the one who is going to achieve, and then her mother marries poor and undramatic Frank, who in ten years produces two offspring and a stream of surprise bestsellers, with barely a twitch to show for it.

'How's the Citizens' Advice Bureau?' she asks.

'Eh? The Citizens . . . oh the Citizens. Yes well those. Yes I gave them up, gave the poor buggers right up, oh years ago now, before you were born. How old are you now?' Unlike her mother he has kept his Leicester vowels.

'Well, actually Markus, I'm twenty-two. Are you sure it was then? You were working there last time I saw you.' She pauses, tactfully. 'A few years ago, at Mum's house? In Bath?'

'Yes. Hmm. Well, maybe, maybe. All over now, finished with, done. No more advising citizens, hey. No, what I'm doing now is much more interesting.' He glares suspiciously to right and left, like a Disney villain.

'Oh, really?' asks Anna politely, trying to keep incredulity out of her too-bright voice. As far as she knows from a few dark comments from her mother, and her grandmother's warning silence, Markus lives off a small fee for Nature Notes from a free local magazine, and ill-afforded subsidies from his parents. What could he really be doing, with . . . idiosyncrasies like these? Teaching primary school children?

'Come closer,' says Markus.

Must I? She watches crystal spittle flying over the table as he smacks and gobbles his lips. But Markus, despite his bulk, seems easily hurt. For some people, she realizes, London never happened. He must be still bleeding from the shock.

She joins him at the sink.

'I'm a *store detective*,' he confides, *sotto voce*.

'Really?' says Anna weakly. She struggles to avoid an image of Uncle Markus trailing shoppers round Selfridges, while they nervously clutch their handbags and try to attract Security.

'Yes. Oh yes. On an informal basis, as yet. But oh, I have plans.'

'Ah,' she says. A filthy beige telephone clings half-way up

the wall, like a resting snail. Is he in fact – and perhaps she should borrow his phone to call her father, right away – trying to seize shoplifters entirely of his own volition? She casts about for a change of subject.

'So – what are you cooking? It smells . . . unusual.'

'Try it.' Markus smiles complacently.

She takes the blackened spoon. 'Really? Now?' The pan spits maroon mud pools.

'Sit down then,' Markus pouts, and turns back to the pan. Obediently, Anna sits. The quiet spreads like gas. She scratches a spinachy fleck from her plate and tips it over. On its underside a miniature long-haired man, pectorals and triceps impressively outlined, embraces the words:

Sampsonite Ceramics
Hotelware
Super-Vitrified

Muscles deep in her uncle's back flick and shift efficiently as he reaches for a plastic colander. Over its edges pasta shapes pour like sightless fishes. 'How's . . . ah, the, your, you know, father? Eh? The golden boy. Mother's pride. Eh?'

'I think he's . . . fine. In fact, he's very well.' Now might Nemesis strike her father's fragile head. Thrown by Markus's unexpected declaration of hostility, she flails like a blindfolded swimmer for the shore.

'Do you . . . cook much?'

'Ah yes.' He lifts a finger, as if in admonition, then taps his forehead, hard. 'I've got it up here. Oh yes. Natural talent. Not like the other two with their black designer pasta and their authentic Moroccan hand-carved tah-*jeens*.'

It's almost a shock when he mentions his sisters. Markus

is so very unsleek; can they really all have shared the same womb-space? It's hard to picture that household: the determined, careful parents, the three English-accented prodigies. When did Markus become like this? Was Anna's mother born that thin? What did Stella do before she discovered smoking?

Now is her chance to ask. But after the complicated business of serving, Markus is flicking and blinking so hard that the plates are in danger of skipping from his hands. She snatches them, helpfully. 'Thank you, Markus.'

He nods, and begins to eat, head still jerking, eyes down. She dips the tines of her canteen fork into the dark and clotted surface, expecting hare's blood or a shocking slap of sugar. It is tomato, and delicious. She shuffles it around her tongue, unable to trust her tastebuds, like a foot flinching from the burn of icy water. Then she notices black fragments at the bottom of her bowl. One has an attachment that may have been a leg. Numbly she finishes her mouthful, keeping her tongue away.

After a pause, during which she surreptitiously grinds the darker shapes to form a base for their limp fellows, Markus looks up. His bowl is the cleanest place on the table.

'Plenty more to go, girl. Just like your mother.'

'I'm not like Mum usually,' she says, trying to sound indifferent. 'It's just – well, I'm a bit tired.'

Markus watches her, breathing audibly through his nose. Is he waiting or thinking? The silence begins to grow, sucking the air from the stuffy kitchen.

'Did Mum never eat?' she asks eventually. She watches his stubby fingers patting the table-top, making private patterns.

'Well, not much, no, not at all. Always been proud of her stick-like physique, yes. Puts all her energy into cooking it, yes, does Magda, or zooming up to check on London. Poor girl; wish she'd stop.'

Anna tries to lasso back the conversation. 'Did you always get on with Mum?' she asks. If they have this talk; she and Markus – and maybe even Stella – will forge a new closeness. Together they will expose whatever padlocked secret her mother hoards in the dark. He won't have heard of the Glasses; she'll have to retrieve Stella's ring alone. But the letter?

'Markus, Mum never tells me anything. Come on; didn't you secretly prefer Stella?'

She smiles at her uncle in new complicity. He'd be much less bad-looking if he cut his hair; her mother should have told him.

'Well, no,' says Markus. 'We got on as much as – very different, me and Stella. The naughty little sister. Oh yes. Magda's more . . . we were friends, us two. More careful.'

'Aren't you still? I'm surprised, Markus. She's so . . . controlled. I'd have thought—'

'Be careful yourself. Dangerous, that one.'

She smiles politely, as if she needed warning about her mother, then launches herself. 'I can't help being curious, you see. They always act as if they get on, but— well, Mum keeps hold of her, Stella's, keys, which I'm sure Stella hates, and Mum is *obsessed* with knowing when she'll be around, and it's mad, really, and I don't know if I'm supposed to be getting involved, and I don't want to, obviously, but sometimes I really think there's something important. That they're keeping something from me.'

He looks at her, a flat closed glance of private history. Then, abruptly, he begins to laugh.

Anna stares at his large yellow teeth, the saliva twanging

between his jaws. A tear creeps over the bridge of his nose and down below his nostril. Eventually, with a sinking series of '*hoo* hoo' noises, he subsides.

'*What?*' asks Anna, discomfited. 'Markus, what *is* it? God, it's like growing up Masonic. What are you all being so coy about?'

Markus begins to laugh again, then catches his niece's eye, and stops.

'Lord, girlie, you've really got it, that look,' he says. 'She could corral grown men in minutes with that sphinxy stare. Has your mother ever told you you're paranoid, eh? Eh, Anna?'

Some sort of dust seems to have settled on her itching skin. She scratches her neck and tries not to look sullen. 'Many times.'

'And has she ever told you there's a secret?'

'Well, no. Not exactly – no. But it's sort of implied. You know.' Now she's under the 40-watt spotlight of Markus's alarming kitchen, it's harder to frame vague but penetrating questions than she had imagined.

'Aha. OK. Yes. There we have it.' He clasps his hands on the table and rocks his chair back against an enormous pile of bone-brittle newspapers. 'Now. What do you think the problem might be?'

'Well,' she says slowly, 'it could be anything.' If she approaches her suspicions slowly, Markus may unbend. 'I mean, I don't think it's Stella's personality. Everyone likes her. Even Dad – at least, he always emerges from his study when she visits. Like a hermit crab.'

Markus rolls his eyes.

'And Stella's always nice to Mum . . . relatively. It's as if she's bravely making the best of a bad situation, but doesn't quite understand it, and Mum's always civil but there's nastiness underneath . . .'

'My my, you have been muddling over this one, haven't you, my little Sherlock? My my yes. And has it occurred to you it might be very simple?'

'I *know* that.' With an effort she reigns her condescension in. 'I used to think it must be envy – I mean, everyone goes on about Mum being beautiful, but Stella is too, isn't she, in a completely different way. Her eyes, and her skin – everyone stares at her. They can't help it. She and Mum don't even look related . . .'

Markus fails to rise to the bait. Anna relinquishes her lifelong theory about Stella's disgraceful adoption from a nomadic Magyar tribe.

'So it might be just be that Mum doesn't approve. Living in Paris, not caring about expensive curtains, her sex life.' Markus gives a particularly vigorous twitch. It's now or never. 'Or you know maybe it's more concrete. Something Stella has actually done – to Mum, or to someone important . . .' Anna had resolved to keep the two puzzles separate, but now, at her only chance to question him, they messily collide. 'Do you know someone called Glass, Markus?'

Markus crashes his chair to the floor and rears up. Anna jumps: the lines where his hair should start are furrowing and regrouping at incredible speed. 'Anna. Dear Anna,' he begins, blinking hard and fast, 'this isn't really my place, you know, not at all at all. You should ask her, you must. I don't want to speculate: private matter. My God, no. Enough, I think. Please.'

'Oh. I'm sorry.' The air shimmers with invisible reproach and blighted opportunity. He is waggling his head from side to side like a toy. 'Have I upset you, Markus?'

He waves his hand at her and begins to clear their plates. 'No, no not at all no no. But sticky territory, that one. Yes. Not for me to encroach.'

She stands to help, but he shakes his head, more vigorously. She watches for a few seconds, then begins again.

'It's just that if I should know—'

'No, Anna. We've finished with that one. Finished.'

Their dinner is over. Markus's bubble has been breached; now everyone they both know, every memory they could dredge, is suddenly taboo. It is barely evening, but Anna pleads tiredness. Markus stands in the doorway as she looks for her bag.

'Is it safe round here at night?' she asks him.

'Not for muggers.'

He misses his cue to walk her to the Underground station, join her on the Tube, come back to the flat for a night, or two, and dent the gaping quiet. What does he expect her to *do* with this half-opened secret?

'Bye then, Markus. Thank you. Can I . . . can I come again?'

'Quite. Yes, quite. If you're good.'

As she slams the front door behind her Anna decides to take control. If she just lets herself look round, instead of treating the flat like a shrine, all her imaginings will be laid to rest. To think she used to envisage infanticide, extortion, a drunken pass at Stella's own brother-in-law. Now she understands that she would never stoop to squalor. Her sin is wilder, darker, much more thrilling. What future shock is waiting in the wings?

I will find it, she promises herself. If there is anything to know, I will work it out.

The sitting room is scattered with photographs – blank gold-faced Virgins, a woman waving from a rowing boat, Stella in flares running past a rain-glossed sculpture, and at a birthday party surrounded by men. But their backs are barren. Under every quiet surface truth falters, out of reach.

Anna takes the birthday picture from the bookshelf and looks closer. No date on the back. There are too many candles on the cake to count. She examines the face in the fragile square for jewellery, laughter lines, but it is ageless, suspended in an amber drop of candlelight. Stella is laughing, head turned towards a pair of men by her shoulder. They are light and shadow, grinning, charcoal-eyed. Either of those men might be Richard, she realizes – and catches herself: I must ask Richard. He will have an answer.

The taller of the two is unremarkably good-looking: neat thick hair, mouth curving, eyes moderately round. He is an acquaintance from college, someone else's boyfriend; surely too obvious to be Richard himself. Surely she would never fall for him. But the face of the man on the left, the one on whom Stella's gaze forever rests, is half in darkness. There is nothing to see: a pale plane of cheekbone, a hooded, dark-lashed eye. One slim arm rests on Stella's shoulder, palm upwards, creased and open. But the space between them is incandescent. That eye is smiling at the sight of her.

Anna looks closer, and starts.

It is a woman.

*

She takes the photograph to the sofa, and leans back, barely breathing. The air burns. There can be no doubt, despite the short wing of hair, despite Stella's extraordinary look. The narrowness of the arm and hand, the eyelashes, the smoothness.

Her thoughts are whirling too quickly to control, like surging floodwater. She closes her eyes. Is it possible? Why has she never known?

But what, on reflection, would her mother have said? Isn't this exactly what she would do: keep it dark and hidden, wait until it went away? Never expecting that her daughter would uncover the truth.

This is it; you've found the secret. Now it's time to sleep.

But she cannot sleep. She will not sleep. Her room is hot; her mind will not be quiet. The air seethes: eyes, and skin, and open waiting palms.

Seven

She ricochets around her bedroom, discarding and retrying garment combinations like a mythical blasphemer condemned to endless fashion suffering. Her first day at work begins in fourteen minutes; this is a disaster. This morning, however, Anna's waking brain is wrapped in a fleece of calm. If others can survive submarine disasters, plagues of frogs and towering infernos, surely she can handle this.

Lolloping down Gower Street, encased in a virtual skin of sweat, she tries to prepare, intelligently. Opinions on current fiction? Her mind is swept clean. Why does she want to work in a bookshop? She is an idiot savant without the calendar-mind. She will have to smile and hope they're gentle.

And the other thing? The lightning strike she's trying to ignore? That she'll have to deal with when – if – she returns.

It's like being on a helter-skelter, familiar faces whirling past through mercury tears. Through the hi-speed surround-sound blur she glimpses, and loses sight of, novelists – both dead and alive – she had imagined meeting, street names she remembers from films starring Michael Caine, her own hands, childishly plump yet crazed with wrinkles, hovering over the till. She is introduced, and reintroduced, to full-timers, part-timers, a sales rep and the cleaner. Every conceivable type of customer expects her to know exactly what they want. Briefly, in the Staff Only lavatory, she puts her head in her hands and imagines being a baby penguin, stranded among strangers on a breaking ice floe, the only fluffy bird-chick unsheltered by its parents' knobbly claws. She listens to the sound of her paper-bag survival breathing and longs for a glimpse of a face she knows. Send me an unfavoured cousin, someone from primary school, she thinks. I am surfeited with strangeness. I cannot handle this today.

But with that thought the picture shifts: the dawning of perspective. She can, and she knows it. Somehow she'll learn who some of these people are, and send unrumpled faxes, and won't blush with confusion when faced with an invoice. Next time someone asks for Ondaatje, Seth or Oe she will know the shelf. Wait to develop the film in the dark, she instructs herself. If you can just survive this, at home you can start thinking.

She tries to. She really does.

Wilf is a character manager. If Anna's life were being filmed (playing herself in cashmere and knee boots), Armistead Maupin would cameo. He has a moustache like silver fox fur, an obviously extensive pastel wardrobe, and flirts with everyone, even professors. When his name is mentioned among a brief teatime huddle of his juniors, everyone sneers knowingly.

'What?' she asks. 'Isn't he – well, easy to work for?'

'It's not that,' says the tallest of the male assistants, who has a blond Merchant Ivory fringe and a clumsily supercilious air. He has already, twice within Anna's hearing, drawled 'at Oxford'. 'He's just, you know, melodramatic. In my opinion.'

'You mean . . . he's gay? Isn't he?'

They all laugh, as adults do at infant spelling errors. 'Yes,' say the blond boy, half closing his insolent eyes, and makes an opaque reference to a book launch the previous night, at which Wilf had been out*rage*ous to a gate-crashing actor. Anna smiles at each other face in turn, trying to follow, unable to ask. No, it isn't that he's gay, they assure each other, flopping their wrists. It's that he's *so* queeny, so impossible, so absurd.

Wilf is Anna's only adult homosexual. At college she'd had David, who looked like a beautiful baby and had the soul of Zsa Zsa Gabor. When they weren't holding hands and noisily window shopping, David was learning to use his claws. He had begun to cheat on her with a vicious celebrity daughter, who used her younger brother as bait. They fought; he'd left notes in trembly orange ink on her door; but by Easter they'd divorced.

After David there was Si, the acne-crazed son of a military wife-beater, who declared himself gay, then bi, then straight again. When he began his second round of gayness her sympathy had begun to flag. The night they fell out, her chaste friendship with Luke, who was talkative, caramel-eyed and claimed he could ice-skate, was reborn in a pool of Bulgarian Merlot. By the time it went back under, Si was bi again, with a diminutive spun-sugar girlfriend. Anna had kept away.

*

Now she watches Wilf covertly, a list of gardening books unchecked in front of her. Does he have a boyfriend? A plumpish older man with glasses who mothers him; a dark boy who has his friends round too late and helps himself to the Scotch? Is he happy? Is he glad to be gay?

Is anyone?

Maybe, one day, she will confide in him about Stella. Or better yet, drop hints and see if he follows, a pink-kneed runner through a trail of paper petals. She will offer clues – how Stella dresses, her cutlery choices – and see if he catches on, watch for his nostrils scenting the air. Surely he'll be able to tell, won't he? He must know lots of . . . friends like her.

But Wilf charms in bright flashes, and moves on, leaving barbs floating through the air like thistledown: '*Please*!' 'You *wish*!' His answers to her anxious enquiries about order forms are firm but impatient. She fumbles in their wake, guiltily relieved that Iain, a light-eyed Welsh part-timer, is given even shorter shrift. Dreams of a novelty friendship, cathartic admissions at the Groucho, swell and multiply.

He is fascinating; she has never seen an adult male so palpably aware. He acts as though at any minute his dream man will come into the shop and catch him in the middle of whatever he's doing. She smirks, then catches herself: isn't she also always waiting? Isn't *her* every second the moment just before; every spontaneous skip and smile preplanned? She is prepared, constantly, to be caught unawares. By what? By love, of course.

The terraces are bonfires of evening light. Above her, impossibly, a seagull shrieks. She's heard that squawk before – what can it be doing here? Who can she ask? She squints down

Shawcross Street, but it is empty. Her brain is running a new soundtrack, a song her mother used to play: 'every time I see you, standing there before me; I get a kick . . .', and above her, only a few metres away, that photograph and the letter are waiting. Her feet slap the pavement like metronomes.

Yet, as she climbs the stairs, what she longs for is a floating emerald in the hallway. Her mind is folding away from the bookshop's flurry, leeching courage into the stair carpet. Here again is her other world, stuffed with fears and portents and enormous silent discoveries. She is becoming one of those children locked in cupboards, thinking shoe boxes are their mothers, communicating with coat-hangers and the distant traffic. She needs a conversation.

Anyone would do. It could be Sophie, or Helen, who left a message with Anna's mother: '*She's* having a wonderful time, apparently, and says do you remember Peter, apparently from Glasgow? It seems they're – well, they've met up, and she says Glasgow's marvellous, which personally I doubt . . .'

Or her father, with another concerned but distant heartbreaker: 'Hello Infant it's me; just to say have you rung your bank yet? And did you work out how to turn on the freezer? Beak up, sweetheart.'

Or Sasha: 'Sis, it's me, hi. Poppy and Butch say hi? We need to talk – no, Mum, nothing. That's it. OK. Seeya.'

Or her mother again, assuming she is not waiting, hawklike, at the kitchen table for her daughter to mount the stairs.

Or one of the Glass women, ringing to enlighten or berate. Perhaps the woman in the photograph.

Or Stella, unimaginably.

Or Richard.

*

'Hello, Anna? It's me, again; I was just wondering whether Stella has rung – about, well, any of it. If so – or if not – could you give me a call? 342 3782. Thanks.'

His voice is absurdly low; a volcanic rumble: the product of haywire hormones and a caveman slouch. Then she notices a new yellow light: REPLACE TAPE.

This machine is her nemesis. She is certain to break it. Soon no one will be able to leave messages at all. Stella will return and discover a telecommunications wasteland instigated by her niece.

Should she ring Richard? She could ask Stella, but it's hardly an emergency, and the photograph precludes a casual chat. Should she just go ahead, given that he may be the sometime boyfriend of her aunt? What if she asks a perfect, incisive, question and he crumples, weeping, fatally reminded of a love he could not share? Her fingers slither damply on minutely convex buttons. She makes herself a promise: if you manage not to ask about the photo or the letter, you don't have to ring any of Mum's friends tonight.

A voice; deep but human.

'Yes?'

'Richard? It's Anna. You said to call.'

'So has she?'

'What? Oh – no, she hasn't.' If she had, would Anna tell? 'She sent a postcard though.'

'Really? And?'

'It was quite vague about dates.'

'Of course.'

'Can I help, at all?'

'Well, it's about this play on Friday. I did want to take

her there; it's the sort of thing she claims to like. You know, Gallic and complicated, dark throbbing symbolism.'

'I think I read a review.' Maybe he'll take me, she thinks. 'That *is* her kind of thing, isn't it . . . do you often go to plays with her?'

He laughs. 'Well, not what you'd call regularly. But sometimes. When I can lure her out. She did actually say that she wanted to see this one – in the spring, I think, when they announced it. So I bought these, you know, on the off-chance.'

'Yes, she is difficult to . . . well, see, isn't she. I haven't, for ages. She's my aunt. Did I tell you?'

'Mmm. How respectable that sounds.'

'Why does everyone make her sound like Mata Hari? She *is* respectable, isn't she? I mean, she's quite . . . sensible.'

'God, not the Stella I know. Not at all. *Sensible?* Hardly.'

It's hard to retaliate without sounding defensive, or crestfallen. 'Well, no, I didn't mean that, I meant . . . well, you probably know her better than me. Are you . . . an old friend?'

A weary inhalation fills her ear, as if a wave were bracing itself to fall. 'Oh, Anna.' She catches her breath. 'Well, not that, exactly. More a *close* friend; or I was, once. I think I blew it, actually. You know. Anyway.' She can hear his chest expanding, his eyes lifting from the desk, or the open window.

'Richard,' she begins, 'there was one more thing on her postcard. About a woman called Glass. I think a woman. Do you know her?'

'No,' says Richard slowly. 'I don't think so – there was a man, once, I think. Some lecturer friend of hers. Nicky, possibly,' and she hears his voice harden. 'Was it him?'

'Why?'

'I didn't like him.'

'Ah. Well, no, I think it's a woman. Or a family, at least. She needs me to collect something.' How far should she push this? 'I think it's important . . . Do you—'

'Anna, listen, will you do me a favour?'

'Yes?' she says, cautiously. 'What?'

'If you find out when she's back, will you not mention me, but let me know? You don't even have to say I rang. I just need warning, because I'll have to flog the tickets soon, and she did once say that she liked this actor and I just thought she – well, there we go. So you'll ring me?'

'I will.'

Either Stella will ring, she thinks, and I can tell him so, and they can go to the theatre. Because maybe Stella wants that after all. Or maybe she doesn't, and they won't see each other. He might decide to take me instead. Or perhaps *I* will cook Stella dinner: red wine and the night outside, as she tells me all her secrets.

That photograph rests on the bookshelf, its white borders edging into an embrace. She takes it down again.

Could she ask Richard what happened, and what went wrong? She tries to picture his face when he sees this moment, frozen in film. How much does he know? Would the answer hurt?

Could she ask Stella?

She heats some soup and slices bread, weeping tomatoes, crumbling chalky cheese. Something will happen on Friday night.

She tries television; newspapers; a book about child brides from a pile beside the sofa. But her eyes are speed-reading the bookshelves. There are drawers beneath them, and little piles of papers. She might as well give in.

Licking salty crumbs from the corners of her mouth she kneels before a cupboard. She can almost feel the ground sloping away beneath her; once she lets herself go she'll fall until she hits the bottom.

Seven years ago last summer, when the first of her father's unlikely bestsellers had lifted them from mild penury to this, her mother had suggested a holiday – an early stab at living it up. So the Raines had gone to Turkey where, standing on a deck in the sun, Anna tried paragliding. A short man in wraparound sunglasses, tattoos entwined in his arm-hair, had strapped her into a salt-stained harness. Whistling, he tied a rope from her navel to a fraying post on his friend's motor-boat. While the other man climbed in, Anna stood in the sun with her arms outstretched, feeling the webbing tight against the backs of her thighs and the padding like a warm hand on her collarbone. Behind her, splayed on bleached suede planks, lay the red and yellow parachute like a discarded egg-sac, rustling thinly as breezes skimmed in off the sea.

The man raised his arm, and the boat droned away from the deck in a creamy roar. Reverberations from the motor seemed to flow through her flesh and then, as she watched, coils of rope encrusted with diamonds began to spool towards the sea. Four loops remained, then three, then two, and as she waited to be dragged into the waves she was consumed by helplessness: by a fate so inexorable, so immense, that submission was release.

Now, as she stares at the floorboards she sees that rope again. There are other cupboards besides this one, and – she cranes her neck – at least four layers of shelving. It isn't fair on Stella to take advantage of her absence; how would Anna feel if it were her? The motor hasn't started. If she gives in now, where will she stop?

But she wants to, she can't not want to, her hot hand is rising even as she tries to keep it by her side. My body is not my own, she thinks. The doorknob is cool as water; she rests her wrist against it briefly, smoothing it over her pulse. Then she opens the door.

The cupboard is stuffed with paper. Photocopied articles, builders' estimates, press releases, paid bills and packets of wilting A4. It's like her father's stationery cupboard: an urgent, private three-minute thrill, spiced with fear of discovery and of what she might unearth, before the vulcanized rubber bands and tarry biros begin to pall. A receipt for a fireplace; not the one here. Several pages about a football-making factory in Beijing, with 'Constantine? 84 200 679' scribbled on the top in ageing indigo.

The other cupboard is full of videos: 'C4 23/7/93 El Bayadh', 'TF3 4/9/89 Tébessa', 'BBC1 5/3/97 Kasserine'. She sits back on her heels and runs a dramatically bitten thumbnail over the cardboard cases.

No; there are limits. She is curious, not starving. Arms outstretched like a tightrope walker, she lifts from her tight-thighed crouch and stands eye-to-eye with the bookshelves, practising: Kasserine.

The shelves are packed with fading novels, jammed in too tightly to retrieve. She cocks her head and reads the spines: *The Snow Ball*, *The Nice and the Good*, *The Ladies' Almanack*. Such wholesome titles; not at all what she had expected. But then what was she looking for?

*

'Where are the atlases?'

Mona, one of the other full-timers, looks at her sideways through a wispy veil of fringe. Despite the mild weather she is swaddled in a black self-hating jumper and a tasselled skirt. Don't get like this, Anna warns herself. You have to show skin if you want to look normal.

Mona seems braced for flight. Her eyes flick to the door and back at Anna.

'There, aren't they?'

'Where?'

'Oh . . .' She points a moth-ravaged sleeve at the Cookery corner and tries a smile.

'Reference?' asks Anna.

She nods, excessively.

'Thanks.' It's the see-saw effect; beside this startled swaddled mouse, Anna is Grace Kelly. Befriending her will be easy; she'll probably be grateful for Anna's time. Even Mona might have interesting friends.

But as she crosses the floor her sang-froid slides away. There are too many customers for this, and a pile of overdue returns. By the time she has reached the opposite wall, struggling under the biggest atlas like a studious toddler, Wilf's surveying eye is burning through her spine.

Kasserine. Tébessa.

She finds them quite easily. Mostaganem. Biskra. Souk Ahras. Murmured enquiries and the shop bell segue into minarets, turmeric, hookahs and pomegranate seeds. It's a travelogue based on the *Arabian Nights,* Indiana Jones and her parents' Moroccan honeymoon. Wilf is looking her way. Mostaganem.

*

She still hasn't spoken to her sister. At lunch she walks past a phone box and tries to ignore it, thinking: 'She hasn't rung again. How urgent can it be?' But it might be Sasha in trouble, after all, and if she leaves it . . .

'It's me. Where are you?'

'Walking along with Liddy and – hey, Lid, get me one. I can't—'

'Sasha, I'm on lunch. And I've only got 50p. Quickly, tell me what you need the money for.'

'God, sis, all right, hang on. Yeah, ta.'

'Sasha—'

'Coming. All right. OK, it's Cally.'

'Yes, yes, I know. But what?'

'She's, right, she's having another—'

'What, baby?'

'Abortion.'

'Another?'

'Yeah. And—'

'Sash, I'm not paying for that. I can't. I couldn't even pay for my *own* abortion if I—'

'God, sis, not you too?'

'*No!* God, no – I'm bloody careful. When I . . . have a reason to be. Unlike Cally. You are being too, aren't you?'

'Yeah, yeah, course. Look, whatever, Cally needs one. And the reason I'm asking is . . . OK, she's had it. She needed it then. And so me and Butch gave her the cash.'

'You didn't. How? Where from?'

'I borrowed it from Mum, yeah? And Butch sold . . . stuff.'

'I don't want to know. But what did you tell Mum?'

'That it was to buy your birthday present. And Christmas.'

'Oh, Sasha. Oh, you shouldn't have. Please.'

'Well, I did. But now *I* need the cash—'

'Not for—'

'Shut up, sis, no. Nah, it's for Butch. Someone's nicked his guitar.'

'Well that's hardly—'

'Yeah, no, it's really important. It's his livelihood, innit. Sort of. And the thing is, right, it's not his, it's Nev's. Who'll be fiercely hacked off when he hears. So we've like, got to get him another one. Now.'

'Jesus, Sasha. Can't you just tell Nev – I'm sure it wasn't Butch's fault—'

'Seriously, sis, we've got to. It's complicated.'

'Clearly.'

'So what I want is – look, I need Mum to write off the loan, right? For *my* birthday.'

'But why can't you just ask her yourself?'

'Because she's forgotten what I said the cash was for, and then she ended up being with me when I *did* buy your present, right, so now I need her to still forget and give *me* the cash as my present.'

'So you can give it to Butch.'

'Right. That's my present.'

'. . . Right. Christ.'

'And I need you to do it 'cause I've already asked her for some stuff, right, and if I just change my mind it won't work. You need to say it.'

'I don't see why—'

'Please, sis, I really need it.'

'Want it.'

'Whatever. Please.'

'Oh, God, the beeps. All right. Maybe. I'll see what I can—'

'Are you going tonight?' a part-timer asks, showing her again how to work the Switch machine.

'Where?'

'Oh . . . the reading. Didn't Wilf say?'

No, Wilf didn't. She busies herself with Visa slips, shame lapping at the lobes of her brain like warm seawater filling a rock pool. Then she knocks into a pile of leaflets, and as she squats to prevent pages escaping with every hot gust from the open door, she feels herself being looked upon. She glances up at a section of lemon polo-shirt.

'When you've done that could you help set out glasses. She'll be here in forty minutes and there's work to do.'

'Sorry – who will?'

'Maggie O'Keeffe.'

Jesus. Anna has read at least four M. R. O'Keeffe novels, years ago. They are books for consuming in hammocks, thinking of other people's brothers in a kiss of sunlight, knowing that everything was about to happen. And now, in a different way entirely, everything is. M. R. O'Keeffe might take to a young thing like her, to charm and dazzle at orgiastic bookish parties. Anna knows she can do it; all she needs is a forum.

Yet when the last pensioner has headed into the unwelcoming night, the novelist still lingers by the till, telling Anna about the swollen marketing budgets lavished on her literary ex-lovers. Anna is lost in talk of showcards and dumpbins, like a twelve-year-old in the lunch queue pretending to know about blow-jobs. Stella, however, will be impressed when she hears of their meeting.

M. R. O'Keeffe pours herself another glass of wine and begins to describe her affair with a Greek diplomat in 1974. 'So, five glorious months later, he took me for dinner at the Connaught. It was then that I knew it was over. I drew a heart in the aspic on his turbot, and he looked at me with chill indifference.' She describes in sonorous detail the subsequent months of Earls Court bedsits, gin, strange men in damp gassy guesthouses. 'You wouldn't believe the loneliness. I'd go to bed at eight for the dreams.'

'I . . . I've done that,' says Anna. Her cheeks flame.

From under her Lady Novelist fringe the author, now gathering her strewn possessions, looks at her sharply.

'I don't bel*ieve* it.'

Anna smiles, abashed.

'Well, if you want my advice you'll do three things. Go to galleries and look approachable. Accept every invitation. And rinse that beautiful hair in cold water to give it a shine. If all else fails you'd better move to the country.'

Anna thanks her, and as she leaves finds herself wondering if a mild Cork accent would be an asset. She could be Irish here. Of course, she could be anyone.

Eight

As she opens the white cupboard a chill boxed breath, scented with metal and the clayey smell of plasters, merges into the forest steam. If there are secrets here, they are hers for the taking.

After all, what is there to mind about? Even if Stella guessed she was poking around, it's not as if she knows what Anna's found, and has had the sense to add together. How could she object to a little healthy curiosity, a cursory investigation, by her niece? They barely know each other. Surely it is reasonable to compensate in her absence?

Later, lying in the bath, Anna soaps her skin again and tries to rationalize. This is normal, isn't it? Not necessarily likeable, but normal, to be so interested in someone else? Particularly, she tells herself, given every girl's need for an example which, without abandoning the physique of a sagging whippet and her abiding interest in tapenade, her mother will never provide. But something is snagging at her thoughts as she tries to float them guiltlessly above the foam. Is it her disappointment at finding only a blue nailbrush, toothpaste and an enormous bottle of Badedas? What had she expected to discover? She scrubs at the soles of her feet, soaps her back as high and as low as she can reach, runs the water out and starts again, but discomfort still plucks at her shrinking skin.

Moreover, every time, in bath or bed, her hand sinks between her thighs – and is it wise to be doing it this often? – her thoughts return to one disturbing theme. Despite her success in imagining Richard, plucked from her usual throng of shining participants and spectators, something has shifted. Now, even when she pictures herself with him, another image floats across the lens.

When I lean over him my hair is shorter, straighter. This is not my body. I am smiling with her mouth. As recognition hits, Anna's heart lifts in shock. 'Oh God,' she bubbles into the water, sliding beneath it to wash away the slippery guilt.

All evening, despite another phone call from her mother ('Have you rung Marianne? Anna, please. I'm trying to help. How are you going to make new friends and earn enough for a mortgage if you're selling bookmarks? Cigars are an international commodity – and did I tell you that it's the sister magazine to *Sommelier*, which is one of the better wine magazines? So try to be *nice*, Anna.'), and a calming half-hour with *Lark Rise to Candleford*, the air is sticky with distractions. Questions she could have asked her mother plague her; excuses for rooting through Stella's cupboards solidify and settle. Turning her head from side to side on the leaden pillow, trying to cool her face by blowing at her fringe, she makes three resolutions.

I will have fewer baths to avoid stripping my body of natural oils.

I will not entertain unrealistic fantasies about sex with Richard.

And I will not, ever, imagine myself as Stella, or allow her to feature in those thoughts.

Within twelve hours, inevitably, she has done all three.

Friday passes in a sleep-stiffened daze. There are difficult moments: eviscerating bouts of shyness; open customer annoyance; accidental knockings and spillings. Sometimes she becomes so muddled at the till, so unable to remember the most basic information ('Where's the lavatory?' 'Do you deliver? 'What do you have for uncles?') that she seriously begins to doubt her mental development. However, even if she loses them millions, even if she is reduced to eating faulty till receipts, at least she has distractions.

While looking for a sandwich she wanders into a chemist's, smiling relaxedly like a shoplifter. Signs encourage her to Ask Your Pharmacist; she examines the hair accessories, thinking of questions. What is wrong with me? Can London actually make you ill? Am I over-bathing? She reads the list of Bach Flower Remedies and wonders which she could possibly do without. Soon she'll be stuttering at small children, laughing at inopportune moments, seeing messages in telegraph poles. She thinks of Markus, and touches her own sleeve for reassurance, or warning.

Only later, after dragging weekend groceries through the Brunswick Centre's concrete shell, does she remember what Richard is doing tonight. She rechecks the answerphone; he may have rung while she was in the bathroom, or coughing. But there is nothing.

Bastard.

He shouldn't have raised her hopes. All that flirting, 'don't you want to know who I am' and 'do me a favour'. No I don't, I won't. I'm not going to help you win Stella. Even if I knew how.

It has begun to rain. She is briefly comforted: no moonlit walks for Richard tonight. But she is still stuck here and he is presumably there, perhaps with Stella – the centre of all this, the one everybody has to love, or hate. She is sick with curiosity. Stella, she asks the walls, the windows – what is it? Tell me. What have you done?

The walls are the colour of clotted cream. Muslin hangs at the two enormous windows. A door shuts off the alcove: of course, a little room of Stella's own. Streetlights suffuse the room with a salmon glow. She finds a switch, and her vision floods with gold.

The air is threaded with the scent of wooden boxes and silver and Stella. Some women, like Anna's mother, trail behind them artificial clouds of green and flowers so intense that everything picks up a trace, like possessions tainted by heartbreak. Others smell more faintly, yet still so entirely of themselves that rooms echo with their touch, their lost presence. Anna's attempts to smell herself have invariably failed, except when dirty or excited. But she may be one of those scented people. Whatever she fingers will bear a sign.

She crosses to the chest of drawers opposite the bed, where a mirror slides copper light from a side-lamp to the floor. Beneath it a coin glints like a tiny flame. Stella wore a gold ring in the garden. Of course. A signet ring – no, a wedding band. A thin ring with a flat . . . how could she have forgotten? Could it be the one that was lost?

Everything has become tangled and muddied. She closes her eyes for quiet and then, with a leap, she opens her mind.

This, it seems, is what she knows:

a) N. Glass is a man. Nicky Glass.

b) Whose family hate Stella, and won't give back her ring.

c) A woman loved Stella. Loves her.

d) Stella did something Anna's mother hates.

e) Only something of this magnitude would Stella keep a secret – otherwise, surely, she'd have explained why she can't retrieve the ring herself. And only something this . . . this shocking could fully explain the rift between her and Anna's mother, Markus's panic, the Glass women's civilized fury.

Like a queen surveying her terrain, Stella's tragedy is spread out before her. An almost-wedding ring, given – perhaps after the birthday party – to Stella, sealing a secret passion. Discovery, and family crisis: Magda's terrible letter; perhaps more. Then the nameless woman – sister, daughter of Nicky Glass? – leaves, in torment. The ring, thrown aside in their final row, shivers in circles to rest beside the bed. Now, ignored by the woman's jealous relations, it languishes, while Stella, proud and beautiful, weeps alone in Paris. Waiting for Anna to deliver it.

She is standing, transfixed, like a priest in a syrupy rhombus of light. If someone walked in now, they'd leap entirely to the wrong conclusions. Anna's only looking for explanations, after all; just the rest of the letter, another photograph, the key to this simple family mystery. There is no subtext.

Here are her things:

A blue bowl washed with bronze, filled with earrings: hoops the size of a fingernail, glass jewels, gold. Anna lifts a hook and touches a miniature cherub, suspended from a starry sphere.

Bottles: Guerlain; a ridged bottle with a stained French label. She lifts the stopper and inhales the ghosts of roses.

A dark lipstick; a Lancôme mascara, Very Black. She strokes the lipstick over the back of her hand, streaking it with war paint.

A Nefertiti collar of necklaces hung over the mirror: intricate silver; a dusty amber string.

While her body roams like a child in a garden, scenting, touching, tasting bits of twig and leaf, her mind is a cartwheel of roaring thought, picturing them here together. She closes a warm palm around the amber beads, and is about to lift them when she hears a noise. A black taxi is idling, just outside the flat. She holds her body still and invisible beside the window. Any second now the front door will slam, and she'll hear footsteps, and Stella will be in here, in this flat, like a comet. If it's her, she isn't with Richard. If it's her, she'll find Anna in her bedroom, looking for skeletons.

But the taxi does not pull away, and instead of footsteps there is only Anna's breathing, very fast and shallow, billowing the curtains. She closes her eyes against the glass, against the dark night waiting to pour in. Time passes; there is no miracle.

The bed is enormous: a low bank of embroidered white cotton. She could lie back on it now and, when she rises again, smooth over the sunken places until it looks untouched. Instead, quickly, she tours the room, searching for traces: threads from her clothing, breath in the mirror. Then she walks into her own bedroom and shuts the door. Until the moment when darkness slides over her eyelids and her thoughts atomize, she has a flat white world to consider. As she pulls off her clothes her skin is singing.

In the morning when, body damp and mind half-melted, she finally leaves her bed, only a sudden car-horn reminds her of the world outside. As she races to work a pheremonal cloud seems to swarm after her, like killer bees chasing a starlet in a headscarf. However, as evening approaches no one suggests meeting for a drink, or asks her to a party, or is, realistically, likely to. A pub is mentioned, briefly, but she has no heart for beer and Hula Hoops. She had expected a Sunday lunch invitation, at the very least. But it seems they all, even flinching Mona, even Kirsten, Wilf's taciturn deputy, have somehow developed weekend lives. Unless she makes an effort, or her mother refuses to stay away, Anna will be a deaf-mute by Tuesday, flailing an arm's length from her rightful life.

However, even as she shuts the front door behind her, the next forty-eight hours, already solid as a golem, lurch and dissolve. At the bottom of the stairs, glowing in the communal half-light, floats a pale rectangle. Unless it belongs to the still unseen neighbours – who surely before long, perhaps even tonight, will overcome their shyness and invite her in for a lasting urban friendship of interesting risotto and enormous bacchic lunches – she has post.

She steps slowly towards the doormat, like a reluctant

bride. Only when her fingers touch the edges of the card does she allow herself to notice Stella's writing.

'Richard it's, it's Anna.'

'Oh – hello.' On the back of her lids a picture is frozen: herself in the bath, water rhythmically lapping. 'You've just caught me,' he says. 'I was on my way out.'

'Oh, well, I . . . mustn't keep you.' She pauses minutely for reassurance; he offers none. 'Yes, well I was just ringing to say . . . I have some information. Well no, not that, exactly, but—' Her social skills are ossifying. Any minute now he will secrete a little dollop of condescension, and her composure will dissolve. 'About Stella.'

'You haven't, have you? Really?' Obviously Stella wasn't at the theatre last night. Anna arches her back and smiles as Richard says: 'Did she mention me?'

Now he's the supplicant. She wants to laugh. 'Well, no, she didn't. But she wrote to me; it arrived this morning. I've been working; I haven't had a minute. It's sitting here on the rug.'

'What does she say?'

'She says, as far as I can remember, "Dear Anna, As it turns out I'm stuck in Paris for a while longer, but will come as soon as I can. Blah-de-blah, Stella."'

There is a pause, filled by tapping and one tired sigh like closing bellows. Then he rallies. 'Not one for rambling, is she, your Stella. Nothing else?'

'No – not really.' She twists mystery into the end of her words; an apple-green lovelock, barely noticed.

He waits for more; his mouth opens with a small wet click. 'Anna. I have an idea. Why don't we – well, you've done me a favour. She let us know rather late, but there we go. Now, why don't I buy you a drink? As a reward?'

Startled, she makes a sound as if being gently strangled.

'No, really. It's the least I can do, given your willingness to act as my – announcer, I suppose. I'm just . . . keen to know when she'll be back. You know, so we can make plans.'

'Of course,' she says smoothly, her mind sprinting. 'So . . .' Drinks parties, birthday parties, intimate dinners for two, or three. If he asks for this weekend better not sound too grateful. Pretend he's just one on your impressive list.

'Yes, so, a drink? Perfect. Say . . . well, why not Tuesday? I've a friend pencilled in but – never mind. OK?

What if he is hideously pockmarked? dwarfish? blond? 'Yes – yes.'

'Good. So, when would suit you? Seven-ish, at Florian's in Soho? Do you know it?'

'Well, not exactly, but I'm sure . . .'

'Geek Street, or no, is that the other one. Never mind, I'm sure you'll find it. Listen, I'm horribly late. So, see you then.'

'Yes. Great. Bye?'

'Bye, Anna.'

— Geek Street? Surely not. Eventually she finds her new *A–Z*, inexplicably lost despite the neatness of the flat and her scant possessions. Nothing under Geek; she tries Geak, Gee and Ghee before turning to Soho and moving her fingernail slowly over every little lane. D'Arblay; Foubert's; Glasshouse; Beak. Greek.

— He said 'us'. Conspiracy has joined them, like private

detectives in a sixties farce. She will make a poor colleague: she has searched envelope backs and Post-Its for her aunt's telephone number, but it has gone, as cleanly as if written in lemon-juice. She will have to find a way to ask her mother for it again, although she can already see the frown of irritation, the wounded silence into which her request will sink.

— And all that business about 'willingness' and 'reward' and 'your Stella' – is he being blind on purpose? Surely he can see *why* she's being so helpful – it's hardly for Stella's sake, after all. Isn't it obvious that Richard and Anna should meet?

— If Stella wasn't at the theatre she can't be interested in him, or surely she would have answered his message and come back. In Anna's new life as a pensioner, her evenings full of timewasting and inflated reminiscence, *she* wouldn't ignore an invitation. Stella must have other preoccupations; she's independent, but not careless, despite what her sister says. Now, whenever Anna thinks of her face it's that rapt gaze in the photograph – her eyes, her certain smile, the open hand. The ground has tilted. If Stella doesn't want Richard, who does she want?

Nine

By Tuesday it is all under control. She has imagined their goodbye kiss so many ways that there is no smile, no look, no faint pressure to which she will not be attuned. She briefly considers keeping herself pure and fresh for work, but decides she needs to be sexually tranquillized for their meeting, not a jittery skittering celibate. Then she eats three slices of toast, to line her stomach, and cleans her teeth twice. For forty-eight hours her bag has contained the following items:

1 mascara, frequently tested for dryness and clumping.

1 lipgloss, for that suggestive sheen.

1 note to self: CHECK. It's intentionally cryptic, in case they reach the bag-rifling stage of drink-fuelled intimacy. He may assume it's a transatlantic banking reminder; instead it is short for CHECK UNDERPANTS, itself code for GO INTO LOO SOON AFTER ARRIVAL AND DAB TINY BIT OF CUNTIC JUICES BEHIND EARS. It is supposed to drive them wild; in any case, she likes the smell.

She buys an expensive sandwich for lunch, to make her feel wantable enough to want. Coronation chicken drips on to her black trousers – the sort of thing Stella might wear, though probably not with this strange brownish shirt – but with scrubbing the mark mostly disappears. Even artificial fibres are conspiring in her favour. As she walks back to the bookshop, licking snippings of coriander from the corners of her mouth and wondering how long it will be till they start meeting here, she rehearses saying 'Oh, sorry, but I truly can't come out tonight. I've got a date' to admiring glances and Wilf's companionable ribbing; they're allies now in the race for happiness.

She ducks into the office to retrieve a customer's forgotten catflap ('Don't ask,' says Wilf), and the telephone rings. Suddenly she knows it's over: Richard has realized his mistake, Stella adores him, there's no need to meet her niece. Bravely, she meets her fate.

'Hey. Anna?'

'Sasha? What are you – this is work, Sasha. You can't just—'

'Calm down, sis. You're hysterical. Anyway, Mum said it'd be fine to ring.'

'Did she.'

'Listen. Any news about the guitar? Nev's getting itchy.'

'Revolting thought. No, none; look, sorry. I've been meaning to, but there's so much—'

'Oh, come on . . . You're just moping around the house, aren't you, feeling mournful and watching Stell's porn collection.'

'She hasn't—?'

'For God's sake, Anna. As if. Don't be pervy. Look, please can you talk to Mum. I really need the cash. Nev's literally a monster.'

'Sash . . .'

'Yeah. Hang on, Butch is just— stop it, darlin'. Not the baby. Six months is way too young. Anyway . . .'

'Are you there?'

'Yeah. *No,* Butch.'

'Sash, just tell me, you know how Mum and Stella are funny?'

'Like, weirdos?'

'No. Well, yes, but you know – with each other?'

'Durr. *Yes.* Have I got eyes?

'Well, yes, obviously. I mean, what do you think it's about?'

'Dunno. Mutual hatred. Huge row. Something.'

'What, an actual huge row? Or just maybe?'

'Oh God, no idea. Actual, I think. About that girl. That man. You know.'

'What? What girl? What man? What?'

'You've lost it, sis. Relax. I dunno, I said. Ask Mum.'

'Sasha—'

'Gotta go. Butch, he'll *choke.* T'ra.'

Slowly, Anna stands, rapt with indecision.

'What's happened to you?'

'What?'

Wilf is bristling at her through the doorway. 'Catflap?'

'Sorry? Oh, here. Sorry.'

'You all right?'

'Yes,' she nods. 'Just feel a bit . . . strange.'

'Right,' says Wilf, striding to the door. 'Don't puke on the signed copies. And hurry up.'

Swiftly, Anna dials her mother.

'At last.'

'Hi, Mum. How did you know it was—'

'Your number came up on the little window.'

'But how—'

'Oh, shh. Of course I know it; Directories told me. Anyway, Marianne—'

'Mum, look, sorry, but I've got to run. I just wanted to ask, um, what are you getting Sasha for her birthday?'

'Various things. What are you getting?'

'Oh, drugs I think . . . Mum? Mum, that was a joke.'

'Hilarious.'

'Sorry. OK – I don't know yet either. So I wondered . . .' She can feel Wilf approaching. Her brain empties like a cup. 'How about . . . us both buying her something together?'

'I hardly think that will work, Anna. Besides, I've already promised—'

'Well, yes, but you see I spoke to her . . . this morning, and she said she wanted, um, some CDs and things. Some music. So—'

'So when she tells me what it is, I can buy it.'

'No, it's not like that – it's . . . bands you won't have heard of. Still recording. Um . . . why not just give her the money?'

'No, Anna. That's hardly festive. Anyway, it's between me and her.'

'Mum—' Wilf is on the other side of the door. 'Got to go. I'll ring.' He enters as Anna dives to the floor, and begins to scrabble for imaginary receipts.

She must ring the Glasses, one more time. If she could arrange a meeting, she might identify the photograph woman, the source of Stella's suffering. There's so much to find out, Anna's at risk of forgetting the ring.

*

By six o'clock she is ready. She doesn't even care that no one has asked her plans: it's best not to intimidate them. Quite soon, possibly, they will be drawing her attention to the handsome stranger waiting for her in Health and Fitness. 'Oh, that's my boyfriend,' she will reply airily, and keep him waiting just a little longer as she fields demanding customers, while tightening the leather straps on her weekending case.

She strides down Tottenham Court Road, smiling intriguingly at lamp-posts, looking up through her eyelashes at passing strangers' backs. Her stomach follows tremulously some metres behind.

The front of Florian's is large and bright and crowded. Men in shirtsleeves hold up fingers by the bar and sweat; handsome boys in shades with cigarettes laugh and shout in Italian with long-haired dark-tanned women, all little unseasonal T-shirts and visible hip-bones. This doesn't seem the sort of place Richard would choose; and if it is, she now realizes, how will she recognize him? Even if he is unchanged since the photograph – which may, of course, not be Richard after all – even if she finds him, she can hardly confess she's been snooping around Stella's shelves, memorizing her life.

Her only hope is to get there last, and trust he's on the lookout for a young female relative of someone with red hair. She crosses the street and stands beside a pink Indian restaurant, watching the door for a thick fringe, for dark eyes, for something Stella might once have liked. To distract her from the motorbikes and loaded stares of passing men, she lets her mind slide sideways, to Stella's face as he'd trace it with his finger, assessing the features she's almost sure they do not share.

Time passes, slow as sleep. At twenty-past she walks through the open doors of Florian's. She looks at every man in turn, warily – just enough for each to respond if they are him, without encouraging random attention. None seem possible: she fast-forwards and sees herself, so obscured by the advances of a sinuous Casanova that Richard misses her, actually does not see her, and both are doomed. She pushes through to the back of the bar, barely glancing above the torso of most of the men. He won't be wearing that little top – too shiny. And nothing in minty green. He would have to appeal to Stella; not that he's here for her, but she did once like him. Maybe still does. Exactly how jealous, Anna wonders, would Stella be?

At the back of the bar is a spiral staircase, a DNA twirl in tortured bronze. She should try upstairs, but what if at the very same moment he is fighting through the lower room? A blink of his long lashes may momentarily hide the stairs, and again he will miss her, and again will lose their chance for bliss. Instead, she will scoot up quickly and then, in the time it would take for him to walk slowly through the bar, she will race back down and weave out towards the front, where he will catch her as he emerges, despondent.

However, as she reaches the top of the stairs, her plans realign. The upper layer is darker; here are small tables, tiny spotlights, grown-ups smiling and leaning close. Here, surely, is where he wants her.

She can't begin the whole process again, cannot time her re-entry to be late but certain. She will have to wait here and hope he's just delayed; hope that, as she toys alluringly with the china ashtray, he isn't crafting some dark humiliation for her to nurse, still oozing, in the night.

She asks for a drinks menu; rearranges her knees and elbows to suggest composed, even fond, impatience; turns her face in becoming profile from the stairs. As the waiter approaches a second time she looks up and sees CINZANO in scarlet neon; she orders one on a whim. As she waits she tries to rid herself of the fear that any second now, due to nervousness receptors in the table-top or a simple visual assessment of her bitten fingernails, she will be exposed as an impostor and asked to leave. 'What made you think,' her interrogator will ask in cruel Sicilian accents, 'that we would take you for a desirable adult? Let alone a convincing Londoner? It is laughable. Enough. Go back to the playground where you belong.'

She sips at her bitter drink, and wonders how to drag Richard gently off the subject of her aunt, should their conversation stray that way. He can hardly want her still if, as seems fairly likely, he is about to begin a major romance with her niece. She tries, and fails, to identify precisely what he has said to suggest he still fancies Stella. Perhaps it was projection: Anna's selfless hope that he might yet long for – let's be honest – her ageing spinster aunt. Who deserves romance, surely, even from a man her niece might easily reject.

And here he is. A man is slaloming slowly towards her from the stairs, half-smiling, eyebrows raised. He's fine, just that; tallish, and darkish, unworryingly good-looking; the man in the photograph come to life. Just, somehow, not quite what she had hoped for. Not what she had hoped for, at all.

'Are you – Anna?'

She smiles, as much from relief as friendliness. Why are

you late? 'Richard.' She holds out a hand, irresolutely; he takes and waves it briefly in his own. Smiles again. Well, she thinks, that's the first hurdle.

He sits, decanting newspapers and wallet and phone and change from his pockets. 'Stuck in a meeting; couldn't find a meter. Sorry.' Is that enough? Does she now forgive him, or do real women bide their time? 'Can I get you a drink? Oh, Martini?'

There's no point pretending she likes it; it's too disgusting to be truly chic. She makes a face. 'C-Cinzano.' Her mouth is dry. 'I thought I'd be experimental.'

He smiles. 'I see. Another?'

'Oh God, no. Something else. A vodka and tonic? Please.'

'OK. And I need cigarettes.' He stands and walks away, patting his pockets.

She thinks: he can't be doing a runner, surely; he's left his stuff all over the table. Unless he's so desperate he'd abandon his jacket and phone. I could have a quick look, just to check for signs of ongoing Stella. Photographs in his wallet, perhaps, or hearts around her name in his diary. He'll think I'm trying to steal his change.

If only I hadn't said 'experimental'. He might think I'm into restraint and catsuits – which I'm not, of course, I'm fairly sure I'm not. Is vodka and tonic a young drink, or is it transparently sophisticated? I'd better avoid the subject of age; after Stella he isn't going to want a juvenile. In fact, probably best to bypass her altogether, even if there's no one else to cross-examine. It may be Stella who has brought us here, but she's nothing to do with it now.

There are footsteps just behind her. She turns, resolving not to ask a single question, not to make a leading comment, not to give, in fact, the least encouragement to any talk of Stella. If he still has crush-vestiges he'd better lose them. Anna could hardly be less interested.

'Do you smoke?'

'Only sometimes. Thanks.' Her lungs flounder under the first hit; she's very out of practice. She tightens her cindery chest and waits for the coughing urge to pass.

'Me too. So, you're Stella's niece?'

In her surprise she opens her mouth and a curl of undigested smoke burps out. 'Oh – did I say? Yes, I am. Do, do I remind you of her?' Suddenly she realizes how pleased he looked when he found her: this, of course, must be the reason. She gives him an amused and subtly wayward smile, practised – but not to the point of staleness – in the bathroom mirror.

'Not much, no. Well, I suppose your hair, a bit. Not otherwise, though; definitely not your eyebrows.'

She lifts a hand; they don't feel ruched. 'What?'

'Oh, sorry, no, not that. Just that hers are so extraordinary. Have you not noticed?'

'I don't think . . .'

'You must have. They're very arched. Naturally, I think, but they're a terrific shape. Next time you see her, have a peek. I'm sure she'd be thrilled.'

'I will.'

He smiles, and wipes a red drop from the edge of his wineglass. 'I'm sorry. You must think me very rude.' He has a trace of an accent: her mother would know. 'I breeze in here, horribly late, and start comparing you to your relatives. In a good way, of course. But forgive me. Let's start again.' Something about his encouraging smile, or his beautiful peacock tie, or maybe his way of leaning forward, makes him someone she could almost trust. His forearms are lightly muscled; something which, usually, Anna cannot resist.

'So, Anna, how are you? Any news since we last spoke?'

'Do you mean . . . Stella?'

'Well no, no, how about in general?'

Oh God, I've been crass, thinks Anna. Like me, he's decided this is nothing to do with her. Or maybe he is in terrible pain; he's desperately in love with her and now I've made it worse. Perhaps I could staunch his wounds. Do I want to?

'Oh. Sorry. OK.' She sucks air unattractively through her teeth; something she has never knowingly done before. 'Well, no news as such – I've been working – in a bookshop, at the moment – and um . . . you know. Just being around.' She sips her discarded Cinzano lamely, like an alcoholic borrowing other people's drinks. He looks a little like someone famous. 'Sorry, what do you do?'

He smiles, mid-gulp, and she wonders whether he feels, like her, the oddness of this evening. He's like a friend already; it's as if they're past the stage of being serious. Is it a date, necessarily? It feels more like a meeting of distant colleagues – simultaneous discoverers of a cure for cancer, the third sex, alchemy – who have an hour to decide whether to crack this one together.

She looks down at his hands, strong, emphatically hairy, and imagines how those fingers would feel on skin, inside her. Her irises burn with scenes already envisaged.

'I'm a journalist. On the *Economist*.' She smiles in a politely interested manner as he fully explains – even nice men do it – the exact importance of his job.

'And do you enjoy it?' she asks.

'More than I used to. I'm very interested in Islamic relations with the West – and now I'm concentrating on it.'

'Like Algerians in Paris?' The gods are smiling on Florian's tonight.

'Exactly.'

The area around the bridge of his nose is oddly attractive: his forehead, his smudgy brows, the slightly stunned set of his eyes. 'So it's quite dangerous, at times,' he is saying, 'but to be honest I prefer that. You know, Boy's Own Adventure. No one *wants* to grow up and work in an office, do they?'

'I suppose not,' says Anna. He *does* have an air of a boy enjoying adulthood: tousled, interested, perhaps a little selfish. He lacks the worn look a man his age should have. 'So – is that how you two, you and . . .' It's absurd to ignore the third guest at the table. Already they are gesturing towards where she would sit.

'No – well, yes, sort of. We both had some terrible trouble in Tangiers and ended up at the British embassy on the same day. I hated her actually – she said I smelt. Which I probably did. Still . . .'

He trails off. Anna is trying to extract her lemon with a fingertip and misses the beginning of his stare.

'Do you all have that hair?'

'No – just me and her. She's my mother's sister.'

'Really? Is your mother . . . quite young?'

'No. Not at all. Much older than Stella, in every way. She—'

'To tell the truth,' says Richard, 'she doesn't talk much about family – well, not to me. But then she's probably never mentioned me to you.' He fiddles with his cuff. 'Has she?'

His front tooth is chipped, which, unexpectedly, adds to his appeal. Is that what Stella would have thought when she first saw him – despite his smell? 'I – oh yes, probably. I honestly can't remember. We usually discuss, well, different things. Our family, I suppose, and her work . . . How long have you known her?'

'About . . . eight, ten years. After she'd called me smelly, and I called her filthy, which she was, you see, she still somehow managed to charm me, irritatingly, and – it started. The being friends, if that's what you mean.'

Anna frowns – is that what she meant? Then she remembers the photograph. It has grown so much in her mind – has taken on music, and smoky colour, and movement whirling around that look – it's almost as if it has nothing to do with Richard. But that face – the other one – is definitely his. There is heat in her stomach and a swoop of sexual vertigo. This means she wants him; she knows she wants him.

He is swirling the last of his wine round the glass, watching translucent tendrils slipping down the sides. 'Well, that's quite enough about *her*. Would she devote the same time to us? I think not. Now, tell me how you like London.'

She tells him briefly about work; given that the flat is now taboo there isn't much else to say.

'I worked in a shop in the holidays,' he tells her. 'God, years ago. It was hell. Budgens – my parents had just split up, and I decided to go to Paraguay. Don't ask. I lasted about a week; raised £73. I didn't get to Paraguay.'

'Ah,' says Anna, wondering how Stella helped soothe his pain. 'Well, I'm hoping to stay a bit longer than that.'

'Right.'

They have stalled. He coughs. A blush spreads through the air between them. 'So, given that – well, it's not why we met, but it was involved – *is* there any more news, um . . .

about Stella? Plans for arrival, you know, red carpet requirements, things like that?'

Anna smiles. She can't stop smiling. 'Not exactly, no. I told you about her postcard – held up, back soon. That's about all it said.'

'So she could be back at any time, I suppose?'

'Any time.' He has proper lips, not just a flesh-coloured slit. She looks away for a waiter and imagines kissing that mouth, imagines him feeling the softness of her own.

The waiter stands beside the table, dishcloth lightly draped over a muscle-knotted wrist. Richard looks up. 'One more please. You?'

'Another for me. Vodka and tonic. Thank you.'

'I used to like vodka – well, I'd drink it. And then I saw what they put in it. Oh, no, sorry,' he exclaims, seeing her face fall. There is a heavy feeling in her chest: cirrhosis? 'No, I mean in Russia. Shoes and things.'

Winsome horror is hard to achieve but she does it, or nearly. 'Oh – enough. Please.'

'Forgive me. Anyway, where were we. You were saying . . . so what are we supposed to do? It must be odd for you, not knowing if she's about to breeze in when you're in the bath.'

'Very.' There is a pause; they both toy assiduously with their paper coasters.

'It's just . . . sorry. I must stop going on about this. It's just so frustrating trying to get anything out of her.' Anna smiles, and leans forwards encouragingly, close enough to notice how short his nails are cut, how his forearms are furred but not Neanderthal, and wonders if she wants him quite enough.

He rubs at his knuckles and looks at her. 'It's funny, you

know, meeting someone who knows her so well. You see, we used to have – well, we were friends. As you know.'

She smiles, in such a way as to suggest she has not considered what he may be about to say, but will welcome and soothe it, whatever it may be: a *Little House on the Prairie* look.

'And then it sort of, I suppose it – we had a thing. A sort of on-and-off thing. As you do.'

She nods. 'Yes – I can imagine.'

'And it went on for years. You know?'

'Yes?'

'And I never quite knew where it was going – I mean, what were we? Were we – you know – lovers, or friends who happened to do that, or what, exactly?'

'And?'

'And she seemed fine about it, and so did I, I think, and sometimes it was quite, well, intense, and sometimes not, and she had other people – we both did.'

There is a pause. He taps his jacket pocket for cigarettes, offers one. They are lightly crushed.

'So what happened?' asks Anna, wondering what exactly he means by 'people'. 'Is it over now?'

'Well, that's it – I think. I never quite know when it *is* over, you see. So I'm never sure if I'm supposed to be being in touch, or staying away, or what to expect. And I don't mean that she's making it like that – at least, not on purpose. Not necessarily. It isn't as if we've discussed it, exactly, or I've said what I want. Or even *know* what I want. It's more that I don't know if Stella wants . . . this, and don't want to blow it all by asking the wrong question, and suddenly not be who she thought I was, or something. If you see what I mean. Hmm.'

'And what do you think she wants?' asks Anna, bending closer.

'God only knows. What do you think? You're a woman, practically related . . .'

'Actually related.'

'Quite. So? What does she want, do you think?'

'Richard. I – it's hard to say, to be honest. I mean, she's so private, so sort of . . . self-sufficient. It's easier to see what *you* want. If you don't mind my saying so.'

He looks appalled, then self-conscious, then embarrassed by his lack of disguise. He ducks his head. 'Oh. Is it?'

'Well—'

'What do I want?'

'You want her to come a bit closer, so you're not in constant suspense for her card, or her call, or her sudden unannounced arrival at your doorstep. You want to know how much of what you thought you had, the connection, is really there, and how much is your imagining. I suppose some of it is . . . sex, and most is her manner. It's silly, really, given that she isn't that special-looking, and sometimes she can be a cow . . . .' She pauses, horrified and impressed, but he is smiling. 'What? What is it? Don't you agree? I'm sorry if that was – out of place. You see I just . . .'

'Shhh, Anna. It's okay. No, really – in fact, in a horrible way you're right. But it's also that – I hope you don't mind my saying this – I do keep thinking "really, it's amazing, they're not a bit alike", and then you say something *bold* like that and suddenly you could be her sister. Or even her, a long time ago. To some extent, of course.'

Of course. He does have a certain indefinable sexiness, thinks Anna, even though, obviously, they have nothing in common.

'Which reminds me,' he says. 'Did you hear from Nicky Glass?'

With an effort, Anna pulls her mind away. 'I . . . well. Actually I was meaning to mention it to you.'

'And?'

'I did – well, I tried. I spoke to another woman, who was reasonably friendly, until I mentioned Stella.' Richard is looking with interest at the ashtray. 'And then she wasn't. And I wondered—'

'How weird. Why did you ring her, anyway?'

'I don't know if it's anything to do with your Nicky at all.' An obscuring instinct surfaces; she prods the table. 'In fact, I'd imagine not. No one's mentioned him so far. I called because Stella left something there: a ring. I imagine she lent it to one of them. And she's asked me to get it back. But no one . . . it sounds like chaos there, and no one can be bothered to look.'

Richard leans back. 'Well, I'm glad that's all it is. Stella tends to breed complications . . . So, I don't see the problem.'

'It's just that I promised Stella I'd try to get it back. And so far I'm failing.'

'Right. Have you considered cat burglary?'

Anna's small duplicity has surprised her. She laughs, a little manically. His smile wavers. There is a terrible pause.

'Did you see her much when you were growing up?' he asks politely.

Her opportunity shrinks and is extinguished. 'No, hardly ever. So of course when she did visit it was always ridiculously exciting, you know? Like, "Stella's coming, so she'll give us whisky, and laugh at Mum's headmistressy friends, and bring us an African penis-sheath." I think it was the not-knowingness that got us – she might describe her periods in enormous detail in a shop, or insist on calling us all "Fanny" in public. And of course our mother was always braced, which made it more exciting . . .'

'Why braced?'

'Oh, you know – for the destruction of family life, I suppose. For What People Think. Stella telling the neighbours she was a she-male, or a nun in Special Branch. And Mum would always complain about her to our father, Frank, and you could tell he was hardly bothered, or she'd moan on the phone to her parents – we'd hear it – and she'd just get frustrated. I think she thought Stella could do anything and then just dance her way back into everyone's favour. It's true, too; it isn't really fair.'

'I know. God, I know. So often she's said something incredible – I mean, really appalling – and I've thought "That's it. Keep away from me". And then I'm back. I hate that I do it – but I do. Bloody Stella-for-star.'

Anna grins. 'I always think of that. Or Melissa from *Thirtysomething*, with more bite.'

'Sexier, too. Or the Devil.'

'Exactly. That's it – despite it all you want her to like you – well, not that she doesn't already, in your case. Or in mine, to be fair. I mean, we always used to get on, generally. In fact, we've always been supposed to have a sort of . . . special bond—'

Now she sounds like a schoolgirl. And, to be honest, it's harder and harder to recall any sign from Stella that this is indeed the case. But it *feels* like the truth. After all, she did offer the flat. And even if it is an exaggeration, Richard must be glad Stella likes her, just as she, Anna, is pleased that Stella likes him. They are all each others' sort of people. How nice that they can now be friends.

She looks up, and discovers that Richard is gazing right at her. He is pouring himself through her eyes. She smiles, but the moment does not break. He simply keeps on looking.

Anna has never fully understood the point about eyes. Books, even people, make extraordinary claims: that through them one can anatomize the soul, can see it flash like a magic lens. But romance aside, what can you really see?

She sees the residue of love, but it's as much in his anxious smile, his torn cuticles, the little piles of coins ordered and reordered in front of him. Only residue, of course; of course that is not why he's here. It isn't Stella he wants.

And Anna wants him. Yes, definitely. He's really quite desirable, if you like that sort of thing, which, she suddenly realizes, she does. She stares back.

She thinks: his forearms are delicious. What's that little white bobble under his eye? Is he going to kiss me? I suppose he is quite sexy; he concentrates on everything I say. And he's unexpectedly interesting. If only I could stay here, talking to him, indefinitely. We really do seem suited.

His stare slides through her body: dry throat, radar nipples, zephyrs in her stomach, melting gold between her thighs.

How long is he going to look at me? Is one of us supposed to say something now?

'Anna?'

'Yes?' This is the moment that will change her life; the one when, as their friends will fondly tire of hearing, they just knew.

'I really ought to go. It's getting late.'

'Oh. Is it?' she asks stupidly, and the spell is broken.

The grown-ups have all gone home. There is almost no one left on Florian's upper deck. He offers to pay; she protests weakly, then lets him. This is so far outside her experience, personal or borrowed, that she is unmoored. In the wings other personae – femme fatale, Timotei maiden, amazon, bluestocking – tut and pick their nails, waiting for their entrance.

'OK then?'

'OK.' She smiles bravely. She will wait for him to do whatever it is that grown men do to seduce girls like her. If this doesn't happen I will combust, she thinks. He moves past her, and then, as if finally hearing his prompt, he leans back and holds out his hand.

His fingertips are the epicentre of a spinning funfair world. It is only as she reaches for his hand that she realizes it's not for her but for the waiter, he's showing the waiter that he's left a tip, and her stupid pink-knuckled paw is floating in the air like a rudder, a fatally overlooked danger sign. She looks at it as one would a stump where, until a second before by that threshing machine, an ordinary limb had been. The world rushes back to fill the vacuum.

Slowly, very slowly, in the objective knowledge that this is the worst solution she could possibly have found, she stretches out the other arm beside it and clenches her hands, as if Florian's of a Tuesday night is an ideal spot to exercise. She extends and stretches her fingers, then smiles, as if a cramp has been relieved, and lowers her arm. Her nerve endings sing chorales of embarrassment. Then, only then, does she look at him. He has looked away.

Silent swearing is not enough. The time for blushing is long past. All she can do is follow him to the top of the stairs, to put that fat-and-blood-coloured hoof on the shining cochlear rail and walk herself to the door.

'Well, it was a pleasure,' he says, smiling, adjusting the

collar of his jacket. The star of Bethlehem clicks on above her, did he not see it? Am I safe? Further handsome boys in T-shirts, together with their friends in fresh-cloned waves, caw and chatter on the pavements. 'Where do you go from here?'

She cannot even pretend that he said 'we'. 'I – Bloomsbury. You know, Stella's flat.'

'Oh yes. Stupid.' And he gives her an impenetrable look. 'We'll get you a taxi.'

And he does, miraculously, using some sort of internal cab-sensor as yet uninstalled in her. He tells the driver 'Shawcross Street', and smiles at her through the open window as she struggles in.

'Richard, what will I . . .?' She needs to prolong this moment for something to happen; to postpone the point of knowing it will not.

'What?' A wisp of Stella narrows his eyes, a 'let's get back to the grown-ups' look.

'Nothing.' She forces a smile back through the gap.

'OK. Well, good drink. And very good to meet you.' He pats her hand where it rests, a web of paper cuts and biro scars, on the window-catch. 'We'll be in touch. Yes?'

'Yes . . . thank you, Richard.'

He waves at the taxi-driver. Then he is gone.

Ten

'Mum?'

'Hello. Did you get my message? Who was that extra-ordinary man at your shop?'

'Mum, you can't really . . .'

'He sounded like Princess Margaret. Anyway, Anna, I have no time for this. Those lovely friends of Andrea's, the McCauleys, are coming round—'

'Aren't they the ones where she's still allowed to sleep with her ex-husband?'

'—and I still have monkfish to collect. It's a miracle I've found it in this primitive backwater, so I'm not about to let it rot. Now, concentrate. You're supposed to be ringing Andrea. I've set this up for you, so stop pretending you've forgotten. And have you heard anything at all from Stella?'

'. . . No.'

'Make sure you tell me when you do. We're going to find you somewhere to stay, if you aren't capable of it yourself. The last thing she'll want is you moping underfoot. Right?'

'OK. I won't. I mean, I will. Mum, I know you . . . can I have her number again? So I can ask her?'

'Wasn't once enough?'

'Well, yes, obviously, but I can't seem to . . . it's gone.'

'Not now, no. I'm in a rush. I'll ring her myself if I have a minute. And ring *me* if you hear.'

She will not let it lie. Despite draining social commitments, most evenings she finds time to telephone Anna with impractical requests ('Darling, just pop to Van Cleet's in Kensington for me, will you? Just a curtain rail – not that heavy. You can bring it when Stella's back.'), or information about train times, or wheedling, or threats. Anna, vainly, tries to turn the tables.

'About Sasha's pres—'

'OK, Anna. What's this about?'

'Nothing. Nothing, Mum. Seriously. It's just a hunch—'

'Nonsense. You're both lying. Tell me now.'

Mentioning Cally is out of the question. Her violent boyfriend, window cleaning, once stole Andrea Lefschitz's silver pen, and Anna's mother visibly winces when her name is heard. And so Anna changes the subject, and every subsequent conversation dodges and flits around the money, like a half-guessed vice.

Her attempts to escape become increasingly spurious: a trip to the Chinese takeaway ('Forty minutes? That's fine, I'll just sit here.'); a late-night search for toe-dividers; even a Polish real-time film at the local arthouse cinema, where she is ignored by every donnish couple sharing flapjacks and Appletize, and weeps becomingly but alone throughout the second half.

And so she misses another silent call from an irretrievable number.

As she replaces the handset she imagines Richard in the belly of an old hotel, uncomfortably perched in a glassed mahogany cubicle, fumbling in his trenchcoat pockets for change. Or wedged, shirt-sleeved, between till and peanut dispenser in a bar so loud the tables have pulses, ignoring the cheering friends at his elbow, trying to find the words he needs to say.

Time for a bath. She has never felt so clean, or so dirty. She should lock the front door in case her mother comes knocking, but what if Stella arrives unannounced? She leaves the bathroom door ajar and steps into the water.

It must have been Richard; and why not? She is young, and arguably pretty; she is neither raddled nor a virgin; she is fairly clever, and until recently had a life. She can make potato salad, dive and name the kings and queens of England. What more could he want?

Days pass, slow as crystals forming. Like a sleepwalker she mixes up forms and names and numbers. It is dangerous to wake her.

One evening she takes the 'Tébessa' video from the sitting-room cupboard, wishing she could ring Stella and ask whether she uses channel 6 or 0. She anticipates cheering scenes of village life, simple charts giving Reasons for Conflict, luscious and complicated feasts. Something, in any case, that will help with Richard.

She has considered, at length, the possibilities.

Either: he never wants to see her again, due to A) a minor but appalling gaffe – the way she sat, the style of her shoes, a problem with Cinzano, or B) her patent immaturity, dullness and lack of personal charm.

Or: he has been so thoroughly captivated by her girlish

ways, sensitivity and powerful sex appeal that he is, even now, wondering where to take her for their honeymoon.

Both, surely, are inevitable, and this crash-course in the socio-political problems of North Africa is merely a safety-net. While alternate images of spinsterhood and conjugal bliss loop before her eyes like a truth-telling lava lamp, she prepares for the single fact or observation which, when casually dropped into conversation, will catalyse their love.

However, to her surprise Stella's film does not feature pyramids, dark goateed men in white pyjamas, bustling village scenes or obscenely glistening figs. Instead, teenage boys march shoeless through desert, decrepit shepherds are shot for their lambs, and girls breastfeed their rapists' fair babies. Anna's mouth hangs open. She pushes aside her chicken sandwich with a toe.

Yet, as the film progresses she finds herself moving closer and closer to the sofa's edge. There is something curiously familiar in the air. Unable to sit still, she crosses to the window, runs her finger through the dust on the bookshelves, wipes a space on the round table-top and observes her reflection marooned in its syrupy depths. Perhaps she should do some cleaning. It is only as she kneels on the floor that she finally notices: the voice is Stella's.

The room is full of her voice. Anna's mother, of course, could identify the proportions of Leicester, Bloomsbury and Paris, like a tea-taster calibrating tar and spice. But she has not thought to pass this to her daughter. Instead Anna, too shocked to absorb the narrative, lets barely connected consonants sift across her skin, while her mind darts from her aunt to her mother's hidden letter, and back again. Then, just as she is considering retrieving the birthday photograph, as a visual aid, Anna sees something on the screen which makes her pause.

In the sun, on reddish earth outside a low and dirty concrete building, a man and a woman are arguing in barely audible French. The bonnet of a filthy truck cuts across the corner of the picture. Beside the man's blue epauletted shirt, the woman's dingy cotton looks disreputably crumpled, as though she has been sleeping on the floor. His heavy accent is faded out as the voiceover explains: '. . . he is telling us "no", despite our papers, despite the assurances we have received. He is armed and aggressive' – here the hidden camera pans down towards the hardware at his waist – 'and the border police have often clashed with reporters, sometimes with fatal results.'

Anna finally allows herself to recognize the woman on the screen, and a chill drips down her neck. The man begins to gesture with his gun. Subtitles patter quickly across the dust.

I'm telling you, woman. And don't give me that look. Show some respect. Do you know who you're fighting with?

I have the papers. Why are you playing with me? Come on, let me through. You have no right to do this.

You don't tell me what to do. Now leave.

Oh yes? Or?

Or trouble. I mean it. Fuck off.

What did you say to me?

Filthy bitch.

Anna waits, dry-lipped. Despite the shaking of the camera, and another noise, which may be someone starting up the jeep, she has heard a trickle of steel in Stella's voice which the man cannot have missed. Anna wants to say 'be *careful*', to climb inside the screen and lead her away from that isolated building and his snarling and his gun. It's like a Bond film: you know who will win, but the odds seem stacked, and the villain's weapons are always to hand.

On the screen Stella takes a step backward. Only the tip of her nose and her jaw are visible. She opens her mouth, and as she speaks, more calmly now, another subtitle materializes under her feet.

> **Listen. I think there has been a misunderstanding. None of these papers matter. What does matter is that I am a close friend of Commander Ashrawi in Algiers. A *personal* friend. And I am sure he would be very happy to hear that you yourself have let me through, and most unhappy to hear that you have not. If you don't believe me you can telephone him and check. His direct line is 67383519. Are you ready to let me through now?**

There is a pause. The guard stares at her, then smiles. 'Yes?' she asks him, and he nods, and, head down, leads her to a door. The screen fills with a shot of trees in the dusk below heather-coloured mountains, and the voiceover resumes.

'Commander Ashrawi is the most corrupt and brutal police chief in Algeria's recent history. However, his name is known to very few outsiders. I have never met him, and would not rate my chances if I did. This time I was lucky. Others have been less fortunate.'

The screen goes blank and, before the credits begin, a white sentence appears in the darkness.

> **In memory of Daniella Glass, 1953–1989.**

Eleven

That week she does several things that she should not.

1. Her mother telephones again and this time, as she bends crone-like over the machine, Anna decides not to answer. Despite her utter lack of evening contact, there is only so much she can endure.

'Anna, are you there? Surely you're not out? Now, I bumped into Marianne Brooks, and she says you still haven't rung her. Anna, frankly I don't know what you're playing at. Do you realise that *Cigar* is sold in Harvey Nichols? Don't waste this. I want you to ring her tomorrow.

'And can you let me know when you're coming back to Bath, please? I know Stella must be about to pop over, and as we have discussed, you can't stay there when she does. I'd give you her number, again, but perhaps it's best in person. And if you'd done Andrea the courtesy of a call you'd know that she has something very special for you. OK? We have to talk. So ring me. Hope you're surviving.'

If she had picked up the phone she could have responded, however weakly. Could have demanded the number, or waited for a breath and inserted 'What do you know about Daniella

Glass?', like a lever between tectonic plates. But now, more than ever, she needs her mother out of the way.

All the next day, during which Wilf praises the blond Oxonian in a staff meeting and Anna, chagrined, remains untipped for greatness, she tries to work out the best possible time to call. As well as the obvious elements to consider, the shopping trips and martyrish errands, perhaps she can control the flow of information in other ways. Soon she is beaming signals at passers-by through the window, their likely book-buying plans dependent on a web of chance and her own volition. The gods, who seem more numerous and malignant in this part of England, decide to play. She finally calls; her mother is out. Anna leaves a busy person's message, full of background noise and harassed promises. She has discharged her duty: now the ground is clear.

2. She tugs open the wardrobe door, and closes her eyes at the scent released: smoke; incense; skin. Stella's clothes are hanging in a thick and silent row, waiting to be brought to life. Steady as a magician, she extends her hand and blesses woollen folds, velvet and cool linen: aubergine, slate, chestnut and olive; glides her fingers over creases like furry blades, waxen silk, tiny blouses washed to a cornflour touch.

Where does one buy clothes like this? Anna's Adulthood fantasies resurface in a thicket of swinging hangers. She could help herself, but as she stares into the blackness at the back of the wardrobe, above the empty necks and waists, she glimpses a tragic future as an Aunt Impersonator. What if she met one of Stella's friends, who would finger a hem and ask uncomfortable questions? Or if Stella herself found a collar-hair with a telltale wave, a more hesitating red?

Her sigh subsides among the plastic skins. Even Stella's

fashion decades, which in her sister's wardrobe show clear as tree-trunk rings, are undetectable. She is not about to stumble across dresses nametaped for another woman, baby slippers or a confession of murder. There is no secret history here.

3. Her least favourite regular, an unconvincing academic with a bouffant libido and breath like gherkins, asks her to recommend 'a fetish book, but tasteful'. Anna puts down her stapler. She looks at the bridge of his nose and into her head, like a nightmare rider, drums the command 'Leave and don't come back'. She knows she must smile, and ask politely exactly what kind of fetish, and direct his attention to the Taschen postcards on the rack. But she cannot. 'Oscar,' she says, smiling at the blond Oxonian. 'Can you—?' And she keeps her smile until she has locked herself safely in the staff toilet.

4. The blond Oxonian suggests lunch in the park. Anna declines, instantly, and submits to an afternoon haunted by the friends he might have led to.

5. She obtains from Uncle Markus, despite his dark assurances that he is very busy, Stella's number. It's simpler that way. She devotes herself to not memorizing the number. By morning it is scored by diamonds on her bones.

6. And last among these ill-advised and dangerous acts is a memory. For days now it has nibbled at the edges of her brain, fed by silence and dangerous liberty. She runs a bath and climbs in: the safest place. Then she lets it start.

*

Anna stands in her father's workroom, ankle-deep in family history – dusty duffel coats, wallpaper, rollerskates. She tries not to think about spiders or the telephone. Very quietly she eases a can of oil from a metal-filled drawer and drips it on to the grey block on the workbench before her. She holds the knife firmly by the handle, cautiously by the tip, and begins to push it across the sheeny surface of the stone, as she has seen her father do. She has never prepared to this extent, never spent calm minutes getting ready. There is a shocked pleasure in knowing she will go to these lengths now. The blackened oil wells up before the blade.

She wipes it carefully on a ball of Kleenex. She doesn't want blood poisoning, after all. Testing its sharpness on the edge of a paper scrap, her heart begins to race. It will work much better than the blunt kitchen carvers, the pencil-sharpener blades, the scalpel she hasn't dared steal from school. It is temptation and fear. She holds the knife tightly in her hand, stretches out her right arm and slices, firmly, gently. The freckled skin gapes. She is bleeding fast. The nervousness has gone: there is only pain, and alertness, and release.

Short but deep. Anna mops the blood dropping down her white forearm with the cleanest tissue and holds her cut together, blowing to help it dry. This time, one is enough. The knife will be ready when she needs it next. She washes it quickly in the basin and creeps upstairs to the warm empty kitchen, the blade behind her back. The drawer barely squeaks as she closes it, her arm beginning to throb under her school sleeve. She finds Savlon and a plaster; now she needs it to heal, discreetly. It doesn't feel like punishment or self-hatred. It gives her comfort and courage. It's a relief to know there's always this.

*

And now Anna, prone and bloodless in the shivering water, strokes the lines on her silver skin and counts again, her secret number. She is capable of anything – anything, it seems, but revealing these. Until now. Maybe Stella will be the one.

Twelve

This has been a busy week. Like the discoverer of a new and jealous god, Anna has been wandering Bloomsbury like an augur, divining good omens, inventing obeisance. As yet no postcards, messages or large raffia-tied bunches of long-stemmed flowers have arrived, but she knows they will be coming. The air around her has thickened; it hums tight with portent.

She walks along Torrington Place, hoping to discover a delicatessen or Portuguese coffee shop she may have overlooked. It has been a stressful day of misplaced deliveries and unpopular shift realignments; Wilf was ratty and everyone else, though bonded, was tense. Anna has begun to consider cigarettes, and is searching her little rucksack for change. She looks up and there, just by the postbox, rounding the corner into Habitat, is a pair of legs in unbecoming wine-coloured tights. Attached to the legs is Andrea Lefschitz.

Anna stops in her tracks, like a shot animal. She begins to edge backwards, her eyes on the right angle of concrete and glass, every sinew braced for the moment when Andrea, alerted by a primeval sabre-tooth-detecting sense to Anna's horrified stare, looks back around the side and spots her.

Anna rocks back on her heels, turns, and begins to run, but it is not until she hits a kerb and wheels round into Gower Street can she begin to believe she is safe. And it is only then, as, lungs subsiding, she begins a winding route home, that she realizes her mistake. Andrea has probably watched Anna's entire escape through the Habitat window, ducking behind rust-coloured armchairs and rattan storage units until her quarry relaxes her guard. Of course her presence isn't coincidental. Anna hasn't been ringing her mother, let alone Andrea. It was only a matter of time before they became proactive, and Anna tripped over a tentacle.

She considers phoning her mother to confront her with the truth. But she will never admit to spying, and any new hostility will tighten her grip. Anna will have to be very vigilant from now on.

At work, of course, she could try some befriending. Relations with Mona have not transcended silent coffee, which at least leaves Anna feeling charismatic, like a youthful Jackie O. Hilary, an anaemic part-timer who can't handle credit-card transactions, having once choked on a Visa as a child, seems to be falling for Welsh Iain, who is amusing, but actively plain. Kirsten, the deputy, disappears in her lunchbreaks; the blond Oxonian claims that she cycles 'home to Hackney'. And Wilf goes for a power walk, or eats his ciabatta roll in the staff office, reading the *Standard*, with his ears tight shut. What Anna needs is a confidante: someone to help her decide what to do. At this rate she will have to track down Andrea, take her by her thin-skinned arm and lead her off for a résumé.

There is a row of self-help titles in the bookshop beside

Fantasy. Like Mary Whitehouse from late-night television, Anna keeps away.

Richard still hasn't telephoned. She resolves and reconsiders constantly; there is so much to discuss and she is, after all, not hideous. He should be calling her. In the stillest centre of the night she imagines standing in the street outside his house, calling to his subconscious as he sleeps: Riiichard, Riiiiiiiichard, you love Aaaannnnna. You want to fuuuuuck her.

And then she finds an excuse. She has been lying on the sofa, daring a key in the door. When the telephone rings she jolts like an adulterer. But it is her mother.

'What was it you said Andrea has for me?'

'She has very kindly, Anna, said she's considering letting you borrow Beccy's room while she's in Florence. Although unless you ring her—'

'Please. Jesus. I don't need a room – I have a lovely one here. Honestly, I don't need this.'

'Anna, I'd say you're hardly the best judge of that. Now, about your sister's birthday—'

'Oh – I mean, have you, has she spoken to you about it at all? I don't know—'

'Of course she hasn't. I *know* she has a plan. If you'd just spit it out we'd all be happier, wouldn't we.'

'Really, Mum,' says Anna, with the sudden confidence of a decision made. 'There's nothing. Trust me. She does just want some complicated music thing – nothing either of us would understand. And listen, another thing. I meant to ask you – do you know many of Stella's friends?'

'Well, no. They're hardly—'

'Because, you see, I found this picture, this little postcard, really, sort of fallen off the wall, and I bent down to pick it up and just by chance I glanced down and happened to see the name on the back as you do, and it wasn't one I recognized and out of curiosity I wondered if it was someone you knew . . . Daniella Glass.'

Her mother is very quiet. Anna begins to tap her foot nervously against the table.

'Is it? . . . I mean, I know you don't like chatting about Stella, but it's just I'm—'

'Listen,' she says, and Anna's foot stills at her voice. 'I don't know what you've been poking through, and I don't want to know. But that is a private business, and believe me, you are better off out of it. I don't want you discussing it, either.'

'With who?' cries Anna. 'Whom *can* I discuss it with when you're all so clammed shut about her? You'd think she's a criminal from all this ridiculous silence. How do you expect me to be uninterested if everyone acts like there's some huge secret?' Her eye creeps across the sitting room to the birthday photograph.

Her mother's voice is strained. 'Why are you so fascinated, Anna? Why can't you just let it be?'

'Because . . .' She tries a different tack. 'Because this is how you brought me up – to be curious and inquiring, and . . . there's something Stella needs me to do. Just a little—'

'What did she say to you?' demands her mother.

'Nothing. I just . . .'

'Enough. Look, there's a simple answer to your question,'

she says with a sigh, and Anna waits for the sentence that will change everything, the confirmation of what she knows is true. 'The Glasses are – were – good friends of ours. Of the whole family – me originally, because I was at school with Daniella, and Mum and Dad loved her, and Nicky was a distant friend of your uncle's, and when they married Stella became a friend too. You knew them, and their children, but only as a child yourself, of course. And . . . and unfortunately. Unfortunately Daniella died. Of cancer. And . . . it was terrible. So,' and her voice rights itself, 'it's quite a painful subject. But a simple story. Better – well, better not to mention it.'

'Okay,' whispers Anna, but she knows her mother is lying. Her careful phrases are pinched and shaped by the secrets she is keeping. Even if Daniella did die as she said, even if she was married, Anna's heart knows what really happened. Poor, poor Stella. This is a far from a simple story.

'Richard?'

'Anna. Hello. Any news?'

She hadn't thought of that, but now she's calm enough to lie. 'Hmm. You mean, of Stella's arrival? It's hardly her style, is it? I mean, I wish it were, but we're both in a bit of a limbo, aren't we—' Please, she prays, don't let him ask me to ring.

'So there's none?'

'No. Sorry.'

'Never mind. It's good that – that you're there. To report. Otherwise – well, for all we know she could have returned in splendour months ago.'

'I know, with dancing horses, and we'd be none the wiser.'

'Exactly. Just as long as you let me know as soon as there's anything, I can relax. So, how are things? I enjoyed our . . . meeting. Very much.'

'Good. I mean, so did I.' Quickly she opens the telephone book. 'Richard, can I ask you something?'

'Of course. Well, probably.'

'Do you know anyone in . . .' her finger traces quickly to N. Glass. What if he makes the connection? 'In NW5?'

'Round Tufnell Park? Or further? Why?'

'Because I . . . I have a friend who's, well, moving to NW5. Soon. And she asked if I knew anyone who – what it's like. You know.'

'I do. Well, it's quite mixed, I suppose. I knew someone who had an amazing house in Kentish Town – huge. Revoltingly adult. But some parts are much scruffier – you know, I think Stella had a bit of a run-in there, once.'

'What? How? What?'

'Oh – nothing dramatic. At least, not for Stella. I think she got on the wrong side of someone – more than one, actually. Hoods, probably, knowing her, or the CIA—'

He seems to have forgotten about the ring, and so, for the moment, has Anna. 'No, please, tell me. Who was it really?'

'I don't know, Anna. To be honest I wasn't convinced – they're out to get her all over the place, but in Kentish Town? All I know is she likes to give it a wide berth—' his laugh turns into a cough. Anna combusts patiently, but he has nothing else to tell her.

When Wilf calls to her from the office Anna is so surprised she closes the till on her sleeve, and has to ring through and cancel an imaginary purchase before she is released. She long-jumps half-packed boxes – how did she find the number? who could have told her where I work? – and finds the receiver in an open drawer. Its curly wire is frilled with rubber bands.

'Sorry – hello?' The wire twines affectionately round her finger as she begins to pick them off.

'Anna?' asks a woman, tentatively amused.

'It is – yes?'

'Ohhh,' the voice exhales in a rush, as Anna fights a damburst of disappointment. 'I couldn't tell, you see, it's been so long. Your mother said . . . Oh, sorry, yes, it's Janey. Warner?' Janey Warner. Of course.

Janey Warner was at primary school with Anna's mother. She wears cords in self-effacing forest shades, pouchy at the knee, and House of Fraser cotton crew necks. As her mother puts out the fattening biscuits for one of Janey's visits, Anna likes to comment on their sweetly enduring friendship, and Janey's husband's hugely salaried job near the head of Channel 4.

'Oh, Janey. I . . . How nice of you to ring. Did Mum . . .?'

'Yes, she did. Well, no, she didn't actually *tell* me. Gosh, what a muddle.' Her voice is vaguely Northern ('*Yorkshire*', according to Anna's mother); how could Anna not have known it?

'So . . . how are you? How's, um, Richmond?'

'Well, you know, still surviving.' She laughs gaily, and Anna winces. 'Anyway, yes, Magda, who sent a message – where was it? oh yes "so-and-so's staying in your room [it says "Smeggy" here but that's hardly a name, is it?] but let us know when Stella's coming to London and I'll clear him out" – whatever that means – anyway, she said you were in London yourself and, well, finding it a bit of a struggle, really, so would I like to ring you? So naturally I said, yes, lovely. Although I doubted I'd catch you – I know how it is. My girls tells me.'

Janey's girls and Anna are diametrically opposed. The Warner daughters all have perfectly straight mahogany hair, precise lipliner and colourfully entangled boyfriends. They left Bath Girls' for St Paul's where, the mothers agree, they have since flourished. Anna's mother reports on their successes at the dinner table: '—apparently she's found a loft in Tribeca – no, not an attic, Sasha – Frank, explain – and her script's gone into production. Anna, why don't *you* launch a website?'

While her offspring apparently sprang Venus-like from the open pages of *Marie-Claire*, Janey is a fifties secretary, rife with things her best friend will not tell her. Anna has often wondered how she feels about her diamond-edged daughters, and smiles encouragingly at Janey whenever the girls are mentioned. Now, perhaps, in London Janey will break down and confess that they are stuck-up cows and Anna, dear Anna, is the child she wishes was hers. Anna's new role will be friend to adults – wise and comforting. What does Janey know? Her mouth twitches.

'Well, yes . . . obviously I've got things to *do* – I'm at work now, for a start [*'Magda, it's Janey. I rang Anna; she sounds very busy and successful'*] – but I've only just arrived, you know.'

'And how,' asks Janey, voice dropping, 'are you coping in that *flat*?'

'Oh . . . it's – what do you mean?'

'Well, Magda says it's not at all a place for young girls. In fact, you know you could always come here if you need a place – we could find you a sleeping bag, and I'm sure the girls wouldn't mind – they're never around. Magda suggested it, but of course—'

'OK, Janey. Thank you. But it's not . . . necessary. I'm – Mum shouldn't have asked.'

'Never mind – I don't mean now, anyway. We're going to Singapore on Thursday – something for Paul's work, he's being very coy – and then we won't be back for weeks – sort of an extended holiday. It's for our twenty-fifth.'

'What? Oh – anniversary?'

'Yes.' Janey's voice lifts in tragic middle-aged excitement. According to Andrea Lefschitz, Paul Warner has affairs.

'Did Janey Warner ring you?'

'*Mum.* I can't talk now. I'm at work. We're not really supposed to . . .'

'Rubbish. If I want to talk to my daughter, what can they do? And don't they have better things to do than monitor your phone life?'

'Well, they might . . .'

'For God's sake, Anna. I just rang to ask you a quick question and it's turning into a seminar on workplace ethics. Now, could you please tell me if you spoke to Janey?'

'Yes – sort of.' Her mind works quickly, in circles. 'She rang – here – and was very friendly but they're going away. Didn't you know that?'

'Of *course* I knew, Anna. *Every*one knows where Paul's taking her. God, they're hardly keeping it quiet. If your father would only think more commercially *I* could be stopping off in the Gazelle d'Or, not Janey Warner in her sensible plimsolls. Paul's so *sweet.* And so successful. I wonder how he finds the time.'

There is a contemplative pause, during which her mother presumably considers her past, present or future relations with boyish but powerful Paul. Anna grits her teeth. 'But Mum, that's really not Dad's field.'

'Anna—' and her mother's voice is suddenly Victorian, hung with invalid children and the weight of the fading world. 'Anna. When will you – either of you – learn that the nation is not agog for many more novels of Gothic sleuthing. What they want is something new – something *sexy* – and your father is the man to give it to them, if only he could lift his ill-brushed head from thirty years of decomposing research and look around.'

'Like what?'

'Oh – really. I don't know – I'm hardly the expert. Medieval nature, or paintings, or something. Food. Cigars. But oh no. No, it has to be bones.'

'Well, no, not exactly—' Her mother will harry him to his deathbed. She'll be a sad wrinkled widow-woman subsiding into shabby gentility on the proceeds of her little shop, and how will she like that?

'Anyway, darling, if Janey rings again, or *any* of my friends, try to be a bit more welcoming, will you? I'm doing all I can to find you somewhere else.'

'Mum, really. Please stop. I don't want to move. And what's all this about Smeggy in my room?' Smeggy is the most pitiful of all her sister's friends. As his passion for Sasha increases, so too do the spikes, plugs and feathers with which his acne-contoured face is sown. No one can bring themselves to tell him that nickel-plating won't win Sasha's heart.

'Well, poor Smeggy has been evicted again, or something, and he needs somewhere to stay. Don't be such a dog in the manger, Anna. He won't hurt anything.'

'But he looks so . . .' She wants to say infectious, but this conversation is dissolving; she needs to regain ground. 'Anyway, I still don't know when Stella's coming back – I'm sure it won't be for a while, at least. And even then I don't see why I need to stay away. Can you just tell me,' she says, and swallows, noisily, 'what exactly is your problem with me staying?'

Across motorways and silted rivers, mother and daughter sit in exactly the same position: one foot impatiently swinging, opposite eyebrow raised. Between them, beneath a blanket of roots and chalky soil, barley sugar cables crackle with clashing wills.

'I don't have a problem,' says her mother fiercely.

Anna unsucessfully tries to straighten her back. 'I – you won't give me her number, and you're trying to evict . . .' She is speaking as fast as she can. 'I am big enough to—'

'How dare you—' The door bangs open against a life-size cut-out of Eric Bristow. Wilf sticks his silver crewcut through the gap.

'Christ, Anna, there you are. When you've quite finished there's a queue half-way to Vauxhall. *Could* you please . . .' He strides off, leaving the door wide behind him.

'Oh God – Mum, I really have to—'

'Don't think,' says her mother darkly, 'that I'm going to let this go.'

And then, without warning, the future steps closer. On Friday she returns home to a message. It is from an unknown man.

'Stella, are you there? It's me – it's Jakey. I've just got back; it was *awful.* Really. I know you've been, but I couldn't believe it. And when we saw that bastard who ran the place, he tried to beat up my cameraman; he said he remembered *you.* Listen, next time you do orphans, I'm going first. Anyway, are you around? Ring me if you want some company. And Jane says hi.'

She owes it to Richard to let him know. She spends hours in preparation, like a geisha: bath in case he says 'come over', tidy the flat (impressive items uppermost) in case he rushes round himself. Will the message make him jealous? Revive Stella's flagging appeal?

Upstairs, before she dresses, she has one last bid to calm herself. Under her hand, which could be his hand, her nipple is hard as unripe fruit. He may have done this here before, only a door away. She tries to separate the sensations of her breast and palm. How does it feel to feel this flesh, to be stroked by him, to be him stroking her?

It isn't, she discovers, very difficult to imagine, after all.

And when she goes back downstairs to ring him, shaky and flushed, she hears a noise in the kitchen and smiles to herself even as her heart catapults. She knows she is rosy, a delectable niece, and Stella unexpected is better than not at all. As she skips her hand down the banisters she straightens her crumpled shirt, and prepares for welcome.

But not for this.

Andrea Lefschitz is standing in burgundy velour at the kitchen table. They jump, glower and right their expressions in synchronicity.

'Anna!' she exclaims. 'I thought you were out. You're looking very . . . vibrant.'

‘Thank you. I . . .’ Andrea’s ray-gun stare has her pinioned. ‘Were you . . . can I—’

‘I was looking for a pen.’ Speechless, Anna hands her a biro. ‘But I don’t need one now, obviously, since you’re here.’ Her bulging blue eyes are fixed on Anna’s face, the magenta spreading towards her neck.

‘Did you . . . was the door—’

‘I just dropped by,’ says Andrea, lowering her eyes to Anna’s bare feet, ‘to leave you a note.’

‘Ah,’ Anna nods. She keeps her hands behind her back and tries to smile at Andrea, who is removing a thread from the hem of her mac. Raindrops gleam in her thin hair. ‘Saying . . .?

‘Your mother mentioned that Beccy’s away?’

‘Oh. Yes, she did. But I explained, Andrea, you see, that I’m fine here. Really. It’s very kind but—’

Andrea stands like a battleship figurehead. She barely blinks. ‘Well, I was in the area, and Magda asked me to let you know that it’s free from next Thursday. Just give me a ring and I’ll show you where everything is.’

‘Truly, I’m fine. It’s very sweet of you, but—’ Andrea, indifferent, is already heading for the hall. ‘I – the door wasn’t open, was it? I didn’t hear you come in.’

‘Your mother gave me her key,’ says Andrea, casting a final look around the kitchen. ‘I said I’d check up on you.’

‘Oh,’ says Anna.

‘How fortunate I did.’

Anna, head in hands, leans against the doorway. Her bones are shrinking from her flesh; with every second her embarrassment deepens. What if Andrea had decided to look upstairs?

What if Anna had been rereading her mother's letter when she arrived, or telephoning Richard, or in Stella's room? She thinks: my mother has ruined my life. And then she notices another green light on the answerphone.

Even inanimate objects are conspiring against her. As the tape rewinds she tells herself that at least someone will think she goes out.

The someone is Stella.

'Anna, sweetheart, it's me. I seem to have missed you; are you behaving? I wonder where you can be. Now, listen, two things. I suddenly remembered: I'd been meaning to buy a picture for your room, make it a bit less boarding-school. Unless that's a look you like, of course. So, I wondered, would you? I'll put fifty pounds in the post, so why don't you nip down to Museum Street or somewhere and find yourself a print; something gorgeous. Not birds. I'd do it myself, but I'm filming naked Moroccans all this week, and at the weekend I – well, never mind. It's not for public ears. Get the picture framed if you can with the money; if not I'll give you more. And don't you dare tell Magda. She thinks everyone's Trojan when it comes to presents.

'Also, I'm definitely now coming back in about three weeks' time; around the seventeenth – either the Friday or Saturday. Don't worry: only for a couple of days. I'll see you then. Hope you're making the most of things in the meantime . . .'

Thirteen

'So it's definite?'

'Well, yes, I think so. "Around the seventeenth" – isn't that Friday?'

'Roughly. So, she's coming. She says.'

'Do you think you'll see her?' asks Anna.

'Yes – well, I should think so. Possibly. I suppose it depends on what she – we both want. And if there's time. You're sure she didn't say anything else, apart from about the picture?'

Anna hugs herself. She is full of delicious secrets. 'No, Richard. But then she wouldn't to me, would she? Like "Please ring Richard, whom you haven't met, and tell him I'm on my way" – I mean, I might *steal* you.'

They both laugh immoderately. Anna, now gripping the doorframe for support, wonders if her heartbeats are audible. To fill the gap that follows, both begin to speak at once; she waits; he goes on. 'This week has been a nightmare: I had to rush to Romania to cover the riots, and my big report's due in next Tuesday. I meant to ring you back, actually, but there wasn't time.'

A smile hovers by her mouth which will not be frowned

away. 'And *I* was going to say that I'll have to find the picture before she arrives. Otherwise she might think I'm ungrateful . . .'

'Any thoughts about what you might choose?'

'Oh God, I don't know. I can't even think where to begin.' Andrea has left her mind a mess. 'I've just had a bit of a drama, actually.'

'Really?'

Almost too late, Anna realizes how much she can't explain. 'Never mind. About the picture – do you know where I could find one?'

'Not really. I've a few ideas, but . . . Do you ever find that when she does something like this, it's almost more unnerving than when she's vile?'

'Well, not . . .'

'I know other people do. They expect her to be shocking, or staggeringly rude, and then she comes over all sweet and generous and it just *floors* them. I expect your mother hates it.'

'Well, yes,' she says. How strange that he remembered. 'You might be right. She probably does. But, still, you know, it's nice of Stella. And it's good she doesn't think I'll lower the tone. I might choose a picture of kittens.'

'Embossed.'

'Well, yes.'

'Or a painting of minarets in an attempt to please.'

Anna laughs, anxiously. She has to ask him, somehow, but her mind is stone. Then, like a miracle, Richard says:

'Look, Anna. What are you doing next Sunday?'

'Nothing,' she says, stupidly. 'I mean, not much. Why?'

'Well, why don't I help you look for that picture?

We could have lunch at that restaurant on Museum Street – you know, the dark one with the fish – and then wander round the shops. I think they'll mostly be open, for the tourists.'

'Really? Oh – lovely. I mean, oh, yes. Let's.' Is she losing the ability to communicate? What if Museum Street is miles? Or if there are two, and she waits for hours outside the Museum of Minor Catastrophes, while her romantic future dies in Trafalgar Square?

'Anna?'

'Oh yes, sorry. So, when shall we meet?'

'One-ish? Say one-fifteen, outside the first print shop you come to on the left when you're walking *from* the museum. That way, if one of us is late, at least we'll have something to look at.'

'Well – OK, if you really think we'll find each other.' She imagines sliding leaves of sunlight, an Edwardian meeting: bowing, park benches. Maybe she will wear a hat.

'Of course. I'd spot you anywhere. So, one-fifteen next Sunday. Are you sure? You don't sound very decided.'

'No, sorry, I didn't mean to.' Anywhere? 'I'm sure. I'm absolutely sure.'

Everybody is in pairs. Sophie, her most self-sufficient friend, has written from Poland to say she is seeing a botanist called Marek, who meets her after classes with posies, their English names memorized, and plays songs of heartbroken gypsies on his sister's guitar. Sasha has dumped Butch for selling her kitten, and is now sleeping with Eric, a tall tarot reader wanted by the CSA. In urgent need of comfort, Anna phones her at two-thirty from work when, Sasha confides, she is still wiping Eric's sperm from her chest.

Acquaintances send postcards describing embryonic happiness with Andean primary school teachers and Spanish engineers. At lunchtimes Hilary and Iain leave the bookshop together, holding hands. For their millionth wedding anniversary, Anna's parents go to St Paul de Vence. Even Wilf has taken to having long phone calls with the office door shut, and keeps disappearing early with bottles wrapped in orange tissue paper.

It's such a waste of a perfectly good libido. Anna stalks the flat like a successful ascetic, transcending all carnal embraces except her own, her dreams plagued by devils with familiar faces.

She worries, in strict rotation:

— What if she misheard the day? And leaves him so wrathful that he ignores her apologies?

— What if she's on the phone being harangued by her mother when he rings to cancel, and the answerphone somehow drops his message? Anna has now claimed to have lost Andrea's number twice and to have tried it (engaged) once; her mother, who has not mentioned their row, will not listen when she demands or begs for a reprieve. Marianne Brooks is mentioned every second phone call, and her father came on the line especially to remind her to ring Markus, despite a publishing deadline ('He's in there all day with Queen Fredegonda and the Bishop of Tours,' reports her mother, 'but who's going to read a murder set in an abattoir if the cover is brown and yellow?'). Worst of all, despite a heated conversation about Andrea and the key, her mother will not drop her relocation plans. Anna lies in her quiet bedroom and imagines squatting at Beccy Lefschitz's, in a nest of Calvin Klein body-sprays and little cardigans.

— Why didn't she tell Richard about that other phone call? She has to tell him; she promised she would. That 'hi' from Jane was surely just a sugar coating; 'Jakey' is so obvious, with his hazelnutty voice and his 'my cameraman' nonsense and his infantile name. What would Stella want with *him*?

— Can she make Richard help her with the ring? Anna knows she's stuck without him, but it's her task: her's alone. She is trapped.

— How can she even begin to ask him about Stella? What if he breaks down? What if he doesn't know? However, unless she begs her mother, Anna has little choice. By the time Stella arrives, she has to know enough.

— Will Stella even be here when she said she'd be here? She is now virtually en route for London. The flat must always be ready, just in case.

— What is going to happen on Sunday at lunchtime? Will Richard just interrogate her and expect her to find her own way back? Or will they romantically stroll, parasols twirling, through bright cold air and trampled plane leaves, to bend over woodcuts and watercolours in darkened studios? Will Richard expect her to listen endlessly to details of his tragic romantic history? Or will he suddenly press a great verdigris-weeping doorbell and lead her into a notoriously secret hotel, where amid Irish linen and infinitely discreet room service he will finally, exhaustively, masterfully but gracefully, do to her almost all she has ever wanted?

She has prepared every room for Stella's arrival. One alone remains to be checked.

The bed is plumped and smooth as cream; the wardrobe shuttered as a confessional. She intends only a quick inspection, a search for spoors and wrinkles. But once she has examined every surface, has straightened the rug and re-angled the mirror, she cannot quite make herself leave. The door on the opposite side of the room, above the sitting-room extension, is bare and closed as the gate to Wonderland. Surely it is her duty, as niece with initiative, to investigate, briefly, the space behind? If it contains a dripping tap, or a stray rotting pigeon, or simply too much dust, it would be better dealt with.

Of course, it is a bathroom. She touches the milky porcelain gloss; sits briefly on the edge of the bath, turns the cold tap not quite far enough for water. 'This is where her head rests in the bath; this is where she washes her hands,' she intones silently, like a celebrity bathroom tour guide. 'You will notice that there is a bidet. This demonstrates either an active sex life or a time spent in France.'

There is a cupboard in here too, and so she opens it; she might as well. But what she finds there leaves her no more satisfied than before: three mashed toothbrushes, cleanser, combs, cotton wool, foreign deodorant (Lady Speed Stick), Nurofen, Night Nurse, Elastoplast, regular tampons, body lotion (Clinique). She finds a small cut on her knuckle, rips open an H-shaped plaster and presses it onto her skin. It was the only interesting one; what if Stella notices it's missing?

Or comes back tonight and, as Anna steps back from her welcoming embrace, spots the salmon-coloured patch and guesses where she might have been? She leaves it on: a souvenir.

Her insides are hot and clenched with the need to pee. The door is open, and she shouldn't, of course she shouldn't, but of course she does. She sits on the icy edge of the bidet, and as a gammony smell rises from the stream between her legs she worries about the causes of her mild breathlessness, her flush.

How can all this looking not have produced evidence? A sign of Richard's presence, or someone else's; drugs, or dying person's medicine? Where are the diaphragms, Super-Plus sanitary towels, embarrassing adult ointments, *anything* to suggest that she is normal, that her life is as messy as everybody else's?

It's almost as if she is hiding something. Anna turns on the fountain of water, checks for yellow drops on the china, shuts the cupboard and closes the bathroom door. Her senses are stingingly alert; Stella has never been one to keep her word. Why shouldn't she come back early, for a meeting, or a date, or simply on a whim? Anna walks to the chest of drawers and smiles at herself in the mirror. If Stella came in now she'd see Anna in the doorway, and they could smile at each other's reflections in the mottled glass. She listens, but the house is still. To her left and right are the yellow squares of other windows; anyone could see her here. She crosses the room and pulls muslin across the glass. Then, enclosed, she opens a drawer.

But there are no secrets hidden among the trousers and T-shirts, no hidden key. Even the anomalies – a dusty-smelling beige cashmere V-neck, a horrible mango-coloured shirt – are so annulled by the other successes that Anna begins to suspect them of invisible virtues. Too baffled to continue, she pushes the drawer closed with her foot and flops back on the bed behind her.

When she opens her eyes she can just see, at the bottom of the large picture-framed mirror, her fanned-out hair, dark terracotta against the duvet. She shuffles up until her face appears: incipient double chin, ordinary nose, lids and eyebrows and look-at-me hair. With more wriggling she can see most of her body: sinking thighs and hips in floppy black trousers, rib cage, stomach and two soft hemispheres in thick pink cotton, shoulders and pale open arms. This must be how she looks in bed. Is this why Stella has it? Deliberately and with effort, Anna pulls a screen across her mind.

She lies very still, watching herself with eyes which, at this angle, seem more hooded and sleepy than before. Stella, realistically, will not be back until the seventeenth; Andrea Lefschitz has had her visit; her mother, surely, will stay away. Still holding her own stare, she takes the hem of her top and lifts it over her hot white stomach, over her bra, up as far as her neck, and pauses. Silence. The fabric lies in unflattering wattles on her chest. She pulls it off.

The black wired cups of her bra rise and fall, rise, and fall. She reaches behind her back and unclips it. Her breasts are blancmanges: round, white, edible. In the chill air of the bedroom her nipples pinch and thicken.

She runs her finger down towards her navel, where her trousers have left a bunched pink blur. The hairs on her skin sense everything. Silence.

Still watching her eyes, her mouth, her arms in the mirror, she slides one hand inside the waistband of her trousers. As this hand moves lower, the other drifts slowly up: over her stomach, waist, chest, the dunes and inclines of her thirsty skin. She is behind the glass, and then she is outside it, watching the other woman in the mirror as she is touched into life. Features float and recombine: white body, mouth, red hair, transfixed together by her gaze. The glass burns. Anna is lost in an alchemy of unknown familiar flesh; a new found land.

And then, suddenly, her hands stop moving. With a terrible flare of consciousness she sees where she is and what she is thinking and what she has almost done. In the great gilt mirror her mouth says to her eyes, 'You cannot do this.' Reflection and flesh, hands and breasts and hair and skin return to their proper places, and the unimaginable retreats behind the glass.

Patting the duvet for her strewn clothes, staring open-mouthed at the face in the mirror, she hoists herself from the wasted bed. On the carpet is a flat black alarm clock, face averted. She turns it with her toe; twelve hours until Museum Street. Clothes hang from her hands like bunting. She tries to stroke deep creases out of the duvet cover, but they will not lie flat. There will be time in the morning.

The reflection has followed her to bed. She should sleep but, even with eyes tightly closed, in the black below her lids she still sees gold against the glass, pale flesh moving, gently. Think of Richard. Only him.

Fourteen

It is twenty-nine past one and Anna is trying to cross Russell Square. At the lights her ankle right-angles on a paving slab, and now she limps like a disabled greyhound vainly trying to stay in the race. Despite hourly wardrobe assessments for over a week, and a fifty-minute clothing crisis (too small, too loose, too dull, too young, too square, too almost-trendy, too ugly, too *dirty*), her chosen outfit (short but bunchy skirt, calf-concealing boots) is inevitably a disastrous mistake.

She is late because:

— At the last possible moment she had decided to use Stella's coffee-pot for a stylish (if he asks) emergency caffeine-boost, but the perished rubber seal had seeped and spat, and the coffee boiled to nothing on the hob.

— Meanwhile she had set her heart on a lucky layer of Stella's mascara, and had brushed the little dried-up wand with her own toothbrush, cleverly impregnated with eye makeup remover. This had removed it all over Stella's sink. By the time Anna had applied the oily black to her lashes, eye makeup-removered and rinsed toothbrush and bathroom, and pinched her cheeks for natural colour, she was already past the point of desirable lateness and into snow-blind panic.

— And then she had remembered the crumpled duvet and spent minutes stroking, bashing and eventually rolling on it, leaving it flatter but still as tumbled as before. She will wash and replace it, praying Stella stays away till then.

The air is gelid and shimmering. People flow towards her like broken ice in a thick and tepid sea. Her movements are swaddled, and her mind creeps slow as glass. She is in a post-coital haze of her own devising, and Richard must be the last to know. She stumbles again as she crosses Great Russell Street, just before the sleeping pharaohs. Richard will require concentration. This time, however hard he tries, she must steer the conversation from Stella, from Paris and eyebrows and unpleasant personal characteristics. Yes, she thinks as she finds the street, this is just about us. He wants to see me. And I'm longing to see him, naturally.

There is no sign of him. She must not look at her watch; it's uncool, and will depress her. She forces her eyes away, keeps her wrist deep inside her ill-chosen sleeve, and then magically her arm flies up and she has noticed it is twenty to two.

She deserves to be shot, or gored, or eaten alive. Normal human intercourse is plainly beyond her. She will be fit only to dandle her sister's oddly named infants on her withered spinster knee, or to appear in low-budget Carlton documentaries (autumn leaves, thistledown, empty swings) with other Women Who Missed Their Chance For Love.

'Hannah?'

'Yes!' She whirls round, to smile at a fat man in a flat Burberry cap, surrounded by his evident wife, hair dyed Foreign Matron Blonde, and three rubicund trenchcoated sons. They are probably Belgian, and very far from Richard.

'Oh, no,' she says, 'no, I think there's a mistake. I'm not . . . oh, never mind. Sorry.' She points at her watch, grimaces, turns and scuttles up the street. There, looking quizzical and tired is Richard, in a doorway, watching her.

'What's going on?' he asks.

'Nothing. Sorry. God. Hello Richard. I'm so sorry I'm late.'

'You *are,* aren't you. Never mind.' He smiles calmly and, with his hand just under her elbow, guides her towards the kerb. 'It's just over the road; I booked.' His tranquillity is an affront. If he's so easily won, thinks Anna, I'm not interested.

The restaurant is almost empty; dark wood and quartzy autumn light. A very poised waiter, with a wedge-shaped neck like a tense bull, takes their coats, offers bread, pours a neon olive pool on to a saucer.

'I came here with Stella once, who said, of that waiter, "He looks like the new boy in a dance company ravaged by AIDS",' says Richard, picking at a crust.

Anna smiles. 'Not nice,' she says, feeling disloyal. She crosses her hands flat on the paper tablecloth, and watches as Richard looks vaguely around the restaurant, fiddles with the collar of his thick grey shirt, prods a pepper hillock with his clumsy fingertip. Grains of annoyance slip down her spine. 'So, how are you? How's work?'

His attention boomerangs back through the past towards her. 'Mine? Oh, it's fine. Undramatic. I finished that report, thank God, and it went down well. Very well. And now they keep trying to send me back to Romania, but there's also that bombing in Fez – you know, the one that . . . never mind – which is *much* more interesting. So I'm just waiting to see if I can go there tomorrow, which I'd rather do, but it all depends on . . . oh, sorry. Would you like a drink?'

Anna swallows. 'Yes.' She watches, astonished, as Richard mumbles over the wine list. She has seen the world anew. The war between the sexes is over. With one colossal insight, she has solved mutual incomprehension, heartbreak and divorce: men can be in love yet prefer to discuss themselves.

He tastes the wine. Anna follows the waiter's stare to Richard's left earlobe, which is sweetly furred. 'Lovely.'

Anna and the waiter nod their agreement.

'So,' he says, balancing his glass among the broken peppercorns. 'Anna. How have you been?'

Anna, who has just taken an enormous tonsil-sloshing mouthful of Chilean red, smiles, gulps, re-gulps and begins to cough. Her eyes water, her throat burns, and ruby bubbles begin to emerge from her flaring nostrils. Each time she hopes for quiet, the choking begins again. Everyone in the restaurant, including two otherwise self-absorbed 'I'm pretty but he's rich' couples, turns to look at her. Richard offers her his napkin, water, an embarrassed smile. Finally, gratefully, she subsides.

'Phew. Sorry. God. It felt like *drowning.* I don't quite know what happened.'

He smiles, but the room is still silent and Anna knows that if Stella were here she would glare at each in turn, or perhaps offer her own comments, until every greying and chestnut head had turned away and left them.

Fixing her eyes on the menu's spiky show-off writing, she tries to gather her thoughts. Her cheeks cool slowly; her blood subsides. Richard asks rhetorical questions about the food and leans precariously back in his chair to catch the waiter, while Anna covertly inspects his hands and wonders what he and Stella did after they'd eaten – here, and everywhere else.

The waiter muscles over.

'Anna?'

'Oh, sorry. I haven't quite – maybe the artichoke ravioli thing? And then the . . . brill? No, the duck. Oh God, no, the brill. Do you know?'

'And I'll have – well, I wasn't planning to have a starter.'

Anna's heart falls; too late, she goes for playful. 'Oh no, you *must*. It's so . . . ungrateful not to.'

He grins at her. She imagines her touching his lips with a fingertip, a clean crescent of nail. 'OK then, I'll have the Caesar Salad. And then the Rosemary Lamb Shank with Flageolet Beans.'

As if a stagehand stood by her shoulder, slotting vision-tinting gels between her retina and the world, so Anna's perception changes again. She has always nursed a private prejudice against ordering food by its full menu name. Now she begins to reconsider – is his hair quite short enough? is his shirt rather dull? would that profile become annoying? – and it is only as she begins to anatomize, query and dismiss the buttons on his cuffs that she hears the echo of her mother.

Richard reaches the end of a story about a diplomat on a plane with some internet porn, and Anna smiles and nods and prays that he won't suddenly ask her about downloading websites, or ask her to draw a wine-drop diagram of the net on the tablecloth. And then she realizes who he's talking about.

'. . . does she?'

'Sorry? I . . .'

'Stella. She doesn't have email.'

'No. Well, I don't expect so. She's not really into that sort of thing. Is she?'

'You never know quite what she will be into.'

Like a pair of newborn babies their eyes blur and unfocus, lost in cybervisions of Stella, face lit by a nightmare aquarium gleam.

The glass door opens and two young men in polo-necks, black and camel, are led to a corner table. Anna half-smiles – they might be her neighbours – and turns back to Richard. 'Now,' she says, brushing a little rockery of crumbs and snowy salt-flakes from her side of the tablecloth. 'We're not here to discuss her, of course, are we? Tell me about . . . oh, your week.' She stops. 'Although I suppose you have.'

He smiles awkwardly. 'What have *you* been doing with yourself?' Anna feels a blush start, but he does not seem to notice. 'Any picture ideas?'

'Well,' says Anna, 'no. I mean I've thought about it, occasionally, obviously, but it's so personal. What I like might be . . . inappropriate, or – you see, I've never actually bought a picture before. Except one for my parents, years ago, which they secretly hated. Both of them, which is quite a feat as they have wildly differing tastes. So, no.'

'Ah. OK. Well, afterwards we can have a go. Wander about. I'm sure we'll find something that she . . . you'll like.'

'OK.'

'OK. I'm trying to give up smoking.'

'Really?'

'Yes.'

'And how is . . .' There is almost nothing to talk about. They are strangers, inappropriately familiar, like a pair of duellists accidentally meeting before the dawn. The waiter, who has been laughing and mock-dancing with a waitress behind the bar, approaches their table with two deep white plates. Perhaps I should be a waitress, thinks Anna, drinking from her refilled wineglass. Her entire body is longing for someone, even an irredeemably camp waiter, to put their arm around her waist. Lack of bodily contact is turning her into a shrinking hag, a block of ice, a leper. Maybe she should carry a bell.

'How is it?'

She has barely noticed. Her brain and tastebuds reconnect. 'Gorgeous. Like a beautiful artichokey cushion. Do you want to try?'

'Please.'

She deposits a slice on the chaste lip of his plate. 'What do you call that? When they only give you one? A raviolus?'

'A raviolo, maybe.'

'Yes. How's yours?'

'Well, it's very . . .'

'Caesary?'

He gives her the look long-reserved for inexplicable women. 'Probably. Nice wine.'

They have descended to the world's most secretly boring subject. 'Yes.'

'Hmm.'

He knows nothing of Stella's other life, she suspects. His usefulness is limited. The crunching of Cos lettuce fills their silent space. She concentrates hard on the crimped edges of her ravioloid, but her mind is an empty spinning ball, filling with cutlery clinks and the crushing pressure of having nothing at all to say.

Then, suddenly, they are speaking: 'Richard'/'Stella' overlapping, entangling, like unsuccessful dubbing.

'Sorry – go on.'

'You first.'

'I was just . . . did you call me Stella?'

'No. I mean . . . no. I can't have. Did I?'

'Well, yes.' He looks stunned, and guilty. 'I suppose you . . . you might have been going to say something like, oh, "Stella is allergic to artichokes", but that isn't how it sounded . . . You *know* I'm not Stella. I don't look like her. Do I?'

'Like Stella?'

' . . . '

'No.'

She nods, and moves her knife and fork to five o'clock. The air quickens. 'Right. So . . . what were you going to say?'

'It doesn't matter. Look,' he says, moving his own cutlery two centimetres to the left. 'Is it that you really can't bear to discuss her? I know you're probably sick of the subject; I don't want to be a bore. It's just – well, you know her, to an extent, and . . . listen, can I speak confidentially?'

'Of course,' she says, wondering if anyone ever says 'please don't.'

'Well, I've decided . . .' He inspects his palm, then takes a sip of water. Anna offers mental suggestions: to have no pudding; to tell me what you did in bed; never to see either of us again.

'I've decided that that weekend, when Stella's back, will have to be a watershed, if I can find out what she wants. No, I *have* to find out what she wants. This is ridiculous. I can't spend my life on tenterhooks.'

'Right. Blimey. So – what are you going to do, exactly? Ask her? I suppose you'll have to.' They pull matching upside-down grins of horror.

'I know. It's hardly tempting. She's not the sort of woman you want to assume . . . once we were at the cinema, in Kilburn or somewhere horrible. We were watching this ridiculous film about a little child and a puppy, and how they were trying to find a cure for the teenage sister, who was tragically ill with typhoid – I think it had been pouring and we'd needed somewhere to hide.'

The waiter takes their plates; she smiles up at him, but keeps her eyes on Richard.

'Anyway, it was a truly dreadful film. But fairly involving, despite myself, and actually quite moving, at the end. I remember feeling quite choked up, and I'm hardly a cryer. At least not in films.' Anna leans forward, thinking: do you cry because of Stella? 'And anyway, she sniffed. Stella sniffed a bit, and sort of squirmed in her seat, like she was really distressed.'

'Yes?'

'So I whispered, "Oh, poor Stella, are you really upset?" and tried to stroke her hand.'

'And?'

'And in this hushed cinema full of weeping mums and murmuring tots, she let out an enormous snort, and I realized she was laughing, literally shaking with laughter—'

'*No*,' says Anna. 'What, obvious giggling?'

'Worse. Actual blatant guffaws. It was awful. I didn't know what to do, so I grabbed her arm and dragged her up the stairs, these endless spotlit stairs, past all their eyes, and then, just as we were about to leave, she calmed herself.'

'Thank God.'

'And said, in the loudest and most perfectly-projecting voice—'

'No,' breathes Anna.

' "Typhoid's too good for her. And the dog. Richard, take me home. I need sexual intercourse." '

Wide-eyed with gleeful dismay, Anna shivers.

'*Yes*,' he says. 'You see? I can't blunder in there feeling emotional and assume she feels the same. She's horrifying.'

Anna nods, inspects her sliding reflection on a fork-back, and remembers a story her sister told her in which Stella had gone to bed with someone very important at Channel 4 ('But *who*?' 'Sorry, sis, I *did* know, but—') and had asked him *as he actually came* if he was gay.

The waiter appears, bearing two huge plates. Anna, who has begun to feel her mind relax, allows a complicitous silence to fall until he leaves their table, as if he knows Stella too. 'I suppose,' she says as she scrapes the top of a saffron potato with a silver tine, 'I suppose she is. I wish I were. She's the sort of person who spots an infant in a fluffy pink dress, and instead of cooing over it – or worrying about its childhood, as I might – she'd march up to its mother and pretend to be interested in where to buy one, and washing instructions, and so on. I saw her do that once, at a zoo. We were by the giraffes, hysterical, and she kept a completely straight face. She was pretending it was for me.' She tries her fish. 'God, this is lovely.'

'And another thing,' says Richard, between mouthfuls of Rosemary Lamb Shank. 'I think we've hit on a definite feature of Stella.'

Anna tilts her head intelligently to one side.

'She's anecdotal. No, she is. Everything she does is a story. Whenever you meet people who know her – and they do, disgustingly – they always have an amazing tale about her asking Norman Mailer if he wore eyeliner, or how she talked her way into an transvestites' brothel in Rio by claiming to be the Dutch ambassador, or how she pretended to be pregnant and climbed out of an Egyptian jail in her underpants . . .'

'Did she?'

'Well, something like that. Maybe bra and underpants. But you get the idea.'

'I do.' Anna finishes a little pile of lentils and tries to think. He isn't really in love with her. He's just like I am, she realizes: oddly interested, more than he wants to be, although obviously in my case it's research, and family curiosity, and in his it's – well, sex. So maybe I should let him talk, just to get Stella out of his system, and then he can concentrate on me, which obviously is preferable. Isn't it? Her logic is becoming furred, her nerves silting up like rimey cobwebs. She finds, to her surprise, that she barely knows what she wants, let alone how to achieve it.

'Have you been to her flat in Paris?' he suddenly asks.

'No. Never. I wish. Have you?'

'No. Not this one. She had another, in the Thirteenth, but there was some man she took against in the flat above and she had to move.'

'I'm surprised she didn't make *him*.'

'Quite,' he agrees. They beam across the table through a warm fog of mutual feeling.

Anna, noticing an airy daring burning in her chest, takes a big gulp of water and eats a potato. Richard's more fun than I'd realized, she thinks. A flash of last night's mirror catches her unawares. The afternoon clicks into another gear.

'Have you been to Paris much?' she asks politely.

'Not as much as I'd like to. Have you?'

'Well,' she says, sitting back in her chair, 'hardly. Once rather illicitly. I always associate it with that.'

'Oh yes? Illicitly? Sounds . . . diverting.' They slit their eyes at each other, smiling adult smiles.

'It was.' Two years ago, during a premonitory lull with Luke, she and a friend had gone to a party. He was the only handsome boy she knew, and, unlike Luke, could dress. They walked through narrow streets, their conversation threading with suggestion, moving closer, closer still. As they talked, breath smoking and the sides of their bodies magnetic, her veins became air and her blood ran scarlet. Upstairs in the packed and thumping room they shot each other blazing looks, and that night, shocked and silent, they undressed. His hipbones crunched into her like granite, and that was all he did, but the next weekend he took her to the Marais, to his godmother's flat, as his absent girlfriend's cousin. There, deafened by parquet floors, sarcophagal marble and mirrors, they crept silently together. She saw the selfish layer beneath the sweet, and realized she preferred him dressed. Luke wept when she told him and she came back home.

Usually she only remembers the scarlet feeling and its bitter echo, but she's glad for it now. Richard is leaning towards her across the table, looking pleased. Her head feels light and hot.

'Well, what about you?' she smiles, pushing a spare lentil over the tablecloth with the nail of her little finger. 'Come on. You must have been illicit in Paris. That's what it's for.'

He shrugs, keeping his laughing brown eyes fixed on hers. 'Well . . . of course I have. But with your aunt, Anna. You don't want to know about that.'

The expression on her face sets and cracks. 'Of course not.'

Like a painted god, dropped from the flies to intervene in romantic messes, the waiter appears, scratching the back of his hand. An enormous bicep flutters up his sleeve. 'Finished?' he asks kindly. Anna hands him her plate, he calls her 'love', Richard catches her eye and twinkles, and the world twirls back on its axis.

'Shall we have more wine?' he asks, as the waiter returns with two small menus.

'Valrhona', 'zabaglione' and 'star anise' jump out at her, but there must be limits to her greed. 'Why not?'

Her new friend brings two big glasses of wine, and suggests the toffee pudding ('Or shall we share a Spiced Plum Tart?' asks Richard), and as he brings their spoons the talk drifts back along the Seine. They drink, and lean closer, and he tells her about horrible things Stella has done or said to managers and producers and to him. Anna says without meaning it 'I must just go to the loo', where she sits spinningly in a curved wood stall, thinks about everything he has told her, flirts with herself in the mirror, and strolls back upstairs to seize her chance.

'But it's not as if she loses all her friends, is it? I mean, the flat is full of postcards and books from them. And photographs.'

'Oh, you've had a look at them, have you?' A challenge curls underneath his smile.

'Yes, I have. Don't worry, none of you naked with piglets. I've just, you know, glanced at the shelves. As you do. Nothing very interesting.'

'Who did you see?'

'Do you mean did I see you? *Richard.* I don't know. Maybe. You've a bit of bread on your shirt.' She leans across to flick it, keeping her eyes low as her finger brushes his warm chest.

'Don't be difficult, Anna.' He grabs her finger and grins. 'Is there one of me?'

'Let go and I'll tell you. Thank you. No, all I've seen is a photo of a party, with Stella in it, and she's smiling at a man. Who could be you. I think he probably is. It's about, oh, ten years ago. That's all I have to say.'

'Really? And what am I doing?'

'Looking friendly. You're by the cake.'

'And what's she doing?'

'Smiling . . .' The picture floats before them like a mirage filling the room with everything it has made her think, and do.

'At?'

The hairs on her arms rise, and shiver. She looks past him, towards the bar. 'Not you.'

Between them the air stiffens, then relaxes, like egg whites slowly whipped. He exhales through his nose and leans back with a muscular click. 'Oh well, it's hardly the first time. Tell me who, then.'

How can she describe that cheekboned curve, that frozen gaze? She lifts her head. 'It's hard to see. Just the corner of someone's face. And a sort of . . . stare, between them.'

He nods.

'I think it's a woman.' She says it in a small voice, eyes averted. Will he be horrified? Or go quiet and puzzled, as she is, and store it in his huge mental file of things he doesn't know about Stella, where it will drip and grow in secret, bleeding into his dreams?

'Oh really?' He sounds oddly sanguine. His face is amused. 'Description?'

'Well . . . as I remember, quite thin, bit older than Stella, short dark hair.'

'Eyes?'

'Sort of hooded?'

His smile broadens. 'Oh, I know who *that* is.'

'What?' Despite the alcohol, which is making her want to lie on the table, she sits up and stares at him. 'Do you?'

'Of course.' He is horribly nonchalant.

'*Who*?'

'Never you mind.'

'Oh come on. You're joking. Aren't you?

'No.'

'Please?'

'No.' He's laughing at her now; she could kick him. 'Sorry, but no. Ask Stella, if it means that much to you.'

She controls the urge to shake him between her teeth. 'Well, obviously it doesn't, really, but I'm just curious. *You* know she does that. She makes me horribly curious. And you, too.'

The Spiced Plum Tart arrives, and as he positions it between them Richard says regretfully, 'Oh Anna, I know. I mean, in general. It's vile of her but she does it so much.'

'Which bit?'

'All of it.'

'Tell me the photograph woman.'

'No.'

She curls her nails into her palm, but the wine has relaxed her; she will watch for another chance. 'Brute,' she says, cutting the tip off the tart as her reward. Bloody fruit lists towards her spoon.

'Yes. Tell me, don't you ever think Stella's vile?'

'If I think about her, I suppose, I do.' Her lids are heavy, but she feels wonderful. She could scoop up the truth with her spoon, if he'd let her; the purple taste is deep as a stain. 'I don't even know if I like her.'

'You know, neither do I. And it's not that she's so very gorgeous, between you and me.'

She tries to look shocked, but her face refuses. 'Oh, I *know.* She gets that terrible dragony look. I've only seen it about once, but it makes you thank God you're not her mother, or her sister, or—'

'Or her spouse.'

'Or her friend—'

'Or her—'

'Lover.'

'No.'

'God.'

They are silent. Anna's glass nudges her hand. Between them the white plate is bloody with plum juice, one frail pastry half-moon floating among the crumbs. He nudges her prone fork with his. 'Go on.'

'I couldn't. Really.'

'You could.'

'Well, I'm not going to.'

'You must. Oh come on, you *want* to. Girls—' she glares at him, but tries to do it good-humouredly, '*women* always want more pudding. It's chemical.'

Her frown splinters and collapses. 'You know that's a filthy lie. Eat it, Richard,' and she lines her fork up with his big knuckles.

'No.'

'Come on.'

'*No.*'

He scoops it up and holds it out to her, eyes intent down the handle of his fork. She pushes his hand aside.

'Take it.'

'No.'

The fork advances. She puts her hand on his wrist and pushes it away.

'Why not?'

'Because.'

'*Stella* would.'

She opens her mouth to reply, and suddenly, like a darting animal, the fork has slipped between her teeth and the last bite of tart is irrevocably hers. 'I hate you,' she mumbles through the crumbs.

He looks delighted; perhaps she has taken this too far. 'I'll get the bill.'

While they wait and talk, synapses dancing with private common thoughts, Anna sneaks looks at his hands and mouth and forearms and wonders where they have been. The scented heat of the restaurant pools beneath her breasts, between her thighs. Richard insists on paying and Anna insists back, until she says overemphatically 'OK, but my turn next time', and his eyebrows shoot up, and as he signs the slip appear to stay there.

'Now where?' she asks brightly as they step outside. The sky is a dirty white, and dry leaves rattle along the gutter.

'Are you cold?'

'A bit.'

But instead of passing his jacket he leads her to a bright doorway and steps inside, nodding to the pink-faced man behind the till.

The shop is glazed with light. Bookshelves stretch almost to the ceiling. In a glass-topped display case by the till, her childhood lies frozen on green baize slopes: Ardizzone, Belloc, spectacled pigs by Edward Lear.

'This way,' calls Richard from behind a bookcase. She rounds the corner and finds him bending right over, peering at a Man Ray hardback.

He looks ridiculous. She tells him so, and he smiles. 'Find anything?'

'Not yet. Where shall we look?'

She points behind them, towards an X-shaped rack of prints. They turn at the same time, bump hips and begin to giggle.

'Shhh.'

'Don't.'

Together they bend over the prints and flick through watery village scenes, eighteenth-century scenes of bosomy vice and flaccid flowers. 'Well?'

She looks up through a reddish veil. 'Keep going.'

He turns over another white board and their eyes fall on a naked dark woman, swathed with absurdly sequinned cloths, pouting into a mirror. The side of her face and the reflection do not match.

'God,' they say together, and begin to laugh again. The pink man behind the till smoothes his long white fringe and looks distressed. They shush each other, with predictable effect, compounded by Richard's impressions of the pouting painting, and Anna's inability to control her giggling. Sternly, Richard leads her to one more rack, but with one glimpse of smudge-faced skipping maidens his shoulders are shaking and she is vainly compressing billows of laughter which emerge, magnificently, from her nose.

'Let's go.'

'Definitely.' They nod seriously, her mouth begins twitching again, and in a tangled roar of renewed hysteria they charge out of the shop and round the corner, where they lean their backs against the grey stone side of the shop and try to subside. As her snorting begins to calm she turns her head, as does he; in an instant, with wide open eyes, they understand, and then their mouths collide.

In that tight roaring space there is nothing but his mouth and gentle waist-balanced hands. The air becomes slithery and alive. Every nerve in her body surges towards him until they seem to merge, until she is merely a female surface beneath his lips and palms. Then something switches, and it is as if she touches that surface, as if twin curves of waist and soft marzipan lips bloom beneath her hands, her mouth. A suggestion of silk, a secret swoop of flesh, new flesh, and, if she looks up now . . .

But it is only Richard, eyes tightly shut. Surreptitiously she closes her eyes again, but the fantasy dissolves as she pursues it. His stubble is scuffing the edge of her mouth, and she has glimpsed his nostril hair. That waist and mouth are Anna's, just Anna's, once more, and she is in Richard's arms, and there is no one between them.

She shifts to the other foot and feels him falter. His face is befuddled, possibly ashamed, until he catches her looking, and smiles. Could he possibly have guessed what she had been thinking?

'Well hello.'

'Hello.'

And the spell is broken.

Neither of them seems to want to linger. They round the corner and walk towards the museum, through afternoon light now rich and strange. Anna, suddenly sober, looks at her feet and thinks of things to say should their companionable silence become uncomfortable. Almost immediately, it does.

'So . . .'

'So.'

'I wasn't expecting that.' I'm trite, thinks Anna, on top of everything else. Would it be impolite to wipe her lip? Her mind is a whirling swamp of improper thoughts and confusing—

'Anna?'

'Yes?'

'I don't think we'll be finding you a picture today, do you?'

'No.' I am lost, she thinks. His voice is rumbling beside her. 'Sorry?'

'I said would you like a cab? You're looking a bit pale.' He nudges her arm. 'Are you OK?'

'No, I'm fine. But perhaps should go. Richard . . .'

'Yes?' he asks over his shoulder, one arm already out to embrace a distant taxi.

'Nothing.'

A black cab squeals against the curb. Richard calls her address into the driver's smoky cabin, and opens the door wide.

'Well . . .'

'OK then. Thanks for – lunch. Ahem.' They smile at each other, but something else flies between them: a spark of panic, or relief. She is almost certain she can trust him not to tell.

'Look after yourself. We'll speak soon.' He puts his hand on her back, and kisses the top of her head as she turns and climbs into the cab. The door slams. She is alone, and not alone. There is the feeling of those other lips against hers, like a blessing.

Fifteen

Anna's mind and body are not her own. She paces the floor, jumps at sudden noises, draws complicated doodles involving initials and profiles and curling Florentine leaves. She leaves messages for her sister, and for sweet understanding Janey Warner, but hides her address book before she resorts to Markus. Twice during lunchbreaks she rounds the corner of Habitat, lest Andrea Lefschitz returns for fabric swatches and decides, despite their fruitless last encounter, that she'd like a long tête-à-tête over cappuccino in the basement café. And most of all she eyes doorhandles, shampoo bottles and aubergines with a view to self-impalation, right through her sizzling skin, into the rolling simmering liquid in her core.

Then, one quiet afternoon in the bookshop, when Wilf is doing the accounts and the tourists are buying dishcloths elsewhere and everyone else, except her, is talking or flirting or having impressive sex, Anna realizes that without discussing this with someone she will go mad. She surveys her options:

a) Mad Mona, who today is wearing a crumpled Polish widow dress and a ring with an inlaid blue glass eye.

Mona does not look like she has hormones, let alone incestuous kisses with an older man.

b) Wilf: the obvious answer. He teases her most, raises his eyebrows most often towards her, and increasingly Anna cannot look at him without visualizing disclosures, his strong arm around her shoulders, encouragement whispered through her tears. But even as she toys with possible beginnings she recollects his pack-ice stare, his thin-set mouth, his utter loathing of personal weakness. If she starts to tell him about Richard he will lose interest instantly. And if she tries another tack, what will she begin?

c) Hilary the weedy credit-card-swallower, who having been dumped by Welsh Iain spends lunchbreaks blowing her nose and reading novels from the Teen Romance section. She has put her faith in Jesus, which to Anna is not an option.

d) Welsh Iain himself. Recently, Anna has noticed something. Every woman he speaks to, from labrador-enthusiasts to schoolgirls in Spiceboots, melts and unfolds at his words. Each of them, like her, goes through stages: from brief condescension, to beguilement by jokes and dry flattery, and finally the belief that they alone have discovered him, that he responds uniquely to them. Her certainty in his secret passion for her had crumbled to dust and dry splinters, and now she avoids him.

e) Kirsten. She has barely noticed Kirsten, the brusque deputy manager, has not shared her Tupperwared lentils in Gordon Square, or discussed bicycle padlocks as they hang up their kagouls. Besides, her fading sandy bob does not inspire confidence; she looks like she's married a sociologist. But this morning they had caught each other's eye and minimally smiled as a waistcoated solicitor lectured them on British bookselling, and now the shop is hushed. This may be her only chance.

'Kirsten,' she says, semi-expertly stacking flyers. 'I . . . what do you think about Hilary and Iain?'

'What do you mean?' asks Kirsten, passing escapees from under the gift books. In her washed-out red sweatshirt she looks more like an ageing youth worker than a deputy Wilf. The blond Oxonian claims she's a vegan class warrior. 'She'll get over him. I saw her making eyes in Superdrug only yesterday.'

'No—' It's hard to explain; what if Kirsten thinks she's fishing for work-place dirt? 'No, I just meant, you know, was it ever a problem that they were working, well, together?'

'No. Not that I know of. Why?' She is leaning her forearms on the counter, smiling vaguely as she fiddles with a hangnail. To Anna's surprise she isn't wearing a ring.

'Well, I just thought . . . you know how it can get difficult, sometimes, when people get involved with each other. I mean, when other people are entangled.'

'Yes,' Kirsten says slowly, keeping her eyes on her thumb. 'Don't tell me, Anna. You're sleeping with him too.'

'*No,*' she exclaims. 'No, God, nothing like that. It's just . . .'

'What?' Kirsten looks up mildly.

'Well.' She scents her chance like a St Bernard: there's life beneath the snow. 'It's a bit complicated. I've got a . . . a friend. Who's older than me. And this friend, who lives abroad, has a friend here, who's also older. They've been having a sort of affair, for ages. But my . . . my original friend, you see, doesn't really want the other friend . . . it's just been trailing along. And I met the friend – the friend's friend, if you see what I mean—'

'Yes?' Kirsten has sensibly abandoned her hangnail, and is leaning against the counter, arms crossed. It's like an ideal school moment: the kindly teacher, the quiet breaktime, all the advice and concern you ever wanted here, at last, for you.

'We met, and, you see, we got on well. Very well. And—'

'And?'

'Kissed. On Sunday.'

'Well.' She rubs her chin with a dry hand. 'That doesn't sound too bad. You've had a kiss and your friend—'

'Friend's friend.'

'Friend's friend obviously isn't so hung up on the – friend. Am I right?'

Anna looks down. This conversation is roaring away with her, and she wants to get off. Kirsten, however, is looking straight into her eyes. 'I suppose so. But that's, that's not exactly what I'm worried about. It's more that I'm not sure that the friend, I mean the friend's friend . . .'

'You mean the one you kissed.'

'Yes.' Please, she begs silently, decide you don't want to hear any more. 'That one. I'm not sure my friend's friend quite wanted, was quite aware of, even, it being me. Are you sure you've got time for this?'

'Yes.'

'Oh. Right. Um, and to be honest, I'm not sure that—well, maybe I sympathized. You know?'

Kirsten does not blink. Her eyes are the colour of rain.

'I think so. This friend of yours, the initial friend. Have you ever . . . kissed?'

'God no. *No.* Absolutely not.' She notices that she is pulling at the skin on her neck, which feels sanded, strangely new. She drops her hand and begins to scratch her elbow. Her eyes dart to the door. Kirsten keeps on looking. 'What? No, I said. I really haven't. Even if I wanted to, which of course I don't, it wouldn't be – appropriate. At all. I mean, I could with the friend's friend, but no, not with my – friend. No. God. Honestly. Why?'

'Anna,' says Kirsten, patting her arm and beginning to tidy the magazines by the till. 'If you want my advice—'

'Oh, I do,' says Anna anxiously. 'I really do.'

'—I'd stop worrying quite so much about what your friend's friend thinks. I don't think that's really the issue. Do you?'

Anna's throat is dry. She swallows hard and stares at Kirsten's lace-ups. 'No,' she mumbles. 'Perhaps not. Thank you.' The shop is in flames, but her skin is suddenly cool. As she moves away and begins aimlessly to rearrange the calendar section, something in her mind turns round to face her.

Nothing has changed. Like a vampire victim, a sleeping spy, an exiled princess, newly acceded to her throne, the surface of her life must stay the same. Meanwhile, underneath her disguise, she is living in another world.

She has started keeping a diary. This is never a good sign. She no longer idles through expeditions to buy a hair-brush, or a spare button for her new grey coat. Instead she races home like a lover, notebook falling open in her mind's hungry eye. She begins going to bed earlier and earlier, unable to prolong the pleasure of slithering her pink bathed legs against the cotton, watching her future skid across the page.

Later, as the night begins to thicken and sleep calcifies her brain, she slides the fat book under the mattress beside her ear, and closes her eyes. All the scenes as yet undescribed, epiphanies bright as starbursts and hidden hot admissions, crowd before her, fighting for attention. She tries to regiment them. She tries to think of Richard.

His silence should be a torment. A year ago she'd think of nothing else. Even when she attempts to focus, piquing her ego and desire with his indifference, it is hard to raise more than a growl of interest. Nightly she sets up his good-looking tired face, his strong flat rough-skinned body, a photofit of parts she has glimpsed and wanted and touched – parts she is sure she used to long for. And each night his gauzy image, through which she can already glimpse a sinuous shadow, is ripped away as Anna steps into her dreams.

Wilf comments on her haggard appearance and lightly asks if she's taking smack. Anna scowls, and then reminds herself that in his lookist culture, sunbeds are the norm.

But he may have a point. It is, admittedly, all she can do to haul herself to work after her nightly exertions, which are leaving her feeling cheap, but powerful. Even the air has a high-octane shimmer. On successive nights two friends announce they are moving to London in the new year, and even as she jubilates she is changing for bed. Kirsten, who since their little talk would probably rather ignore her, giving rise to great blushing fits of horror at what she might have guessed, half smiles as they pass in the corridor and says, 'burning the candle at both ends?'

Anaesthetized by hormones, she has lost the Glasses; Stella's ring is eclipsed. Then an open telephone directory on Wilf's desk reminds her, and in a last-minute access of boldness she shuts herself in the office and dials. She can barely hear the voice over the commotion of her heart.

'Yes?'

'I – hello. I've rung before, actually. I'm . . . my name is Anna.'

'Anna,' the man says, warm but guarded. 'And what can I do for you?'

'I'm calling about . . . it's a ring.'

'Sorry?'

'A ring. A . . . a friend left it with you. At your house. And – well, she'd like it back; very much. So I said I'd help.'

'. . . I see. And this friend of yours. Do you know why she didn't ring herself?'

'I don't,' Anna confides. 'I'm not quite sure of the – circumstances.'

'I see. So you're the go-between, are you?'

'Yes.' She imagines him nodding; he sounds gentle, probably bearded. 'Is this . . . Nicky Glass?'

'As opposed to?'

'Well, I suppose . . . I don't know. Sorry; I know it's all very vague. But you know the ring, don't you?'

'I do.'

'Can she have it back?' She waits. Is he ordering his Kentish Town hitmen to the flat as they speak? Is he smiling through tears at a portrait of his faithless wife? No wonder this has been kept a secret. Stella's buried love has broken his heart.

'I don't see why not,' he says eventually. 'I certainly don't want it.'

'Oh, thank you. Thank you so much. I was afraid I'd fail—' Anna stops.

'I see,' says the man. 'Does she always ask you to do her dirty work?'

'Not usually . . . I mean, this was just a favour. It's not dirty, is it?'

'Never mind. I'll post it to you.'

'Oh – well, if you wouldn't . . .'

'I'd rather.'

'Do you have the—'

'I do.'

'In Paris?'

'Yes.'

'So . . .'

'That's it. No more to say.'

'Well.' Some kind of ending, a speech of thanks, seems called for. 'It's very kind—'

He cuts her short. 'OK, enough. And Anna?'

'Yes?' Is he about, at last, to lift this unnecessary veil?

'Tell Stella, seriously, to rot in hell.'

Anna replaces the receiver, slowly. She closes her mouth and begins to think. It is like swimming through a maze. That night she falls asleep with her mother's truncated letter in her hand.

*

Even now, Stella's perfect clothes are calling to her.

It would, after all, be foolish to waste them. It's hardly likely that a friend of Stella's would enter the bookshop, recognize a garment, and assume the pale beauty by the till was her relative? And if by chance it were to happen, wouldn't it deepen their bond? 'Darling Anna, how extraordinary. If I'd known that you loved chartreuse too, I'd have asked you to Paris months ago.'

She chooses a thin black knitted top with long funnel-shaped sleeves and a wide neck. It is an elegant cobweb, very Stella, and although it must hang better on her, it could be Anna too. All day their shoulders and wristbones sit together, their skin combines, their breasts are echoes. She begins to remember seeing Stella in it once, maybe more. But Wilf raises his eyebrows and casually asks if she has an attic, and Iain repeatedly mentions bats, and she begins to wonder if perhaps it looks less original-sophisticate and more mid-eighties Madonna Goth than she had hoped. It is also, she now realizes, murkily transparent. She walks home, arms folded against her chest, longing to be free of it, but cannot decide how to wash it, or if she should. She leaves it folded in the bottom drawer, full of her.

Then, one morning, another postcard arrives.

> *Anna, Back six-ish on Fri. Will bring dinner. Stella.*
> *P.S. Can't wait to see you.*

Stella will be here before the end of the week.

She is late, of course, and as she races towards certain reprimand she tries to marshal her thoughts. But there is no time for planning when customers are complaining in detail about the glue used in *How To Breed a Better Alsatian*, or shoplifting encyclopaediae volume by volume, or trying to borrow a book. She returns home late, stunned with tiredness, capable only of vetting and displaying her favoured clothes before bath and bed begin to call to her.

And then the act of becoming horizontal, whether submerged or sheeted, realigns her mind.

Thursday, however, is different. From the moment she heaves herself from her seamy bed the day is fat with promise. She leaps over unpacked boxes and meets difficult enquiries with a speed, firmness and tact which even Wilf cannot fail to notice. Her blood is fizzing; her heart beats fast: no time, no time. After so many weeks of counting the hours, she has just one evening in which to prepare.

She spends her lunchbreak in Tesco's, locked in frenzied self-debate. Say she buys dinner for tonight – a theme meal of hummous and falafels – they'll need to eat tomorrow. Even if Stella isn't one for estate-reared feasts like her sister's, she's bound to want food. Was her promise to bring it a subtle test? Anna eyes the glistening tubs of curried ham coleslaw and steak 'n' kidney fajitas and imagines offering Stella, whose face will be teary with gratitude, artful salads of buffalo mozzarella and wood-roasted artichokes, smoked trout, kalamata olives and icy muscat grapes. Hopeless, helpless, she snatches up an ill-matched range of multi-purpose items, and hopes Stella will bring the centrepiece.

Within seconds the afternoon is over. She races back to Shawcross Street, dodging foreigners and malingerers with hawklike precision, her being focused on a single goal. It is only as she slams the door behind her that she notices her silent incantation: don't let her be early; please don't let her be early. It would ruin everything.

She races the Hoover around the flat, heaving it up and down stairs like an avant-garde Land Girl. She scrubs the bath; inspects the plates for washing-up deficiencies; flaps a duster around the sitting room; considers returning some dust for authenticity but controls herself; rearranges her possessions to suggest both mature intelligence and youthful disarray. She eats her falafels so quickly they lodge in her throat, remembers chickpeas produce wind and devotes several minutes to planning where she could fart between work and the flat tomorrow, in case Stella arrives first. Then, as she is moving her more impressive underwear towards the front of her sock drawer she notices a pile of disregarded cookbooks and hares back downstairs to the kitchen with her mother's spare Claudia Roden under her arm. What if Stella rejects her pathetic provisions? She must concoct something in advance. She opens the book at random; like a messiah, Claudia speaks. Moroccan Carrot Salad. Praise the Lord.

Twenty minutes later she is squashing resistant orange lumps with the back of a fork and worrying about the lifespan of cumin. She could consult her mother but it wouldn't be the same, and besides, she'd guess Anna's plans in seconds. Even before they had hung up Andrea Lefschitz would be at the door in combat gear, ready to bundle her into her Merc and zoom down the motorway towards her mother's waiting jaws.

She leaves the steaming bowl beside an open window, does another circuit of the sitting room to check that every postcard and photograph looks virtually untouched, rushes up to do the same to the little bathroom cabinet, and hesitates. There is nothing left to organize.

With a limb-loosening wave of relief she realizes that nothing but a bath and sleep will help her now. Unbuttoning her shirt clumsily with one hand, an eye on her breasts' white swoop and fall in the mirror, she pauses. Her heart beats against hot fingers. Unexpected courage feathers down her veins.

Her towel licks around the rail as she pulls it, and falls at her feet like a gauntlet. Behind the loofah are Aveda shampoo sachets, hoarded like charms. She reaches for them calmly, as if she makes this decision every day. Barely pausing to listen for noises of arrival, she crosses into Stella's bedroom, ignoring surfaces double-, triple-checked, and leaves the door ajar.

The bathroom is cold and very dark. She stands for a moment, watching light from the hall gild the enamel. There is no reason to resist, apart from fear. So she asks herself what Stella would do, and leans through the darkness to turn on the taps.

Steam rises off the water like a sigh. Her skin pinks and simmers. She tries to float her mind tantricly above the surface, but her limbs loll against the curves and will not stay silent. She could think of another body, strangers' limbs in unknown bathrooms, but she is anchored here. There is no point trying to resist it. She lets herself give in.

Eleven hours later, Anna is at the stockroom desk, considering whether her duty as a niece embraces phoning Eurostar to check on train times, when the telephone rings. She answers, unthinking. It is her mother. Her throat tightens, as if during last night's swoon she forgot her natural element and sank beneath the surface. What has she guessed?

Despite Anna's appeals for mercy – the shop is overrun with millionaires and Wilf is helpless without her – her mother grills her remorselessly.

'Are you quite sure? It's very odd. She's hardly *responsible*, but I still doubt she'd turn up out of nowhere, when you're there. It's very difficult when she won't answer a simple message.'

Anna smiles. 'Well,' she says, crushing her voice flat, 'maybe she doesn't mind whether I'm here or not. Maybe she even wants to see me.'

'Oh Anna.' Unexpectedly, her mother's voice softens. 'Listen. She might, I suppose, but she's funny. You know that. So' – the dark fin resurfaces – 'don't make it awkward for her. If you're *sure* that she hasn't been in touch, then just listen out for her message with the dates, and let me know right away. Understood?'

It's easier to agree. 'Can I speak to Sasha?' she asks instead.

'Of course not. Do you think she'd be here? No, she's helping Vincent scrape something off his van. It's something to do with infra-red—'

'Mum, I've really got to go.'

'Right. Well, should you still be interested, I gave Sasha a cheque today.'

'Oh – right,' says Anna absently. 'That's great of you.' As she puts down the telephone, she tries not to think of her mother's face when she hears of Stella's visit. She will feel that something sacred has been broken; Sasha defies her, but Anna obeys. She pushes her fists together like an anxious boxer and vows to be strong. Stella is on her way, and nothing her mother might try to do will stop her.

All day, as she sells and smiles and panics, Anna thinks of Japanese women watching for tidal waves on the shore. The horizon glimmers with impending total change. If Stella says nothing, Anna will. Her future is about to kaleidoscope.

*

Periwinkle light washes the stuccoed terraces. It is seven o'clock. All over the city garlic is being fried, red wine poured, salad torn leaf from leaf. Everyone with strength to think waits for tomorrow to transform their world, with money, recovery, sudden death, a thunderbolt. Lives begin and end tonight.

Anna creeps up on Shawcross Street like a secret at a wedding. Stella will be here already, checking the shelves, sniffing the milk, uncovering the traces. Anna sings '. . . they can't take that away from me', and wonders why they can't. Then, at the last possible moment, she pauses to cross the road and looks up at the house. There is no light at any of the windows.

This isn't necessarily a bad sign. She could be in the little hall, listening for messages, or climbing the stairs, or in her bathroom – Anna's hot fingers fumble with her keys – or . . . but from every other room light would shine through to the street, except Anna's bedroom. And surely she can't be there.

Black clouds snail across the sun. Perhaps she hasn't come at all.

With infinite slowness, Anna shuffles the doorkey into the lock. Stella sometimes does not turn up: for her siblings' birthdays, for family holidays, once to meet her own mother at the station – whenever, Anna's mother insists, responsibility is involved.

Does this count? It may. Stella would never feel tied by a simple date, a small commitment. But, thinks Anna as she stamps up the dark hall staircase, it isn't just that. She wants to see me – it's in the postcards. She breathes her last outside the door, and steps into the flat.

There are no balloons and streamers. No message saying 'out for champagne'. No languid Stella on the sofa, arms opening at the sound of the latch. Just silence, oyster light and deep blood pulsing.

She nibbles at her fingernails, and paces, for the first time in her life. In the window she catches sight of her reflection, tensed as Raskolnikov. She pauses, impressed, then recollects herself. This will never do. If Stella is still coming, if she wants to be here but is simply delayed, this may be a blessing. She will be ready.

Pinker, cleaner, finally dressed in a too-tight black shirt and fraying indigo jeans, feet bare and toenails painted, Anna walks down the stairs, braced for surprise. The door does not swing open, although she walks as slowly as a bishop to the altar. There is no sound of voices in the hall. It is nearly eight, and Stella is two hours late.

Two and a quarter.

At twenty past eight she goes to the fridge. She will be judged on what she is eating at the moment of arrival; what has been bought, what thrown away. Garlic fumes from the carrot salad may leave Stella reeling on the stairs. There is lentil soup, but vegan slurry is not much of an accessory. There is bread, but one of the kibbled seeds is bound to lodge between her teeth, unnoticed by her but blackly obvious to Stella. So she smears hummous on celery. Will she ring? She opens a lemon yoghurt. When will she ring? She scoops up black olive paste with a finger, pours a strengtheningly large glass of wine from one of three lengthily chosen bottles, decides not to boil her only potato and starts, regrets, bins and disguises a strawberry yoghurt instead.

Ten to nine. She hasn't rung.

Anna drifts towards the sitting room and scans the street

from behind a curtain. If only the stereo worked. She turns on the television, picks up a book, rinses her wine glass to avoid having a second glass, checks the answerphone again and collapses on the sofa, arms crossed behind her head. Then she leans up to push the door shut and flops back in the same spontaneous position.

There is a god. Had she left it open she would have been as visible from the doorway as a peephole kitchenmaid. For, as the cloistered quiet closes around her, Anna begins to drift. Her eyes are open but her mind directs another version of this scene, and her body follows. Soft hot waves build and eddy and crest until, eyes startled bright by what she sees, she comes and comes. And there is someone in the hall.

Her head is swaddled in velvet. Her ears, which in the flat seem attuned only to telephones, refocus, slowly, like lilies turning to the light. And then, in a gelegnitic shock, she is vertical, buttoning her jeans, straightening her shirt and kicking her book to where she might have let it fall.

There is laughter; heels shuffle on the kitchen tiles. Her own feet will be filthy. She grasps the doorhandle with a damp hand and takes the deepest breath of her life.

'Stella?'

Sixteen

She is sitting at the kitchen table, in a short smooth leather jacket Anna has not seen before. Her skin is creamier than she remembers, so it is the perfect fall of her hair's longer ripples, and the tilt of her eyes, and her wide mouth, which reminds Anna that this is indeed Stella, and makes her think *of course.*

She brushes back a wave of terracotta-coloured hair, and smiles. But her body remains facing forward, and it is this which makes Anna rip her eyes away.

On the other side of the table, legs crossed and defiant-chinned, is Richard.

Flames leap at Anna's heart. ' "Fool", said my Muse to me,' a voice warns in her head.

Anna looks from Stella to Richard, and back again.

Richard looks hard at Anna, then back to Stella.

Stella untilts her head and smiles down at the table.

*

'Well,' she says, in that dark, forgotten, uncopyable voice. Her neck curves within the oil-black collar; she runs a ridge into the wood with a fingernail. 'Here we all are.'

Richard's stare slips over the curling flop of her shiny russet hair and straight at Anna. He looks as if he's trying to read her mind. Then, just as she is trying to open her mouth, he speaks.

'Anna?'

Something about the inflection holds her. 'Yes?'

'I'm Richard. We spoke. Stella's friend.'

I am not equipped, she thinks. She is tired, and recently orgasmic, and here in the kitchen is Stella, as if she owned the place. Anna needs to be lying on her own on the floor in the dark. Not standing under a bright bulb and playing games with this man, this thieving duplicitous man, who is even now tapping his foot against his hostess's table-leg.

She narrows her eyes at him over Stella's shoulder. 'Hello.'

They pause, suddenly Pinterish. From her position in the doorway it is difficult to read Stella's expression. The slick leather clings to her shoulders like a sealion's pelt. Her trousers are dark cotton, faintly reflective in the light. Out on the flossy edges of Anna's consciousness Richard is standing, suggesting drinks.

'There's nothing in the flat but Bulgarian wine and vodka,' says Stella. For the first time Anna notices a fine web of lines around her eyes; a loosening of the skin below her jawline. She looks tired. 'We could mix them up, I suppose, for sangria.' Her voice smiles at him: a private joke.

This is not a night for reminiscing. 'There is pineapple juice,' announces Anna. They both turn to look at her. 'I bought some. And there's lots of ice.' Her voice is high and young. 'You never know,' she adds, horribly.

Her words hang like fairy lights, precariously strung. Will they light or fuse? She looks at Stella's straight nose, her mouth.

'Wonderful,' says Stella. 'Aren't you clever. And I *love* pineapple juice, hardly ever have it. We'll fight scurvy. Richard, ice.'

He knows where to find the fridge. 'God, it's full of food. I couldn't eat another thing. Stella, could you?'

'Hardly,' she says, picking up her black shoulderbag. 'We had a ridiculous dinner at that new fish restaurant on Marylebone High Street. Everything was encrusted with something else, like skin diseases. And Richard chose some German hock: sugared urine. Have you been?'

'No,' says Anna warily, thinking of her Tesco's shopping: a failed bounty clogging up the fridge. Should she invent a future dinner with a friend? Did Stella simply change her mind?

Smoke laces the air like autumn. Richard is sloshing vodka into heavy tumblers. Stella exhales a milky plume. 'God, what a relief. Bloody fundamentalists. Richard?'

'Not just yet, thanks.' Didn't he say he'd given up?

'And Anna,' she asks, 'do you?' She is grinning disconcertingly. There is a trapdoor here, doom hidden behind either one of the answers. Anna looks at her pale skin, the fine lines like spines around her eyes.

'Please,' she says and, smiling, reaches out a hand.

*

'It's very neat in here,' says Stella as she opens the sitting-room door. 'Haven't you used it?'

'Oh yes, all the time,' says Anna. She sniffs discreetly, but under the smoke the scent of her activities is lost. Nevertheless, Stella plumps herself on the sofa, like Theseus following the trail. Quickly, while Richard is still emerging from the kitchen, Anna follows, flopping beside her on the bookshelf side from where, to her bridling horror, she sees the birthday photograph, face up on the windowsill where she inspected it last.

Richard is calling from the hall. Slowly, steadily, as if retreating from an adder, she sets her glass on the rug and shifts her body so her head is, roughly, between the real Stella and the photograph. Every time she wants her drink or the ashtray she must lean precariously over, but the alternative is suspicion, accusation, discovery. Then she feels Stella watching her.

'Look at you, squirming. Have you got worms? You funny girl, you're blushing.'

Anna looks down at her knuckles and tries to think cooling thoughts.

'Lucky I'm not an upholstery obsessive like your mother, or I'd be tracking your every move.'

'Sorry – why?'

'You've spilt it.'

'Oh *no*,' she exclaims, and sees a pointed stain like a tongue seeping into the deep red of the sofa, under her thigh. 'I'm sorry, God, I'm such an idiot—'

'Forget it,' says Stella, as she tips her head back towards the door and smiles up at Richard, who enters bearing a tray. She has abandoned her jacket, and above her tight black jumper her throat bends in a hard touchable stream, like frozen water. Anna looks away.

'So.' Richard smiles opaquely. 'Enjoying your stay?'

'Yes,' she says, half turning from his dangerous smile – towards Stella, who is smiling too. 'It's lovely. Thank you. How's Paris?' They're drunker than me, she realizes. Should she stay sober, or join in?

'Gorgeous. And stinking. Richard doesn't like Paris, do you, Richard? He doesn't like the smell.'

'Well, I – I didn't say—'

He is flailing; Anna steps in. 'I *love* it. If it wasn't for the smell it would be too sugary, do you know what I mean? Too . . . flawless.' Where is this nonsense coming from? 'It's like a spike.'

Stella laughs delightedly. 'You're right. Absolutely. It *is* spiked.' And she nudges her arm with her elbow. Anna's heart crashes through her ribs. 'It's not the sort of thing men understand, really, is it, Anna? That mix of hard with soft. They like monotone. We like texture. Don't you think?'

Anna takes a huge swallow of vodka and a puff of cigarette. Something is buzzing under her skin. 'We certainly do,' she says, and smiles back. She is one of them, playing adult games. She can do this.

'Have you been lately?' asks Stella, as if it's just an ordinary city. 'You must.'

Anna's mind skids. She hides behind another swig of vodka, and then, quite unexpectedly, is saying 'I went illicitly' as she once told Richard, lifetimes ago.

'Oh *really*?' asks Stella, moving closer. 'With whom?'

Russet doesn't begin to describe the colour of her hair. Vermilion, thinks Anna. Madder. Crimson lake.

'I can't possibly say,' she smiles, and lowers her eyes.

'I'm shocked. *Tell* me. You naughty girl.'

'Well,' she begins, but is cut off as Richard leaps abruptly from his chair by the window.

'Stella, look. Subsidence. Or perhaps a private investigator.' He points to the birthday photograph, looking straight at Anna. As blankly as possible she returns his look. She has to stop him.

'So, um, Richard. Are you a friend from work?'

'I am. Sort of.'

She feels Stella move away. 'Tell her, Richard, about your amazing achievements. He's always winning Pulitzers and medals from poor oppressed countries, aren't you, Richard. They pour their whole GNP into a little bit of metal for his beefy chest.'

'Really?' asks Anna, turning to her, but she is looking at Richard through half-closed eyes.

'Oh yes. He's quite brave. Tell her, Richard.'

'I'll tell her in a minute. But first, another drink?'

'I'd love one, barman.'

Anna holds out her glass as he passes. With his back to them he bends over the round table in the alcove and, as he pops ice-cubes from their red rubber tray, begins to give Anna an account of his job almost identical to his oration in Florian's. Will this be the sum of my evening, she wonders; a slow duel of repeated stories? Covertly she eyes Stella's feet, and is shocked to find she is wearing trainers.

Trainers, she has assumed, are so un-Stella. And she is right. These are truly dreadful: ridged silver nylon, with olive green eyelets and piping and Nike ticks around the heel. Stella looks like she's wearing anchovies. Worse still, Anna suspects, she looks a little bit sad.

If Stella sees her staring she may expect a comment. So

she turns away and concentrates instead on her second vodka, accepts another cigarette, this time from Richard, and tries not to gaze too obviously at the birthday picture now propped up behind his head. They are discussing trips to China and Albania and Madras and into Anna's head like falling snow settles a single thought: that only an arm's length away is everything she wants.

What is she going to do? She squirms and crunches ice and then, quite suddenly, notices there is silence. They are looking at her.

'What?' Does she smell? She tries to read their faces.

'Did you?'

'Sorry – I—'

Richard smiles in treacherous sympathy. 'You were dreaming. We just wondered if you'd worked out about the stereo.'

Her mouth is open. 'The stereo? Did I fix it? No; I thought . . .'

Stella exhales sharply and stands up. 'No,' she says. 'It's just an old notice – forgot to take it off. I wondered if you'd realized. Never mind.'

Anna gapes. All those evenings wishing for background music, humming to herself, pathetically responsive to television theme tunes. Couldn't Stella have told her? Sent a postcard?

'What shall we have?' Stella takes a shoebox of elderly looking tapes out of the cupboard and rests it by the stereo. Guiltily, Anna pretends to look away. So much for her detective work. She could be impressing Stella with her total recall of every song in the box; now there's only mime, or bluff.

Stella picks through plastic cases. 'There's not much here – or not much we would want. Richard, you can choose.'

'Okay,' he says, and goes to stand beside her. It's easy to see why he'd want Anna to be gooseberry, but why on earth would Stella? She observes the shape of their backs and tries to feel calm.

'How about Paul Simon?'

'*No,*' exclaims Stella. Anna echoes, 'No.'

'Elvis Costello? UB40?'

Anna looks at Stella. '*No,*' they cry.

'What then?'

'Well, none of that duff boys' music,' says Stella. 'Find something else.'

'Tracy Chapman?'

'Oh God,' says Stella. '*No,*' shouts Anna, getting into her stride.

'Richard, it's tragic. You're choosing the dregs. In fact, almost unerringly the only ones that aren't mine. Give up,' Stella tells him, putting her thin hands on his chest and pushing him towards his chair. He sits down crossly and fiddles with his laces, attempting insouciance. On the sofa Anna tucks a fat lock behind her ear and tries not to smile.

'Anna? Let's see if you can do better.'

It's like a quest. If Stella asks her to help film war-torn Afghanistan, to master the art of filo pastry, to sweep the Augean stables she would do it; she knows she could. And now is her chance to show her how alike they are.

She clinks the last ice-cube into her mouth and stands suddenly, unprepared for the light electrocution whistling through her veins. Perhaps Richard is trying to disable her with vodka. It's time she took control.

Stella is still looking through the dusty boxes, mumbling like a disenchanted DJ. Anna joins her, trying to recall a single song she has ever heard her praise. There is nothing.

She is about to risk *Paco Peña plays Flamenco* when, like a vision, she thinks of Charlie Parker.

At the edge of the shoebox is *Birdland.* 'This,' she says, and waits for Stella's diamond smile. It is only as she sits back down on the sofa that she remembers where she saw his face: on a biography by Stella's bed.

'Clever you,' says Stella as she joins her on the sofa. She touches her wrist with warm fingertips. 'I *love* this. Truly. How did you guess?'

'Me too,' says Anna, blinded.

The room fills with rising notes, mournful, intricate; a staircase building into nothing. After a few minutes Anna's rapt expression falters and she finds herself wondering when this endless solo will break, and release the tune. Stella rises soundlessly, and begins to make more drinks. Anna watches her in a kind of trance as the doodling music goes on, and on. Finally Stella crosses to the sofa, hands Anna her glass and is about to sit down with her own when Richard's voice splits the noisy stillness.

'What about me?'

Stella's head snaps towards him. 'You? Oh. I thought you hadn't finished.'

'I hadn't. But now I have.' He tips his head back and throws the last of the pineapple juice down his throat. 'See? Could I have another please?'

Stella's back stiffens, but she laughs, low and knowing. 'Sor*ry.* My lord and master. I shall gratefully prepare another, right away. Don't you find,' she continues as she begins squeezing cubes out of the ice tray, 'that most men, even the nicest—' her head turns briefly to Richard '—have an innate cocktail waitress fantasy?'

Anna waits for him to reply, then realises that Stella was speaking to her. 'Oh—'

'They love manfully mixing martinis and flinging things into tumblers, but when it really comes down to it they want nothing more than a girl with a tray and a curtsey. And a tight vagina.'

Anna exclaims into her vodka.

'No, really. Richard, don't you agree?'

'Hardly,' he answers grumpily.

'Well, I do,' Stella replies sweetly, crossing the floor and handing Richard his refilled glass. 'Did I tell you I don't like your shirt?'

'You didn't. But I guessed. You're always very rude about red.' He plucks self-consciously at the fabric. 'It was the only one clean.'

A whiff of supplication sours the air. Stella sits again on the sofa, this time a little nearer Anna. Now it seems the pendulum has swung the other way. 'As I was saying, and while women like Anna and myself may fulfil those criteria, we do so by choice. If at all. No?'

Anna laughs. With every crystal sip, she feels her brain dissolve. 'Definitely.'

'You see, you *are* clever. That's one of the things I like about you. One of the many,' says Stella, as, quite swiftly, she runs her fingertip up Anna's spine and on to her neck.

Anna breathes in sharply through her nostrils. 'Thank you,' she says, feeling her skin heating.

'My pleasure,' says Stella, and sinks back into the cushions. Richard begins an unreciprocated gossip about a mutual friend's elopement with a cranial osteopath, while Anna concentrates on calculating exactly where tonight might lead.

Then Stella speaks, and as she tunes back in, a spark ignites in her spirit-misted brain.

'Oh, one thing,' she interrupts. Stella looks at her askance.

'Mmm?'

'I just remembered. Sorry. Someone called Jake left you a message.' Richard eyes her suspiciously. 'It didn't sound important. Just are you about, and stay in touch. You know.'

'Right,' Stella nods. 'And this Jake of mine, what did you think of him?' Her eyes are almost closed; it is impossible to tell what she is thinking. Richard inspects his hands.

Anna, bold with vodka, decides to speak her mind. 'Really – what *I* think?'

'Why not?'

I'm a grown-up, Anna reminds herself. I look better. Things have changed; we see each other differently now. 'He sounded smooth. I thought, off-puttingly confident. As if he knew you'd ring.'

Stella's eyes open wide. 'Oh, *did* he. Well. Poor Jake. Because' – she reaches out a hand and rests it on Anna's shoulder – 'as we both know, men like Jake are nothing compared to their egos. Cod's roe is more sexy than they are. No,' she announces, pulling Anna gently towards her, 'we don't care about them at all.'

'Who *do* you care about, then?' asks Richard, looking pleased.

'We care about each other,' says Stella. 'Absolutely.' She laughs, her arm now around Anna's shoulders, who also begins to laugh, watching Stella's eyes move from Richard to her, and back again. 'And, of course, about a few very rare and engaging males.' Now Richard is laughing too.

Stella winks at him, and a drop of clarity forms and trembles in Anna's heart. Is she saying these things for me or for Richard? she wonders, but then Stella rearranges her arm across her shoulders, and she instantaneously forgets the thought.

'Look at her, she's so pretty,' Stella says. 'And as for tight vaginas . . .'

Anna twists round her head and looks at her, incredulous. The air is rocket-light: hilarity, hysteria, drink and origami music. She imagines lying down on the sofa, her hot cheek cooled, but knows this would be fatal. There are thoughts only verticality can keep at bay.

As if in sympathy, Richard rises abruptly and begins to roam the room: picking up novels, inspecting postcards, tapping the fingers of one hand against his thigh.

'What, Richard?' Stella asks. 'What is it?'

Richard does not respond.

'Is it our feminine bonding?'

'Of course not,' he replies, a little too quickly.

'Because if it is, you know, you must try to rise above it. We love you too, don't we Anna? But even thrusting career women like to let down their girly hair sometimes.'

She glances merrily at Anna, who tries to smile. A speck of grit has settled in her skull and will not wash away. As she struggles to retrieve the memory behind it, Stella edges off the sofa and goes to join Richard. She touches his elbow, and like a slap Anna remembers her mother, slamming the phone down late one summer night.

'What?' she had asked disingenuously, fishing for drama.

'Nothing,' her mother had growled. 'Nothing' meant Stella. Anna pressed on.

'Poor Mum. Tell me.' And her mother, tired and unguarded, had outlined a story about Stella manipulating their parents, unfair advantage taken ruthlessly. Now, on the sofa, the details elude Anna, except for one sentence: 'She thinks it's just fun; and then she walks away.' As she watches Stella laughing with Richard, two thoughts are born in parallel: obviously dyed hair looks stupid on adults; and I don't want to be her fun.

Richard crosses to the doorway, and as he begins to go upstairs he calls out to Stella, 'Did you ring her back?'

'Who?' asks Anna, trying to dispel the doubts buzzing round her ears.

'Never mind,' says Stella, clicking a new tape into the stereo. Anna awaits relief, but to her disappointment the room fills again with doublebacking rippling notes, similar or identical to those that came before.

'This one,' Stella smiles: 'it's so – great.'

'How do you mean, "great"?'

'Sorry?' says Stella.

Anna sees she has made a mistake. 'I only meant,' she backtracks, '*why* is it great? You see I'm . . . I'm *interested* in jazz, and I just wondered how you can tell that it's – well, better than the one that we just heard.'

'It's just – great. I don't know. Ask Richard. Anyway, Django, what were you asking? Before your new jazz interest?'

Anna begins to pick at the skin under her thumbnail. 'I can't remember.'

'Oh, yes,' says Stella. 'About our friend. Well, *my* friend. Though Richard likes her.'

'Likes her?' asks Anna brightly, trying to restore the atmosphere. 'I thought he liked – you.'

Stella laughs, but looks gratified. 'You're quite right. He does. But that's different. He only *likes* our friend.'

'And does she *like* him?' asks Anna, grateful to have a joke to join.

'Well, yes. But not like that either. Richard isn't her type.'

'Oh.'

'She likes girls.'

Something explodes, gently, in Anna's blood.

'Sorry?' She looks hard out of the window, but Stella's eyes are on her burning cheek.

'You heard. She does. Are you shocked?'

'No,' says Anna, a little forcefully.

'Well, she does. She used to like me, in fact. A long time ago. Not now.'

The air stings Anna's lungs. 'And . . . now?'

'Oh,' says Stella airily, 'she's away. But coming back soon. Looking for romance, I think. She's had enough of difficult Latins.'

'Right,' says Anna, nodding slowly. She swallows.

'Here's a picture of her, if you like. A visual aid. Hello, Richard.' He reappears in the doorway, and as she crosses the rug towards him she passes Anna something.

'Come on, help me make some coffee,' Stella says to him, pushing him back towards the hallway. Anna stares at the upper edge of the glossy rectangle, allowing its white frame to blur until she hears their voices in the kitchen. Even blinded, she knows who she will see. She lowers her eyes and gazes at the birthday photograph.

In the kitchen Richard is saying, quite loudly, 'How do you know? How do you *know*?' Anna, buckling under the weight of questions, floats back and registers the hurt in his voice. Hadn't he said this weekend would be a turning-point? Wasn't he going to ask Stella to make up her mind?

The voices across the hall have sunk to a soothing murmur. If she has told him no, thinks Anna, will she tell him – or me – the reason? The photograph is trembling in her hand: that jawline, the cheekbone, the single dark eye. This woman, not Daniella, is still alive. Despite Stella's presence, something else beats under Anna's skin.

Stella returns from the kitchen alone. 'Where's Richard?' asks Anna blandly. Now is her chance.

'Tinkering. He says the coffee-pot's broken. Actually, I think he's pissed off.'

'What about?' Say something, she orders herself. Ask her.

Stella stares at her from far above. 'Never you mind, little Anna.'

Anna begins to bite her lip again, watching her stroll around the sitting room, apparently reacquainting herself with her possessions. If Stella were blind, she thinks, I could describe the whole flat to her without moving from the sofa. At what point would suspicion dawn – at my total recall of the kitchen drawers? The dimensions of the postcards? Or not until I began to describe the texture of the bedroom carpet, the perfume bottles, the number of paces between the bidet and the bed? Her mind is fraught with questions. Where should she begin?

Richard sulks soundlessly in the kitchen. Perhaps he won't be staying, and tonight may yet be saved. However, despite the vodka Anna cannot help noticing that, in Richard's absence, Stella seems content to drift around the room indefinitely. It is only when he wordlessly enters the sitting room, holding before him a china jug of coffee and three sailor-striped mugs, that she reanimates.

'There you are. *Enfin.* The world was empty in your absence.'

Anna's glower creeps along the rug and up to Stella's trainers. In the dull light in the centre of the room, far from the shaded side-lamps, their colour is even more unpleasant – a greasy aluminium. Stella has begun to tell a story about a colleague's transgressions, but her outrage seems focused on an ancient trespass involving a desk, and it is hard to empathize. Sacrilege flickers quickly: she sounds like Anna's mother.

Oh my God. Suddenly Anna wants a witness: her uncle or Sasha, even Richard; someone else to watch from the sofa, and help her decide what to think. Silently, unnoticed, a cold cell of indifference blooms and settles in her soul.

Is it the vodka which makes her so bold? Scarcely aware of what she is doing, Anna stands and walks to the stereo. She turns the terrible music down. Then she returns to her place on the sofa, and as she sinks again into the ruby cushions she briefly rests her hand on Stella's knee.

The monologue ceases. All eyes are upon her. She grins at Richard, then at Stella, and pretends to be poking a stray thread into the armrest.

'Anna?' says Stella.

'Yes?'

'Nothing.' Stella looks at her curiously, then turns to Richard, who seems to be biting the inside of his cheek. 'Oh Richard,' she says, 'there you go again.'

'What?' he asks, belligerently.

'You know. Looking all sad.'

'Like a wounded hind,' offers Anna.

'Exactly. Is it what I think it is?' she asks him, a playful torturer.

'Depends what you're thinking,' says Richard, already defrosting in the warm honey of her regard.

'You know. Left-outness. *You* want your knee patted. By one of us.'

'I think he does,' says Anna, now on the right side of the game. 'Poor Richard. Maybe one of us should.'

Stella gives a tinselly laugh. 'Well, yes. But it shouldn't have to be like that, should it?'

'No,' says Anna.

'Not on request.'

'In fact,' Anna announces – her head feels clear and strong – 'that's never how it should be. Friendly pats should be untram, trammelled. Uncurtailed. A perfectly normal sign of affection.'

To underline the point, she inclines her knees towards Stella, who, as if by arrangement, puts her hand on Anna's knee and leaves it there.

She concentrates on keeping her leg still, and waits for Stella to say something clever, but it seems that her store of snappy responses is running dry. Now Anna is flying. 'Richard,' she asks sweetly, 'do you like this tape too? Because I can't help thinking it's musical wanking, really. Or, no, flashing. We're supposed to clap and cheer and all he's doing is getting off on himself. Don't you think?'

'Well . . .'

'It's the same with lots of the things we're supposed to enjoy and don't really. Like Henry James. Or public readings. Or grapefruit.'

'Grapefruit?' asks Stella.

'Never mind. Anyway,' she says breezily, 'you see what I mean, don't you?'

'Not really,' says Stella. Anna looks at her in disappointment. In this light, she notices, her hair is closer to marmalade.

There is a pause. She senses Stella communicating something to Richard, but dares not turn her head to see. Then Stella coughs, and says to Anna: 'It's late. You must be getting tired.'

Am I? thinks Anna, and then understands. Stalling for time, she pretends to drain the last bitter sip from the bottom of her glass, wondering if she has a choice. She does not.

'Oh. Right. Yes. I suppose I am a bit.' She hesitates, willing Stella to change her mind. 'OK.'

Slowly, stiffly, she stands up. If she were ten years younger she would kiss Stella chastely, but should she now? Clearly, indefinably, she cannot. 'Goodnight, then.'

'Goodnight,' says Richard, looking away.

'Night, sweetheart,' says Stella.

The room falls silent. They are waiting for Anna. As she shuts the door behind her and begins to climb the stairs she hears them, very quietly, begin to talk again.

Anna cannot sleep. She turns her head from side to side on the skin-scented pillow, unable to empty her mind.

Richard has left. For several minutes, long after Anna had gone to bed, their argument had been almost audible. Then he and Stella had moved into the little hallway. Anna had considered creeping to the top of the stairs to listen, as in childhood, chill with expectation in the realm of adult truths. Instead she turned her head to the bedroom door, neatly left ajar, and strained her ears.

'Stella, I've said why not.'

'But I think you're mistaken. You're being so rigid.'

'I'm *not.* I don't know what you expect.'

'You know what. It's such a little—'

'Stella, it's not. That's the point. You can't just shut off when I'm not . . . convenient, and expect me back again when I am.'

'Come on, you know that wasn't it. I wasn't *ignoring* you – it's just so busy there, and I suppose . . . I don't see why we can't carry on as before and—'

'And what? What have we got?' His voice rose. 'I can't live like this, Stella.'

Her reply was too quiet for Anna's ears.

'I'm not,' said Richard fiercely. 'You aren't fair. And I don't want to be strung along. I said decide, and you've decided.'

'But that's not – I didn't. No, I just said let's carry on like this. You know. It's fun.'

'*No,*' said Richard, his voice compressed. 'No. It isn't fun. We're grown-ups, Stella, have you noticed? It isn't clever any more to take what you like whenever you like. You didn't answer, not once – I was *worried,* Stella. Uncertainty is horrible, and it isn't going to be fun for long for *you.*'

'Don't talk to me like that,' said Stella, but even to Anna's ears she sounded shocked. 'I want you to stay. I just—'

'What? No, stop it. That's not fair. *Stop* it, Stella.'

'Come on, just a little . . .'

'No.' The door catch clicked open, and Richard's voice changed. 'Really. I've had enough.'

'Please?'

Upstairs Anna winced. Stella drunk, and desperate, is not at all what she expected tonight.

'No. I'm sorry. Come on, it's not as if there's a shortage

of others.' Anna could barely hear him. 'Stel, I'm sorry. I just don't want this. I want someone who—'

Anna leaned right out of bed, straining to catch the final damning words. But, even with eyes tightly shut and body supported by her hand on the floor, all she could hear was her own shallow breathing, and the pool of silence spreading at the foot of the stairs.

Then, quietly, Stella closed the door and a few hushed minutes later came upstairs. A small sound as she crossed the landing in the dark. Anna waited. Her bedroom door shut behind her, and the flat was quiet.

Since then, for hours it seems, Anna has been rehearsing what he might have said. Something about trust? Or commitment? Or even, conceivably, love?

Seventeen

Uranium ashes have covered the world. Anthrax has blown in off the sea. Or no, the Thames has swollen and in a surge of dirty foam has buried Hackney and Piccadilly, leaving Bloomsbury's terraces poking alone above the swell.

She wakes to an unfamiliar silence. Then she remembers. In the bald light of a new day she thinks of every variation on last night, and still is left with that ending. It is only when, in the steamy bolted bathroom, she is reconjuring for the third time Stella saying 'vagina' that Anna's other life breaks through the daze. She has a job.

Quickly sluicing her hairs from the bathtub, barely pausing to arrange her more interesting shampoos along the edge, she slips into her bedroom and into yesterday's trousers, yesterday's shirt, then changes the shirt and heads for the door where she pauses, heart suspended. Is Stella even in the flat?

She opens the door and steps on to the landing. The carpet holds its breath. Her gaze scorches through the wood, but Stella's door stays closed. She creeps downstairs, senses iridescent, into the kitchen.

Stella cannot have gone. Can she? Would she have left this detritus of glasses and ash, an open jar of olives warm as living things, a velvet scarf draped like an arm over her chair? Anna leaves the flat, closing the door behind her quietly as a breath.

It is not until she has actually entered the bookshop that Anna notices what she has done. For days she has imagined this morning: idle stretching in white linen after a night of quiet revelations; a croaking call to work and easy pleas of sickness; and then mutual truancy. Instead she has come straight here, somehow already reconciled to real life, to Stella in the flesh.

Today she works heroically, ferociously, slitting open boxes and suppressing difficult customers. Last night plays in a back room of her skull, like a dreamer scaling subconscious obstacles. She pauses in the middle of a conversation about cheese books, heart suddenly stilled: what if Stella tells her to move out? Urgently, she wants to stay.

London seems fraught with possibility. Kirsten asks her to do overtime on Monday: she thinks of a hundred ways to spend the extra money, and agrees. She makes Wilf laugh, ignores the blond Oxonian and flirts with the tall curly-haired clearly gay man behind the Boots counter. She has new power.

When Iain the part-timer says 'Coming to the launch?' she decides not to not-hear him, as she has done before, and finds herself in a faux-Dublin performance space where male authors in brown suede jackets declaim aggressive fiction. After four vodka-and-tonics she is merrily lopsided but knows she's looking good, has provisionally accepted an unknown person's invitation to a party and has decided she does not care where Stella is sleeping.

Returning through the cold Guinnessy night Anna notes

with pleasure that it is late – probably too late to bump into Stella, who will either be with Richard or in bed, alone. But she climbs the Underground escalator stairs in twos, and her heart is catching fast in her chest as she hurries down Shawcross Street, eyes upon the transfixing lemon glow of the upstairs flat.

'Anna?'

'Yes?'

'I'm in here. Come and see me. I've been longing for your return.'

Anna hesitates, then crosses to the sitting room and stands in the doorway, waiting. There Stella sits, legs drawn up beneath her on the sofa, a cigarette wanly smoking between her fingers. In this light her hair is blood-red. She smiles at Anna, eyes almost closed, and pats the sofa beside her.

'So. How lovely. Just us two together.'

'Yes,' says Anna, doubtfully. 'Well – I didn't know you were here. I've been out. I mean, obviously.' She looks down and sees a bare foot, toes unvarnished.

Stella sighs a white stream. 'You lucky girl. I've had an immeasurably boring day. In fact, I need another drink. How about you?'

Briefly, Anna considers going to fetch the vodka herself; apologizing for her desertion; outlining tonight's social achievements. Instead she sinks lower into the sofa and waits for her drink.

'Do you know,' says Stella, kicking the door shut as she re-enters, 'I can't remember the last time I saw you, before last night.'

Anna swallows an icy wave and pretends to dredge her

memory. 'Wasn't it that time in the garden? At home – I mean, in Bath? But before that . . . God knows.' Other encounters – a winter walk, a grandparental birthday, an unexpected term-time arrival – are forcibly muffled, like caged birds with a cloth.

'Well, it's always good to. We don't see enough of each other, you and I.'

Despite her new insouciance, Anna almost gurgles with delight. 'Do you not think so?'

'I do not.' Her eyes smile over the top of her glass, forcing Anna to close her own. It would almost be a relief to separate now for a spell of thinking, like glancing away from fire to catch its green and purple ghost. 'So, tell me. What have you been doing with yourself?'

Anna feels flame rise in her cheeks. 'I don't . . .'

'Enormously important jobs? Risqué friends? Racy encounters with the natives?'

She looks up sharply, but Stella's expression is bland and closed – so unlike last night's particular Richard-smile. A tiger's breath of courage noses into her blood. Instead of asking questions, Anna decides to act. 'Well, actually . . .'

'You haven't!' Stella clunks her glass on the floorboards and turns to face her. 'I hope your mother hasn't bugged the flat. What *have* you been up to?'

'Oh, you know. Nothing . . . well, one thing.' At last they are face to face. She takes a slow sip and observes her: a clump of eyelashes on the far left, a little mole on her temple, the fine lines around her smile. Stella drops her eyes and fumbles for her cigarette packet, then holds it out, an eyebrow raised. Anna lights one, pacing her glee. 'There was one, but I don't know if I should tell you . . .' The delicious nicotine soar begins.

Stella knits her brows, joke-stern. 'I insist. Come on. I can't tickle you, I'm your aunt.'

Anna stares into the corner and tries to make her face behave. 'Well, it was quite naughty of me. Someone I shouldn't have.'

'Really?'

'No. The . . . friend of a friend.'

'Anna. You wicked little chip off the old block. Story of my life, frankly. And?'

'And—' Anna watches her face, but finds nothing but mild curiosity and slant-eyed appreciation. Her story is skidding away from her, like metal on ice. 'And, to be honest, it all went a bit . . . out of control. I wasn't as keen, actually, as . . .'

'As?'

'Him.'

Stella inspects the end of her cigarette and nods, half smiling. 'I see. *Naughty* Anna. Breaking hearts all over London, it would seem.'

Anna shifts among the cushions in a drunken show of modesty.

'And was he a good fuck?'

She concentrates every reaction into one small nostril-flare. The truth will give entirely the wrong impression, so instead she smirks. 'Extremely.'

Stella laughs delightedly. 'Good. Anna, I hope you won't mind my saying this . . .'

Myriad possibilities dance before her. She struggles to find the optimum expression.

'. . . But,' says Stella, flicking away her ash, 'you're not the girl – or woman – you were.'

'Aren't I?' asks Anna, feeling her face fall.

'No.'

'How?'

'Oh stupid girl, I don't mean *worse*,' says Stella, giving her a poke with her bony foot. 'Just like your mother – so over sensitive. No, what I meant was better. Looking.'

'Really?'

'Yes. Sexier, even. You see, I've been watching you.'

Anna attempts to limit her grin. 'Ri-ight. So . . . since when have I?' Only drunkenness prevents her from dancing around the room. She takes another sip.

'Since . . .'

'. . . I started having sex?'

'Precisely,' smiles Stella. 'Always makes a difference. Particularly oral sex, I find.'

Anna explodes, and buries her head in her sleeve. 'Stella,' she burbles, 'you're such a . . . I . . . oh, I think I'd better make another drink.' She sneezes, still laughing, and stands up. 'For you?'

'If you are,' says Stella, and takes Anna's hand in her own. Slowly, watching her face with every movement, she uncurls Anna's fingers, rests the empty glass on her palm and reforms the shape of her hand around it. Like a stupid animal, Anna looks down at her fist, and then at Stella.

'Take it,' says Stella finally, 'and do what you have to do.'

Anna glides into the kitchen like a cloud on casters. Reckless, rakish, utterly confused, she holds an ice-cube up as a filmy lens to the light bulb, leaves the cap off the tonic and pours Stella an extra slug of vodka. Then, on reflection, she adds one to her own.

'Can I have another fag?' she asks, handing Stella her sweating glass.

'Take it.' Curiously energized by Stella's stare, Anna helps herself and stands awkwardly before the sofa, like a petitioner.

'Come here if you want it lit.'

Anna bends towards her, cigarette clownish at her mouth. She breathes the sulphur deep. 'Thank you.'

'Do you think it's raining?' asks Stella casually. Anna strolls towards the window and makes a show of looking, but it is difficult to see past the bright reflection of the room and Stella on the sofa.

'There! Like that!'

'Sorry?' Anna resists the urge to turn. She watches Stella's white feet floating in the slippery surface of the glass.

'It's what I meant before. How you're standing, your—'

'Carriage,' she offers, euphoric.

There is the briefest perceptible pause. 'Your carriage. Precisely. You are changed. Quite obviously. It's the fucking, Anna.'

Anna smiles at her shining self. She barely hesitates. 'I'm not in the least surprised.'

'Really?'

'Really.' She looks down through a sheet of frozen vodka and sees herself bicycling hands-free along a blaze of Tarmac. Her fingers flutter like moths above the handlebars. It's only courage: stop trying to picture it, pick up speed and just let go.

'And why's that?' asks Stella.

'Because of doing such a lot. In the last couple of – three years. You know.'

'I know,' says the voice behind her with a lift, and the cushions sigh as Stella stands. Her bare feet suck softly at the floor as she approaches the window. Anna concentrates very hard on the glass, and the place where her own reflected eyes would be. Stella's hand is on her shoulder. She turns to see her picking a piece of cellophane from her heel. 'I think we both know.'

Anna uncertainly meets her eye.

'God I'm drunk,' says Stella, righting herself.

'Me too.' The hand remains on her shoulder, waiting. 'Stella . . .'

'Yes?'

'*Do* you know?'

'I think I do.' Her hand gives a little squeeze. She meets her gaze. And then, for one long oblivious second, Anna moves into the hot and spinning space between them.

There is a hand on her waist, and her own palm rests on a fluttering curve of skin. She stands on an island, in a storm of fireballs, shooting stars and lightning – a soft electric collision of lips and tongues.

Then, gently, Stella disengages. The new world wavers and is lost. 'Anna.'

She clears her throat and looks up, dazzled, but Stella's face is dark. 'Yes?'

'Oh, Anna.' Anna wedges her nail in a crack in the painted windowframe, and waits, liquifying. Then Stella gives a smile: amusement, and a little sympathy.

Anna digs her nails deep into the ball of her thumb, and forces her head up. 'I—'

'Shhh,' says Stella, touching the side of Anna's cheek with the back of her hand. 'It's OK. Forget it.'

'How? I mean . . .'

'No, really. Just do. It's not an ordinary goodnight kiss, I grant you – but it happens. Both drunk. Don't look so horrified.'

Anna opens her mouth to argue, or appeal, but Stella shakes her head. '*Please*, Anna. It's OK. It's nothing. Shhh. And go to bed.'

'Now?'

'Yes. Now. Definitely.' Stella gives her a little sideways smile. 'I think this has gone far enough, don't you?'

Anna swallows. 'I . . . suppose so.' Her head feels full of air, but her throat is burning. She tilts her neck back to keep the tears in. 'OK. I'll – goodnight.'

As she goes to the door she hears Stella return to the sofa and shake out a cigarette. 'Goodnight.'

She shuts the door behind her, and begins the roaring climb towards her room.

Eighteen

The bedroom is filled with tepid early light. Anna lies on her side, eyes on the door, screened by a cautious arbour of duvet. Her heartbeat drums through the mattress springs.

Two feet away, Stella is in the bathroom.

There is nothing – mere bricks, a milky dab of paint – between them. Piss hits the water in a ringing stream. Anna tries to concentrate on Stella's face.

She does not pause as she crosses the hall, or as she closes her bedroom door and walks downstairs, her bag bumping the banisters with every second step. She makes coffee, eats breakfast, practises acrobatics for all Anna knows, all without a sound save the squeak of the cutlery drawer and a cupboard conspicuously slammed. She does not call her name, or creep back upstairs to press her ear to the painted wood. Anna, listening in her bell-jar, is not at all sure what she would do if Stella did. When the front door is finally pulled shut, a ray of relief seeps across the carpet and up to the desolation on the bed.

Decades pass before she moves: a Pompeii girl, petrified

amid her sheets. Horrified reverberations hit and floor her. She is beached, three-quarters drowned, swamped by every brackish wave. However hard she squints her eyes, images from last night fill her mind and will not leave.

1. Stella's face, after unfolding Anna's hand for her empty glass: merciless, possibly touched with scorn, daring her to react. When she said 'fucking' her look was the same. Does she, Anna wonders, ever not pause for effect?

2. The syrupy wash of red and gold on the glass through which, despite the almost silent tread of feet behind her, Anna had tried to stare, a moment before the world capsized.

3. Afterwards, telling her to go to bed, her sideways look when Anna hesitated.

4. And lastly, always saved till last, the rightness of that small hand on her waist; the cupped curve under her palm; the deep drugging perfume of hair and skin. The bewildering softness. The silken fall.

Her mother's sister.
Her mother's *sister.*
Not just her relative.
But female.
Both, female.
Oh, God, what has she done?

Stella has left, undoubtedly. However, only a prolonged session of tooth-cleaning and kimono-styling can prepare Anna to open the door and begin the long walk downstairs. The flat is hushed but unexpectant. The kitchen is empty. She leans in the sitting-room doorway and looks at the daylit window, at the floorboards beneath their invisible feet. She looks for the mark her fingernail made and cannot find it. There is no sign they were ever there; no proof, save the embarrassment and terror, and an astonishing, bubbling thrill.

Anna is standing in the kitchen, calibrating how hard she'll have to force herself to eat, when she notices a small sheet of paper on the table. Its ripped upper edge is whipped and knotted, like a profligate's ruff. A full second passes before her brain makes the leap.

Stella has written her a letter.

8 am

Dear Anna,

Well . . . that was a surprise. Let's keep it to ourselves, shall we?

You're still asleep, presumably, but I'll be back briefly at 12 to collect some books. See you then.

Anna reads and rereads the note, until the inky letters seem to powder and drift like spores upon the page. Resisting an urge to fold it into her mouth and swallow, she contents herself with a corner and drops the rest in the bin. Then she retrieves it from its bed of coffee-grounds, wipes it with her sleeve and returns it to the table for another round of anguished contemplation. Tears whiten her espresso-scented fingers.

Incalculably later, no less mortified but considering food, she happens to look at the clock. It is ten to twelve, and she will die if she sees Stella.

In three-and-a-half minutes she is dressed. She hesitates by the front door, head thumping, and prays for some extraordinary patron saint to protect her; then opens it – to silence. Then the street door. And finally, lungs reinflating and mind saggy with relief, she clears the end of Shawcross Street, and she is free.

She buys a cinema ticket, examines rails of impossible shiny trousers and dawdles in Virgin Records, ignoring Charlie Parker. She tries not to think of Stella, the answerphone or Andrea Lefschitz's face if she ever finds out. However, every time she closes her eyes, last night's terrifying miracle begins again: the air is alchemy. Her skin blossoms, her stomach flips and shivers, and she is smiling.

By four o'clock there is nothing left to do. As she returns to Bloomsbury's ashen hush, wondering which professor first brought Stella here, she is struck by a new and frightening thought. Now Stella has collected her books and gone, what has happened – what they did – is permanent, complete, like a landslide. She has no choice but to stay calm, limit the damage, and try to build on that barren – or is it fertile? – ground.

She will start tonight. More cinema, inept cooking, a visit to Markus, a lying letter to a friend: her options are endless, but she knows nothing will keep her from a pilgrimage to the sitting room, a long thoughtful bath, and Stella's abandoned bedroom.

Nothing but Stella herself.

'Anna?'

This is the worst of all possible worlds. She cannot imagine approaching, or ignoring, a single aspect of what they did. She needs Stella gone, so that, alone, she can spy on last night, slice and slice again each fragile sentence, exposing the bone and hidden nerve. Perhaps she should flee like a startled burglar, leaving Stella, at the top of the stairs, dusting the paintwork for fingerprints.

'Anna. What are you doing?'

'Nothing. I'm here. Hang on.'

Apart from the shame, and the shyness, and the staggering laughable shock, the thought of seeing Stella now is lined with something new. She walks slowly to the kitchen, where Stella sits inspecting the hem of her brown jersey.

Despite herself, an enormous blush springs up Anna's neck and swamps her face. Should she giggle? Apologize? Acknowledge it or stare her out? Stella's half-smile gives nothing away.

'Hello?'

'Hello.' She forces air into her lungs. Stella's folded arms, her cool gaze, even the line of her jaw are a barricade which Anna is not invited to cross. She hauls her mind into the present, and notices a huge black disc on the front of Stella's jersey. She says the first thought in her head. 'Oh – I *love* your jumper. You look like an enormous doughnut.'

'Great. Thanks so much,' says Stella.

'Oh no, no, I didn't mean that. I meant—' Stella looks over to the window, allowing Anna's eye to travel slowly over the smudge of earlobe behind her hair, along her jaw and up to the curled bracket of her lips. Her lips.

Again, that buried lurch and flip. She leans her head against the door-jamb and waits for the Catherine wheels to subside.

'Yes, yes. Now, tell me where you've been.'

She needs something to do with her hands, and eyes. Conversation is impossible: her synapses are hugging themselves in disbelief. She opens the refrigerator door. 'Orange juice?'

Stella considers. 'Why not. So?'

'Oh . . .' She cannot admit to solitary filmgoing. Stella will think she's gone to seed. So she shoots herself in the foot and hopes for the best. 'The Tate.'

'Did you? What did you—'

'—see?' asks Anna, too quickly. 'I saw – oh, you know. The usual.'

'The Rego?'

'Sorry?'

'Paula.'

Anna misses the crucial word, having been briefly transfixed by Stella's necklace: a little silver key. Probably platinum. A love-gift: a reminder, or a promise. It catches the light with every breath. Should I ask her now, she wonders – but Stella is hers for the moment, and that puzzling mess can wait.

Then she remembers the question. 'Oh – sorry. Um . . . yes. Definitely. Wonderful.'

'Right.' Stella does not break her gaze as she reaches for the paper. 'Pity. I wanted to see it. We could have gone together.'

The terracotta tiles gently buckle. She looks down at Stella's hands, but their associations do not help her. 'Well – well, we could go now – again. I'd be happy to. Now? Let's.' Her mind is rioting. 'Yes?'

'Wait a minute.' She flicks slowly to the listings. 'Tate . . . Tate . . . no it isn't.'

'What?'

'You've missed it. It's body parts now. And Sierra Leone.'

At this point her sister would walk away in a trail of scorn, leaving the victim to fall upon her sword. But Stella waits, as Anna sinks deeper.

'Really? Ah. It must have been . . . leftovers. Or permanent. There were quite a few. And they might, I suppose, have left them there – for storage?'

'I see. And which was your favourite?'

She tries not to blink. 'That's difficult. Hmm. The one with . . . no . . . well . . . the one with flowers? Pink flowers? Do you, you know, know it?'

Stella elides a smile and a smirk. A suggestion of blue flickers in her temple. 'You have your mother's eye. Now, listen.'

'Yes?' asks Anna anxiously. How long can this game go on?

'I'm sick of the flat. Let's go.'

Her mind blooms. 'Out?'

'Where else?'

Breathless, she waits for Stella to find her bag, head for the door, abandon her diary, remember her phone and retrieve it from a splash of milk on the table.

'Ready?'

'Ready . . .' says Anna, longing to change into – what? Tea clothes, shopping clothes, art clothes . . . bar clothes? If so, what sort of bar?

Stella, in daylight. Tiny lines cobweb around her spearshaped eyes. Disdain shrouds the edges of her mouth. The key at her breastbone dances on pearly skin. Anna looks straight ahead and waits for revelation.

'Have you seen your mother much?' asks Stella as they cross the scruffy grass of Russell Square. The air is heavy as wet wool.

'No,' says Anna carefully. 'Not much.'

'Why not?'

'Well, I'm often out,' she improvises. 'And – well, she lives in Bath. She doesn't have to be here.' She glances at Stella. 'I try to discourage her.'

Stella laughs. 'Brave girl. I don't blame you. Does she come round . . . all the time?'

'Well, no. I'm very strict. But even so she doesn't always ask before she—'

'Just turns up? Oh my God.' When she smiles, Stella's mouth is so soft, so private, that it is hard to believe they were standing together, only yesterday, in a nebula of warm breath and tongue-tips and whirling sparks. Anna's stomach swoops.

'Why haven't you asked for your key back?' she asks. 'I'd have thought you'd hate her dropping in all the time. When you're – you know, in residence.'

Stella shakes her head. Anna catches herself wondering how often she washes her hair; infidel. 'I've tried,' says Stella. 'I've been reasonable, over and over again, and still she will not surrender it. It's incredible; like a rat.'

'What are you going to do?'

'God knows. Mug her. Pay you to rifle her bag. I'm sick of it, to be honest. She has no sense of boundaries.'

'I know,' Anna agrees happily. 'It's a nightmare. Her friends are the same; it's like group fostering. I can barely walk down the street without tripping over – have you met her? – Andrea Lefschitz—'

'I certainly have. She's the anti-Christ.'

'—precisely, hunched in a little hideaway spying on me with her periscope . . . Stella, where are we going?'

'Nowhere,' she says, slowing down outside a low white building with circular windows. Behind chipped railings is a patch of park: trees train-set khaki, Tarmac fringed with moulting grass.

'In here?' asks Anna. 'Really?'

'Why not?'

An enormous white duck is poking its beak gently through the railings. 'Stella, look.' But Stella, one hand on a low gate, is looking down at a wizened man in overalls and eyebrow piercings.

'Sorry, love.'

'Excuse me?' says Stella.

'You can't come in, love. You need a child.'

Anna swallows. How did he know that about Stella? And how did he dare say it? She glances at Stella, and the aftershock is greater than the first. Stella's lids are, unmistakably, fluttering three-quarters closed – a habit of her sister's. Anna is transfixed.

'First,' says Stella, snake-staring with a small and worrying smile. 'I am not your love. And second, what are you talking about? We'd like to come in.'

The man shrugs his little shoulders. 'Read the sign.'

Stella gives an exasperated sigh. 'You read the sign, Anna. I simply can't be—'

'It says "no adults unless accompanied by a child". Maybe we'd better just . . .'

'Bollocks,' says Stella. 'Now, listen,' she calls to the man, who is handing out Strawberry Mivis from a freezer by the poking duck. 'I have a child here. What's the problem?'

'That?' asks the man, looking through the railings. Anna looks around for a straggly blonde girl or football-bouncing Sikh, then understands. Her mouth opens in protest, too late.

'Sixteen or under? I don't think so,' says the gatekeeper.

Stella's insult hangs in the air like exhaust. 'Never mind. The point is, you see, I'm a filmmaker. Looking for venues for a piece on London's parks. Presumably you need charitable funding?'

The gatekeeper coughs uncomfortably. 'Yes . . . I reckon. But I don't see why—'

'Well, you're not going to get that without publicity, are you?' She leans closer to the man, widens her blinding eyes and smiles compellingly. 'B-B-C-1.'

'Right,' the man says doubtfully, looking at his child's plastic watch. He's probably a paedophile with a wardrobe of souvenirs. 'Go on then,' he says finally, but Stella is already half-way through the gate.

Ahead of them is an enclosure inexplicably filled with goats and geese and even, in a fenced-off section, three mud-caked sheep. Anna is too surprised to ignore her. 'So you've been here before? For the animals?' A little fleet of slothful bicyclists is approaching along a shaded walkway.

'No,' smiles Stella, bumping her with a shoulder. 'For the brats. Ice-cream?'

Anna looks at her in surprise. Stella doesn't seem the type for 99 Flakes. 'Oh – I'd like a . . . lolly, I think.'

The gatekeeper eyes them in silence.

'Right,' says Stella. 'I'll have a Pineapple Split, and – Anna?'

	Too infantile	Too weedy	Too lardy	Too faux-adult
Cyber-Rocket	X	O	O	O
Mini Milk	X	X	O	O
Cider Pop	O	O	O	X
Cornetto	O	O	X	X

'I'll have a Lemonade Sparkle, please.'

'And what about you?' asks Stella over her shoulder.

Anna cranes her neck, and sees a small shiny-faced child with moon-calf cheeks, gazing passionately up at the ice-cream freezer. It is panting with longing.

'Kid? What do you want?' says Stella.

The child sidles up to the freezer, and quickly assesses every picture with a little circular movement of its head. Then it points.

'A Jumping Jack Frog, we think,' says Stella.

As Anna unwraps her slab of sweet ice she watches the child tear, blow and pull the skin off its lolly with expert speed. It presses its mouth to the green surface and trots away, leaving her fretting about milk-allergy comas. Touched but not quite forgiving, she follows Stella.

'So, what do you think?'

'Of this?' Anna looks over at a long benched row of worn-looking women, corralled by pushchairs and importuning toddlers. 'I think it's . . . interesting.' She has sucked one corner entirely lemon-free. 'I mean – I'm sure it's a good thing.'

'Do you,' says Stella. 'I think it's repulsive. Everything seems to have mange – not just the creatures. Animals are vile close up, anyway. Can't think why toxoplasmosis has such appeal.'

The slow herd of bicycles crosses their path, and Anna sees with a guilty shock that it is a cluster of wheelchairs, more complicated and surgical than any she has seen, and in them children are lolling, heads supported by pillows or bars, tubes at wrists and nostrils. The women who push them are smiling – at each other, at the hopeless children in the trollies, even at Anna, who mangles a smile back.

Stella is almost by the sandpit, oblivious, when she reaches her. 'So why do you come here if you hate it all so much?'

'Oh, revulsion's good for the soul, don't you think?' says Stella, striding on. She walks like she's crossing a desert checkpoint. 'Besides, I thought it was your sort of thing.'

Poison mixed with honey. Anna closes her eyes in a blur of last night, and walks straight into Stella's elbow.

'Sorry,' she mutters, suddenly furious.

'Oh Anna,' says Stella mildly, slowing to light a cigarette. 'You're not still mooning over last night?'

Anna stops dead. '*What?* I . . . of *course.* I mean, not mooning,' she adds hastily, 'but – well, yes. It does occur to me, from time to time. Doesn't it . . . you?' Her fingers leave evanescent traces of lemon on her jeans, as if slugs had crept over her thighs at night.

'You *are* like your mother,' says Stella, laughing. 'Take everything so seriously. Don't—'

'—Jesus, Stella.' The air boils. 'It *is* serious. Obviously it is. It's *shocking.*' She sits down hard on a bench beside some roaming chickens. Their red-and-white legs scratch angrily at cement. 'How can you say that?'

Stella sighs as she sits beside her, crossing her legs away from Anna. 'Cigarette?'

Her breath smells of old tobacco. Anna shakes her head. A peacock turns its back to them and rattles open its display, brown wings patting its bottom like baseball gloves.

'Listen,' says Stella.

But something in Anna has given way, or taken over, and she is steely with outrage. 'No.' She looks Stella in the eye, suddenly tired of her lazy half-lidded stare. '*You* listen. You can't just pretend all that didn't happen, even if . . . even if you wish to God it hadn't.' Stella does not move or blink or in any way demur. Anna's fury hardens. 'It did, and it probably shouldn't have, and, Stella, whatever you may think, it isn't the sort of thing that happens. Between nieces and aunts. Not in London, or fucking Paris, or anywhere.'

Stella shrugs, but Anna keeps staring, determined not to lose her now, refusing to see the smile hatching a foot away.

'So, whatever you think about it, it isn't *nothing*, Stella. You think you can just cover everything in a layer of – well, disdain, and mildly enjoyable loathing and derision. But you can't. You can't disdain this. It happened, Stella. You were there last night.'

Stella's necklace winks as she inclines her head, saying nothing. She waits until Anna breathes. 'Finished?'

'Maybe,' says Anna, refusing to succumb to her smile.

'Well, can *I* just say that – you obviously haven't done this before, have you?'

'How could I?' asks Anna, feeling her treacherous mouth smile back despite her indignation. 'I don't have another aunt.'

'Touché. Now listen. I can quite understand why you're . . . thrown by this. But what I'm telling you, as a woman with wide experience in every – believe me – field, is that it isn't a *bad* thing to have happened. It's no odder than many other encounters I've had when drunk and lustful.'

Like what? thinks Anna. Lustful? Tell me *now.* Instead she says, 'You're not, you know, though, are you?'

Their gazes touch and sizzle. 'Even if I was it wouldn't happen again. Obviously.'

'No,' agrees Anna, unexpectedly limp with relief.

They sit in silence, while a freakishly over-feathered white chicken pecks around their ankles. The little key on Stella's neck rises and falls. Anna watches until her head begins to ache, deciding, finally, to say—

'Is it my key?' asks Stella.

'Can I see?'

'You may.' It is almost weightless in Anna's hand. 'Do you like it?'

Newly doubtful, she hesitates. 'Do you?'

'Well, I think it's from a cracker. So, no. But everything else in the flat is so depressing. Have it, if you like.' The peacock turns and offers a shriek of chemical blue.

'No,' says Anna. 'You keep it.' Her arms are cold, and it is only as she begins to rub them, as her hand glides over the seamed skin that she notices they are bare, her sleeves are thoughtlessly half-rolled, and she is exposed in the white light of afternoon, bold as a declaration. She hesitates; the world will change if she leaves them unhidden. Won't it?

Dry leaves race and patter at their feet. As they watch, the chicken's feathered bloomers begin to crest in the breeze.

'How do you know if it's a hen or a cock?' Stella eventually asks.

'I'd have thought you'd know better than anyone,' says Anna, beginning to laugh.

*

They walk home in the beginnings of rain. Stella tells a long story about running around the Tuileries in a nightdress, but Anna mostly thinks about the chicken. It is only as side by side they climb the stairs to the flat that Anna remembers the ring.

'Listen, I rang the Glasses, in the end. Well, I tried. They were—'

'It's fine. They sent it.'

'Right.' She hesitates. 'Why are . . .'

'God, I have to go,' says Stella. 'It's later than I thought.'

Anna swallows.

'OK?'

'Um . . . OK.' She lets Stella into her own flat. 'Do you need a hand with anything?' she asks politely.

'You won't know where anything is,' says Stella.

They stand at the door. 'Thank you.'

'No – thank *you.*' They smile together in the murky light.

'See you in January, or whenever.'

'Or whenever. Yes.'

'Goodbye.' Left cheek, right cheek.

'Goodbye.'

Nineteen

Maybe she is happy. She closes her eyes in sandwich queues, ducks into the stockroom for imaginary tasks, meanders through dim November terraces, trying, failing, to decide. There is no reason for it at all: she has won nothing, proved nothing, has found no one or herself been found. Nevertheless, hard as she looks at what she has done, she cannot feel weighted down. She smiles at herself in the bathroom mirror and waits for darkness which does not come. Stella herself is hardly the issue. Something has died, but it feels like spring.

And so, when Chantal the newest part-timer says 'Coming to the pub?' she goes, and there in the dark and damp-carpeted hole she is invited, twice, to Iain's flatmate's party. So off she goes with them all to Wandsworth and drunkenly dances with her workmates and then more closely with others including the unnamed flatmate, whom she had forgotten meeting before, and then, rather imperious, she makes him walk her to find a cab where, in full sight of the driver she kisses him back.

'Can I give you my number?' he asks her.

'No. You call me.' She tells him hers once, from inside the taxi. 'Let's see if you remember it.' And she is driven home over Waterloo Bridge, under a sky of milk in ink, lightness in her heart.

'So ring him back,' says Sophie, from a Polish payphone.

'No. Anyway, I don't want to.'

'You're mad – oh. He wasn't . . . ugly?' Sophie, the youngest of a race of giants, each lovelier than the last, can imagine nothing worse: not polygamy, not idiocy, not herpes.

'No. Not at all. I was amazed.'

'Oh I *see*,' says Sophie, beginning to laugh through the crackles. 'You let him kiss you, and *then* – only then – you noticed that he was handsome and chivalrous and interesting, and decided "not my type"?'

'Stop it. Just because I've had . . . unsuccesses does not mean I can't choose for myself.'

'You can?'

'I can.'

'Not your type?'

'I don't think so.'

'So, now it's pastures new?'

'Unimaginably.'

And then, only an evening later, as she climbs the stairs to the flat she hears something which makes her heart freeze.

Voices.

And she is a child again.

*

Adrenaline prickles across her skin like fire. She presses her ear to the door, and her stomach spins.

She could leave, and choose ignorance. Or she could face them and know the worst. She slides her key into the lock and listens; they are almost shouting now, too loud to hear her. With a safecracker's stealth she opens the door and pockets her keys. They are in the kitchen.

If she slips across the hallway and wedges herself hard against the high-rise of books in the corner, she can see all she needs to see of the long blue room: Stella's profile against the window, hair a corona of lamplight. Her heart slows in disbelief.

'—it isn't an *issue*. Why must it be? Stella, there is no *issue* here. I drop by to see my daughter – not something you would know anything about – I find my sister, completely unexpectedly, and I ask to be let in. Is that a *crime*? All I wanted was a quiet chat, and an hour later I'm being accused . . .' Anna tries to calm her breathing to the merest wisp of life as she waits for explanations. It is as if her body has been breached as she sleeps.

'*Christ*.' Stella's face is shadowed ivory, highlit bones and hollows. A flush has spilled over her jaw and on to her neck: a streak of dappled rose, paling outwards like blood on wet tissue. Her voice is tight and furious.

'I've *told* you what I object to. This assumption that you can swan in and take over, just like you do with Mum and Dad. Well, I'm not them, Magda, and I don't need you. I don't even want you in my flat. Let alone muscling in on my affairs.' Stella's jaw clenches tight as a fist.

Affairs? thinks Anna. She cannot take her eyes from Stella's soft mouth.

'Your affairs? Listen to yourself. Your personal life—'

'*Leave my fucking private life out of this,*' roars Stella, venomous. Anna jumps, almost dislodging the top books from the pile. 'How dare you? It's just *envy*,' she shouts, slamming her hand flat against the table. 'That's all it is. You've *never* had a life like mine, and you sit on your skinny arse in Bath – of all places, Bath! – and fiddle and watch and try to control our strings.'

Fury hangs in the air like singeing fur. There is hair in Anna's eyes but she is paralysed.

'Don't speak to *me* like that, you little hypocrite. You've got a nerve criticizing how *I* treat our parents. They need me, Stella, to come for birthdays and help with decisions and sort everything out. But whenever it suits *you* you traipse up there and worm and show off and name-drop and half the time they're lending you money – you know it—'

'—Shut *up* about that . . .'

'—and it's worse than interfering, what you do. It's manipulation, and I won't have you do it to my daughter.'

In the dark of the hallway Anna grits her teeth. A cold film is easing across her skin.

'This isn't about your *daughter*, Magda,' says Stella with infinite scorn.

'Isn't it? Well, tell me something. Why has she suddenly been asking about the Glasses?'

Stella barely hesitates. 'I can't imagine.'

'You're lying,' says her sister simply. 'It was bad enough, what you did – poor Daniella in hospital, knowing what you were doing with Nicky, and then poor Nicky, once you were through. And those daughters . . . do you think that if Anna knew what you'd done she'd forgive it? To your best friend?' Anna's blood is raging in her ears. 'But I've kept it from her, for her sake – and now you're dragging her into all that?

What are you trying to do, use her as a lure to win back Nicky?'

Anna's mind empties. The air feels very thin. 'As if I ever cared about *that* . . .' spits Stella, breathing flames. 'You're just sick at the thought that I'll touch anything to do with you—'

Dear God no, thinks Anna. Please don't let her tell. I will die. Already her heart seems not to be beating.

'—as if I would. You just want to barge in and order me and her around, and she might not be man—'

'Woman,' hisses her sister.

'Jesus – *woman* enough to stand up to you—'

Aren't I? thinks Anna. Stella, what have you done?

'—but I am. And I will. And I'm telling you to go.'

'Listen,' says Anna's mother, and the eggshell fury in her voice makes Anna bite her lip to the blood, 'I am not staying here for you. I'm here for Anna. I don't need ever to come to this shitty flat again.' Stella gasps melodramatically, but she presses on. 'And I'll give back your key, and as you can't even remember to turn your *taps* off when you leave the country, let alone pay all the bills—'

'Shut up shut up shut *up*. For fuck's sake,' shouts Stella, stamping her foot on the tiles, 'that was *one time*. I said thank you, didn't I?'

'Barely,' says Anna's mother, still glassy with calm. 'And the time I had to drive across London at midnight to let you in to screw that . . . *boy*, and the time I had . . .'

'It wasn't across London, for Christ's sake. You were already north. And anyway, that's what you've got the bloody keys for. Because you said you would. Why else in God's name do you think I'd let you have a set?'

Anna's head throbs. This makes no sense at all. Or if it does, and Stella was lying about her key all this time, was she also lying when she said she was leaving? Has she been with Richard since then?

'Fine. You want them?' There is a clinking scrabble, and then her mother's fingers enter the frame, stretching a handful of metal across the table.

'Don't be ridiculous.'

'See? It's all bravado with you, and image. You'll do anything to get a rise – to get what you want. You're a child, Stella, but an old child now, and that act is really beginning to lose its appeal.'

Stella's face is white. Even her rose-juice flush has evaporated in the icicle chill. Any second now, thinks Anna, they will leap at each other and only one of them will win. And perhaps this time it will be her mother.

And then it comes to her, like torchlight on a colour-chart: all the women together, waiting for her choice. Here is Magda: beautiful, intelligent, admired, and better-married than anyone she knows; bored, interfering, and horribly sad. Here is Stella: independent, daring and – face it – sexy, but also cold-hearted and tantrum-throwing and a little desperate. The alternatives include Andrea Lefschitz, who despite a job and spouse is irredeemably Andrea Lefschitz. Janey Warner is sweet and privately clever, but her dream husband is a nightmare and her children bully her for cash. Kirsten from the bookshop eats millet, cuts her own hair and wears sweatshirts advertising fun-runs. Her university tutors were earnest, dour or angry. Even M. R. O'Keeffe, according to Wilf, is an alcoholic.

These are the options, and there is not one she wants to be. Each has found a key and used it, and now holds it towards her, battered and glittering and useless. She is adrift.

No she isn't.

I have survived London, thinks Anna.

I have recently committed the bravest, stupidest, most self-willed act of my life.

I am almost ready.

'Oh, hello,' she says, stepping into the doorway.

Her mother starts. Stella glares. The room is a booming fireball, billowing thunder.

'I . . . didn't you hear me? I just came home. I mean, got back. To the flat.' She keeps her face turned towards her mother who rallies, with a visible effort.

'Hello, darling. We were just – discussing. I popped by.'

Stella's eyes flick to Anna's, shutter-quick.

'Hi,' says Anna, mini-voiced. She can feel her mother watching her from the side, but she tries again. 'Stella, I thought you'd gone.'

'I'm as surprised as you are,' says her mother. 'She—'

'Where were you?' asks Anna.

'With a friend.'

'With Richard?'

Her mother's eyes click between them like an umpire at a bloodbath. Stella's face is cement. 'Yes.'

On the periphery of their locked stare Anna's mother takes a breath. 'We were just chatting about the flat, as it happens. Your aunt was saying that you've been a pleasure to have here—'

Anna winces at the kindness.

'Very helpful,' adds Stella tightly.

'—but,' says Anna's mother, rearranging the keys more artistically against the pepper, 'that isn't really the point.' She pauses, but Anna does not contradict her. 'You're leaning on my coat.'

'Sorry.' Anna moves to the other side of the kitchen and turns on the cold tap too hard, splashing her stomach and the tiles behind the sink.

'My, quite the little housewife,' says her mother drily, watching her reach for a cloth. Anna ignores her. 'So. As I was saying, Stella says it's fine for you to stay here—'

'Oh good,' says Anna, and glances at Stella, whose neck and hands and breastbone have a lunar gleam.

'—but,' her mother continues, 'you can't.'

'Why not?' Stella is looking out of the window, apparently transfixed by a gust of ochre leaves. Is it Richard? Is it the nights of furtive exploration? Is it, perhaps, the kiss?

'Because,' says her mother, rubbing at an invisible mark on her black wool trousers, 'I've spoken again to Andrea, and Becky won't be back from Florence until August. So you're definitely moving in.'

Stella snaps her head round. 'Sorry?'

'It's not a big deal, Stella. No need to *interfere.* My friend Andrea – sweet of her, isn't it, Anna darling? – has kindly offered to let Anna stay in her flat.'

'But—'

'Magda,' says Stella, 'why?'

'Well . . . it's a very generous offer.'

Stella sniffs. 'Yes, but why? Why should she move?'

'It's a gorgeous flat. Very spacious. Anna, you know she designed it herself.' Anna tries not to roll her eyes.

'Where is it? It can't be more central than here.'

Anna's mother drums her fingers against her knee. 'That's not the point. It's – it's in Highgate. It's a beautiful area, Anna; you won't have been. Wonderful shops, and trees, and . . . Anyway, you'll have a sweet little bedroom. And the kitchen's state of the art. I've seen it, of course. *Conran*,' she stage-whispers, eyes wide in a show of excitement. Anna eyes her coldly, urgently casting about for an argument against her.

'Anyway, darling, what Stella thinks isn't really the point. So why don't you just pop upstairs and find your things, while your aunt and I finish our conversation.'

'Magda,' says Stella in a voice varnished with patience, 'you're being ridiculous. Why should Anna move all the way up to Highgate – it's miles, Anna, and full of old ladies – when she can stay here, welcomed, in an extremely covetable flat.'

Her sister snorts, and glares at Anna. 'What is that top you're wearing?'

Now they are both staring at her. Anna looks down. It is a tight raspberry-coloured jumper, pulled on in this morning's spirit of cold defiance. But Stella hates red, and in her presence such edicts regain their force. 'It's . . . new. I bought it in Covent Garden. Why? Do you like it?'

'No.'

'I do,' says Stella. Anna looks up, patently astonished. 'No, I do. I always like red. Don't you, Anna? What taste we both have.'

'Yes,' says Anna inadequately, gazing down at her ruby bosoms.

'See?' Stella smiles. 'We're made for each other. And for the flat. No, Anna must stay here.'

Anna waits for this tug of love to sink in, but something

half-noticed has snagged her attention. She eyes them discreetly: is it their lipstick? The same hairdresser? Has one of them borrowed the other's clothes? Then it hits her, like slow buckshot. She can see it now in the bridge of their noses; in their new or smoothed-out wrinkles; the stretch of their necks and the jut of their chins. They look like a pair of furious swans. They look like sisters.

'Anna?'

Her heart feels vulcanized, muscle knotted like a handkerchief, but her courage has not left her. Carefully she meets her mother's eye.

'Look—', she says, and her hands shake with a lifetime of sullen compliance. She curls them shut. 'I don't *have* to do what either of you says.' Her mother inhales sharply. 'But if Stella's happy, I'd rather stay here – not to defy, or to please, either of you. Although I appreciate your . . . efforts.'

She smiles politely. London flinches.

'Well,' says her mother eventually, vaguely patting the surface of the table before her. 'If that's how you feel . . . I—' Her fingers meet the pile of keys. 'I brought your furry coat from home. Our home. It's in the car – I'll just . . .' She tails off as she leaves the kitchen. Briefly, Anna pities her for the burning holes her sister stares into her back. Then Stella stands.

'Are you going after her?'

Her eyes are veiled with ice. 'I'm going for a pee.'

'Oh.' Anna swallows, but keeps her body intact until she hears Stella's feet on the upper landing. Then she leans limply against the sink, as the telephone, utterly forgotten, begins to ring.

She needs a moment to recover, and now is not the time

for her father, or for Richard. But the voice on the answerphone is sweet, and Scottish, and entirely new.

'Anna? It's – I'm Pen. A friend of Stella's – I spoke to her on Sunday. The thing is . . . there's a book Stella thought I'd like to borrow; one of hers. But she can't get it to me before she goes to Paris, and – well, it's quite heavy. Photography, apparently. Anyway, she thought that perhaps I could arrange to collect it from you? But the other thing is . . . well, it's embarrassing, but . . . I've just come back from Brazil, you see, and I've moved to London, but I don't – I've never actually lived here before. And so, you see, Stella thought – well, I know it's an imposition. You're probably very busy. But as you've been there a while, and all, perhaps . . . we could have a chat – maybe a drink? I'd just like some ideas about where to go – I've been here a week already, and I've not a clue. So . . . why don't you give me a ring – 020 7353 6148 – and tell me if you're free. It would be good to meet you.'

Anna looks up wildly from the answerphone, as from above and below feet approach the kitchen. Her mother reaches her first.

'Who was that?' she asks, dropping a fat carrier bag in the hallway.

'No one. A friend.'

Her mother sighs and opens the sitting-room door. Any second now Stella will stamp into the kitchen, expecting Anna to fetch drinks and soothe and sympathize. It's an exhausting thought. Almost without thinking, she follows her mother in.

'Um . . . thanks for the coat.'

'It's fine. But Anna, frankly I'm a little shocked.'

'Because I didn't want to play poor relations with Andrea Lefschitz?'

Her mother sighs forbearingly. 'I just *feel*,' she explains, 'that it would have been *polite* if you had *informed* me how you *felt*.'

Anna stares. 'I did! I told you all the time—'

'Well.' Her mother stretches from her perch on the sofa arm, and pushes the door closed. 'You may think you did,' she hisses, 'but it wasn't very clear. I'm well aware Stella can be . . .'

'How?'

'Charming. Very. As I know you'll agree.' Anna looks away quickly, but a blush has already begun to spread. 'But the least you could have done was not to side against your own mother.'

'Christ.' All she wants is to collapse, alone, in bed, and her mother's playing Clytemnestra. 'I haven't sided with her, or you, or anyone. I've explained already. I'm doing it for *me*.'

'Well excuse me,' says her mother. 'Although I'd be grateful if someone could explain how my daughter grew to be *quite* so wilful and selfish.'

'You tell me,' says Anna, giving her a look.

There is a thump of books in the hall.

'Fuck. Oh fuck, my nail.' Anna and her mother listen in silence. Then Stella calls out, 'I'm going.'

Anna's mother flaps her hands, like shooing chickens. Anna opens the door. 'Sorry?' she asks Stella, who is stuffing books into a mound by the telephone.

Stella looks up. 'I *said*, I'm going. Before I get attacked again by this heap of rubbish.' From this angle Anna can see a mouse-coloured tidemark where her dye begins. Stella jerks the door open. 'I think the heating needs fixing – you'll have to get someone in. Tell your mother I'll see her downstairs. And Anna,' she says as she begins to walk down the stairs, 'please keep to your bathroom.'

'What was that?' asks her mother, looking around the sitting-room door.

'Nothing,' Anna mutters. She could race upstairs to search for clues, but it is too late now, almost too late to care. Her mother's eyes are shining in the dark. 'Stella said to meet her downstairs, but I don't see why . . .'

'It's none of your business,' says her mother, heading for the kitchen.

'No, it is. Tell me. You're not going somewhere with her?' At least, she thinks, when Mum does *me* favours I don't bother to deny them. 'Oh no – you're not taking her to the Eurostar, are you?'

Her mother pretends to adjust the strap of her miniature navy bag.

'Mum?'

'If I am, that's up to me, isn't it?'

She could just leave them to catfight in the car – but not this time. She passes her mother her coat. 'Listen,' she says, 'don't do it. Why should you? She's always – she's such a bully. And you're sweet to her. I can't believe you've been doing all that – I mean, you're always helping her. I hadn't realized. Why didn't you say?'

Her mother noisily piles china in the sink, but her face is exhausted. Anna resists the urge to go to her. 'It's nothing to do with you.'

'But why?'

'It's how we are. We're set in it.'

'She's foul to you.' And not just to you, she thinks, remembering the Glasses. 'At least you help people. You shouldn't let her mess you around. You don't have to.'

'I said I would.'

'Did she ask?'

'I offered.'

'Well, get out of it. Tell her you can't. Lie. Please. She's just spoilt,' says Anna, with new certainty. Her mother's eyes are wide, but she is almost smiling. 'Go on. Just fox her. I dare you.'

'Don't tell me what to do,' says her mother, hanging her coat over her arm. 'We'll see. Be good, Anna.' She kisses her forehead and pulls the door closed.

Thirty seconds later there is shouting in the street outside. Anna goes to the window and looks down into the tangerine night.

'You promised.'

'I know. But I've changed my mind,' calls a calmer voice, above the sound of footsteps.

'How dare you?' screams the first voice, almost hysterical.

'I dare,' Anna hears, over a slamming door and the waking purr of an engine.

*

'Is that . . . Pen? It's Anna. Stella's . . . niece.'

'Oh – I'm glad you rang. I wasn't sure if you'd have a . . . hang on a minute, I'll just put this fish down.'

'What on earth are you doing?'

'Oh, nothing. Well, you see this little house I've bought, it's got a wee pond in the garden. And I bought a couple of carp – they said they were carp, but I reckon they're big sick goldfish – but I've not had a chance to sort them out all day. So when you rang I was standing in the garden like a ninny, trying to scoop them out of their plastic box and into the water.'

'By torchlight?'

'Well, yes, as it happens,' she says cheerily.

Anna begins to laugh. 'I know, I know,' says the woman, 'but what could I do? Now, where were we?' A distant door slams, and the line wipes clear.

'Well, to be honest I don't . . . you asked me to ring. You're a friend of Stella's?'

'Oh yes,' she says. 'I am, though it's been years. This was her idea.'

'The carp?'

'Oh no. That we meet.'

'I see.' She waits in vain for illumination. 'So . . . sorry – it's been a bit of a frenzied weekend. I can't quite remember what it is you wanted to borrow—'

'Don't worry. I don't know either. It's just that your Stella suggested a book I might want to read, apparently. Though I can't imagine why, from her description. And thought that – if you don't mind – perhaps we could meet so you could hand it over – it's quite heavy, you see – and also – well, just meet.'

'Yes,' says Anna.

'I mean, I barely know where to buy a pint of milk, let alone a light-box, or a season ticket, or . . . you get the picture.'

'I know,' says Anna, unexpectedly charmed. 'I was like that too, at the beginning.'

'Does it improve?'

'Slightly. No, it does. You'd be surprised. What's a light-box?'

'Oh, you know. You pop a murky little slide on and it lights it up beautifully. From behind.'

'Is it . . . for fun?'

She can hear the woman smile. 'Well, it depends on your fun . . .' Anna, losing sight of the shore, feels her cheeks begin to burn. 'So, shall we?

'Meet?'

'Well, yes. I think Stella thought we might have . . . things in common.'

'Did she?' She pauses, fleetingly torn by vanity and confusion. 'Oh – yes, why don't we? Besides, you want that book. Which is it?'

'Oh,' she says, 'well, I don't quite know. She said it's whatever is at the top of the pile by the sofa. So – would you mind having a look?'

'Hold on.' Anna skids into the sitting room and leans over the sofa's far arm to search. Then, more slowly, she returns to the hall.

'It isn't there. I mean, it can't be.'

'Oh.' The Scottish woman seems unconcerned. 'Well, isn't there one that might be right?'

'I doubt it,' says Anna. 'There's only Howard Hodgkin at the Hayward, and some dreary American early art, and the *Observer Book of the Seashore*. And a lot of dusty novels.'

'Tempting . . . well, I can't think which one she meant. Which one was on top?'

'The *Observer Book of the Seashore*, I'm afraid. And it's not even very heavy.'

'Never mind; we'll have to believe her. Just this once.' They smile at themselves, at each other. 'So, where shall we go?'

Anna is trapped. 'Well, there's . . . hmm. Florian's? Or no, no, I don't think . . . there's that pub on Malet Street . . . no . . . I—'

'You know,' says the woman, 'I went to a brilliant place once with Stella. At least, I thought so – she hated it. But it was when we . . . oh, never mind. It's the sort of place you either like or you don't, though, Anna. A bit louche. Sound promising?'

' . . . Yes. Yes, it does. So, where is it?'

'Ramillies Place. Just off Oxford Street. I've been meaning to go since I arrived, but . . .'

'Well, come with me,' says Anna, and bites her lip.

'It's called Bar Barella.'

'Oh God.'

'I know. But trust me.'

'I'll try. Now, when?'

'I'm pathetically free. How about tomorrow?'

Anna pauses, transparently. 'That would be . . . fine. Lovely. Seven?'

'Seven. Okay, so—'

'Wait – how will we find each other?'

'Don't worry,' she says. 'I'm sure I'll spot you.'

*

Anna hesitates on the upper step. An absurdly handsome man like an Indian godling smiles as he skips up the stairs from the bar. Spotlight beams from its swinging sign gleam like minnows in his hair. She smiles back.

'Going in?'

'I think . . . I might.'

'First time?'

'Well, yes.'

'Just you wait,' says the man and grins as he heads for Oxford Street.

Anna watches him go. The darkness ticks with promise. She walks down the stone stairs towards it.

Inside at a long counter, curved as a marble spine, people wave and drink and call at each other like seabirds on a silver shore. A waiter carries two huge crimson cocktails to a pair of laughing women; more cocktails – phosphorescent, palest pink and blue – wink from shadowed tables in booths on the facing wall. Through the dim light and the smoke and shouts and thump of unfamiliar music, Anna scans the scattered groups of drinkers, waiting to be seen. Her stomach swirls. And then, at a table near the counter, leaning back to look into the depths of the room, she sees someone she knows: a slide of hair, a pale perfect cheekbone, one dark eye. And as Anna watches the profile moves, and there is the woman in the birthday photograph, turning to meet her.